THESE LITTLE DEATHS

Embrace the dark parts

Kelsey

THESE LITTLE DEATHS

A Novel

KELSEY GERBER

Winthrop Books

THESE LITTLE DEATHS

Copyright © 2022 by Kelsey Gerber

Designed by Lynn Templin
Edited by Emily van der Harten

The Library of Congress Cataloging-in-Publication Data is available upon request.

ISBN 978-0-578-38368-2
ISBN 978-0-578-38369-9 (ebook)

Winthrop Books
Chicago, IL

Our books may be purchased in bulk for promotional, educational, and business use. Please contact your local bookseller or visit booksbykelsey.com

First Edition: June 2022
Printed in the United States of America

0 9 8 7 6 5 4 3 2 1

To Mrs. Smith, for always giving me access to your bookshelf.

And for my Grandma Pat, the first person to inspire me to write.

"We were revisionists; what we revised was ourselves."

THE HANDMAID'S TALE BY MARGARET ATWOOD

CHAPTER 1

A wisp of cigarette smoke snakes over a man's shoulder and expands into a cloud that envelops Rachel's face. She holds her breath and weaves back and forth across the sidewalk, trying to decide if she should adjust her pace to overtake him or let herself drift back to a safe distance. Glancing at the time, she makes a move to pass him, careful of the spots of ice along the edges of the path. His stride lengthens and rather than speed up to an attention-drawing jog, Rachel turns the corner into an alley. Adjusting her breath to avoid the sudden odor attack of dumpster rot, she wonders if the city has ever considered posting those brown honorary street signs in alleys to recognize the politicians and Chicagoans who have damaged the reputation of the city. *Don't let your mind wander. Focus!*

Rachel keeps her head down as she passes backdoor entrances, loading docks, and fire escapes. There's a loud thud, and she looks up long enough to confirm that it's just a box being unloaded from the back of a truck, prepared meals that will probably taste as appetizing as the wet cardboard they're boxed in. As she nears the end of the alley, a creeping sensation climbs up her back and nestles between her shoulder blades. She twists to look behind her, sure that someone is following her. No one is there.

Emerging from the alley onto an east-facing street, the wind off Lake Michigan barrels toward her, bitter and bone dry. Rachel leans into it, pulling down the edges of her yellow knit cap over her brown curls to avoid losing it to a gust. She should have taken the time to pull on her gloves this morning, but she was too rushed. The next train was coming in 10 minutes, so it was either leave the leftover chili she'd packed for lunch on the counter or figure out where she tossed her gloves when she got home last night. She hates wasting food.

Her chapped hands burn, the cracked knuckles bleeding against the icy exposure, but Rachel bites her lip and pushes forward. She fixates on the fierce pain and then settles into it, welcoming it. It feels deserved. It feels like an earthly punishment and she accepts it, pain as penance.

The office comes into view, all steel and glass against the muted sunrise. The blue glass that shimmers in summer looks gray behind the dreary veil of February. The gray is everywhere. It wraps around every surface until it's the only color palette Rachel can see. She shoves against the gray revolving door and spills into the gray lobby. She presses the gray button in a gray elevator that takes her to a gray 11th floor that houses her gray department where she sits in a gray cubicle in a row of identical gray cubicles, all outfitted with matching ergonomic chairs, Cisco phones, and mesh desk organizers. She was not prepared for so much gray in her new life.

Pulling off her coat, Rachel notices that even her skin is dry and pallid under the unforgiving fluorescent lights. Her yellow beanie seems excessive and vulgar. She buries it in a coat pocket and slings the coat over the back of her chair. The nondescript sweater-denim-boots look she chose today—chooses most days really—blends into the sea of casual office attire surrounding her. Rachel can't risk making friends. Comradery creates cliques, which breed gossip, and in an office this boring, gossip acts as a form of currency, exposing the dark and sinister. Blending in is just fine.

"Hey, Louise, how are those edits coming along?"

Rachel startles. She looks up from the stack of unopened files on her desk, unsure how long she was being observed. A mid-level manager flashes a plum smile over the cubicle wall. Rachel doesn't know her name. It doesn't matter.

"Sorry, they're taking me a little longer than usual."

"They're supposed to be done on Tuesdays, and I'm sure you know it's Friday and-"

"I'll have them done by the end of the day."

"Great! Thanks, Louise." Plum Lips gives the cubicle wall an approving pat, her rings clinking off the metal frame.

Rachel knows she should feel more grateful for this job, but she only has so much bandwidth for emotion, and anxiety wins every time. It keeps her focused, alive. The work is tedious some days, but easy enough to learn as she goes. She's slowly getting better and able to work more quickly. She has to in order to avoid detection. The only thing she continues to struggle with is InDesign, which she'd never used prior to this job. That was one of the many lies on her resume.

Rachel opens a file for a children's book about a zombie and a vampire who are friends. She looks at the original jacket design and reads the notes one of the editors has scribbled in the margins. She pulls up the design on the computer, makes the changes, prints the revised version, and places it on top of the original inside the file folder, setting it to the side. The next file is a book of poems centered on the theme of sex on top of horses. Or with horses. It's unclear from the cover and Rachel can't decipher if the pull quotes on the back are serious or satire.

Rachel leans back in her chair and pinches the bridge of her nose, frowning against the early signs of a headache. She knows she should have applied for simple hourly jobs with duties she was actually qualified to perform. There were plenty of postings for positions that would require little interaction with others: grocery stocker, housekeeper, overnight shipment operator. But this position caught her eye as she scrolled on her new phone. After several nights spent sleeping on a dirty floor, Rachel couldn't resist this small kindness to herself. It couldn't hurt to apply.

The application process had proven to be more difficult than she'd anticipated. Rachel had gone to the neighborhood library with her lease, but a bearded man behind the counter told her she also needed to show a photo ID. She reached into her purse for her license, but then she froze, realizing the names wouldn't match. She felt the weight of her decision to run away from home, unbearably heavy in that moment, and her face collapsed into tears. The man looked around to make sure they were alone, then whispered something about a one-time exception and handed her a day pass for the computers.

Rachel had created a resume, borrowing experiences and skills from the job description. The English degree was true, but the internships were completely fabricated. They were dangerous lies that could easily be fact-checked, but she wasn't going to take the job even if it were offered to her. They called her the next day for a phone interview. Two days later, they had her come to the office for an in-person interview. She'd told herself it was good practice and went. The atmosphere of the office was frantic, and it was clear that they were desperately short-staffed. When Plum Lips offered her the job on the spot, Rachel couldn't help herself.

A soft buzz emits from Rachel's coat, snapping her attention back. For a few seconds, she forgets to breathe. She twists to the side to fish her phone out of the left pocket. An email from her mother. Rachel thought she turned off notifications for email. She makes a mental note to look through the settings this weekend and comforts herself with a reminder that it's only email. If she hadn't changed her number, she has no idea how many texts her mother would send on a daily basis. She does know they would be just as cruel as the emails but harder to ignore.

Her thumb hovers over the phone screen, paralyzed. She closes her eyes and breathes in for four seconds, holds it for seven, breathes out for eight. A thin curl falls forward and sticks to her damp forehead. These emails have turned brutal since Rachel left home, but her mother has disliked her from birth. She's certain of this fact. Rachel's older brother is named Rory because it means king. Regina was born two years later and her name was chosen because it means queen. Rachel means female sheep. Rachel was never given an explanation for her name, but always the afterthought, she'd assumed it was chosen for the alliteration.

Finally, she opens the email - better to just get it over with. It's short this time.

9:28 AM: *I'll find you, you little bitch*

* * *

Rachel reheats her leftover chili in the breakroom, but when it's hot, the ground beef smells like wet dog food and her stomach turns. She holds her breath and walks to an empty table in the corner. Maybe she can force some of the broth down along with a tomato or two. She's already lost 10 pounds since moving to the city and doesn't want it to turn into 20 like the weeks after Rory's accident. Or the time she developed an eating disorder from what started out as a friendly dieting competition between sisters.

"Not hungry?" a voice behind her asks.

Rachel half turns and sees a coworker approaching the table. She never learned this one's name either but thinks of her as Too Old for Bangs. "No, I'm fine."

"Louise, you've been sitting there stirring for the last 5 minutes."

Rachel cringes at the sound of her mother's name. It's a terrible name and writing it on the preferred name line of the new hire paperwork felt like self-mutilation - worse to see it listed as her first name on forms without a background check associated. Hearing it now feels like being branded with an iron. "Left it in the microwave a little too long. Just waiting for it to cool off."

"Been there," Bangs responds while taking a seat at Rachel's table. "Is it chili? It looks better than this tuna salad sandwich I've been putting off eating since Monday."

If it were up to Rachel, eating five-day-old tuna salad in a shared space would be considered physical assault. She takes shallow breaths from slightly parted lips as Bangs opens her Ziploc bag and yanks the sandwich out, blobs of gray falling to the table. The questions come rapid fire between and sometimes during bites.

"So, Louise, where are you from?"

"Small town. You wouldn't know it."

"In Illinois or somewhere else?"

"Somewhere else."

"Where?"

Rachel knows she needs to provide enough information so as not to look suspicious but also not so much that she gets caught in a lie or can't remember her backstory later. She tries to picture a map of the Midwest and the names of those states down the middle. She's heard people call them flyover states. Her mother called them boring. "Nebraska," she says, trying not to end the response with a question mark.

"Me too!"

Fuck. Rachel kicks herself for settling on a Midwestern state. The tuna salad should have been a dead giveaway with its fishy mayonnaise on white bread. Bangs pauses to dust crumbs off her left breast before continuing. "I'm from Omaha, but I traveled all over the state for volleyball tournaments when I was in high school. Which small town was yours?"

Rachel couldn't point to Omaha on a map, but it sounds familiar. She remembers seeing more dots for actual cities along the eastern border of that column of states.

"The western area. Really close to the border of..." Rachel realizes she doesn't know which state or states are west of Nebraska.

A potato of a man, dressed all in a shade of khaki almost identical to his skin, walks into the breakroom singing to himself out loud, and so also to everyone. Bangs turns to look, and Rachel takes the opportunity to knock her plastic container over, chunks of meat and tomato and beans flowing onto her lap. "Shit, I've got to go clean myself up."

She uses a cupped palm to push chili off the table and back into the container. She can't afford to be wasteful, but if she's honest, she wasn't going to eat a single bite anyway.

"Do you need help?" Bangs asks with a tone that suggests she hopes the answer is no.

"I've got it," Rachel says as she brushes what she can off the front of her and into a large trash can. She rinses her hands in the sink of the small community kitchen and shakes them somewhat dry before rushing out of the room. She takes the elevator up one level to the floor under construction. Rumor has it that a big company suddenly moved out and now the suites are being renovated to prepare for new tenants.

It's dark and the sound of drills and hammers can be heard behind frosted doors.

Rachel walks a long hallway that smells like pencil shavings and crayons, a smell that reminds her of grade school and simpler times. Tucked at the end of the hall is a women's restroom, completely ignored by the all-male construction crew. The cleaning staff gave up restocking it long ago, but Rachel brought her own supplies from home. Sometimes the power is cut and she has to use the flashlight on her phone to see, but today the fluorescent lights flicker to life when she flips the switch. The lights hum and Rachel breathes in the driftwood and sea salt reed diffuser she bought over lunch one day and placed in the middle of the long row of sinks. It's almost like being a C-suite exec with a private office bathroom. Maybe that bathroom has a window that looks out to a beach.

Rachel dumps the chili into a toilet and fights a gag as it sloshes into the water, spattering the sides of the bowl. She closes her eyes to flush, picturing a bright granny smith apple or a crisp carrot. Anything but that chili. At the sink, she rinses the container and then dabs at her jeans with a wet paper towel. The dark denim hides most of the evidence, but her shaky hand betrays the reality of what happened. She was careless.

Rachel grips the edge of the counter to steady herself, mostly to stop herself from running. She stares into the mirror at the violet half-moons beneath her eyes. *I'm ok I'm ok I'm ok.* It probably isn't true, but it brings her back into her body and slows her racing heart. She has twenty-eight minutes left of her break. Twenty-eight minutes to calm the fight-or-flight instinct.

She focuses on the counter and its marbled, soft sky-blue hue. It reminds her of the decorative soaps her grandmother used to display in a porcelain bowl next to the extra roll of toilet paper on the back of the toilet. And even though there were never any guests, Grandma took great care in decorating it.

The soaps were shaped like various seashells and smelled like the ocean, or what Rachel assumed the ocean smelled like since she had visited for the first time recently, despite it only being a day's drive from where she grew up. When she finally put her feet in the sand and took a breath, it was better than she could have imagined. It was both peaceful and wild. It had calmed her nerves as she watched her old cell phone sink, tossed as far as she could throw it into the deep blue, the roaring waves erasing her right before her eyes.

Grandma's bathroom seashell soaps were chosen for their color more than their shape. She'd thought they complimented the mauve wallpaper speckled with tiny white flowers. They didn't. Neither did the framed photos of Paris, a city Grandma talked about often but had never seen.

Also on the back of the toilet, next to the shells was a family of ceramic rabbits because who doesn't keep rabbits in the guest bathroom? The baby bunny was Rachel's favorite. It had been shattered and pieced back together with such care that the cracks were imperceivable unless you knew to look for them. Except for the large piece missing from the left ear, but Rachel felt that chip gave it character.

Rachel dips her chin to her chest, searching for the scent of Passion perfume she dabbed on her collar bones this morning. The flower and patchouli notes smell like a church basement on bingo night, but it reminds her of Grandma's hugs, of the only person who ever truly loved her. Misery rises up inside her and spills out in trails along her cheeks. Nostalgia is not helpful. It is a useless distraction. There is no returning home.

Rachel slaps the palms of her hands on the counter and clenches her jaw. Her palms sting. She focuses on the feeling, grounding herself. This is home now, and she knows she needs to focus on the present if she's going to survive. She can't make another mistake like today's lunch. The amount of effort it will take to avoid Bangs now is unfathomable. She'll just have to take it one day at a time, like always.

She grabs the chili container and pats down her jeans one last time with a fresh paper towel. She buries the paper towel in the bottom of the trash receptacle and returns to the mirror. Today, it's Rory's eyes that stare back. Tomorrow, who knows? That's the tricky part of running away from family; you can never truly escape them when you have shared features on your face.

Rachel gathers her curls at the nape of her neck and wraps them in a low ponytail with the hair tie from her wrist. She uses the remaining time of her lunch break to practice her breathing, eyes closed. She senses the lights flicker through her eyelids, but when she opens her eyes, she wonders if it was only her imagination.

Rachel returns to the office and shuffles to her desk. She stares at the new pile of work left for her while she was away. Her desk has become a dumping ground for projects the others don't want to do. She doesn't mind; it keeps her in their good graces and them out of her business. She feels an itch on her wrist where the hair tie was and looks down. A red indentation is left behind like an angry scar - the ache you only notice when all that remains is the ghost of the constraint.

CHAPTER 2

A person doesn't need a clock to know when it's 5:00 PM at the publishing company. The rush towards the elevators looks like an active shooter drill. Rachel slowly organizes the folders on her desk and then the pens and then the highlighters. She isn't a very organized person but uses this time to let the office clear out until she's alone with only the staff who won't leave for hours and won't look away from their computer screens to even notice her existence.

She gathers her belongings and bundles up for her return to the arctic. As she slips past Manager Row, a voice breaks the silence. "Stay warm. I like that yellow on you."

She pauses to give a tight smile and a half wave goodnight. Only Wears Navy looks up long enough to return the smile and then quickly returns to her monitor with laser focus. Rachel hurries to the elevators and berates herself for choosing such a bright hat. If someone so mono-chromatic noticed it out of her peripherals, it was a mistake.

Rachel takes an empty elevator to the lobby and feels her body fold in on itself as she pushes through the revolving doors. Downtown sparkles, the lights twinkling in the crisp air and reflecting off the frozen river. Rachel hasn't adjusted to the penetrating cold of Chicago, but the city still looks like magic at night. That impression dissipates as she descends the dark stairway to the train, holding her breath at the turn in the stairs where the stench of urine is strongest.

Rachel squeezes onto a packed Red Line. Her train car slowly empties as it travels north, and the bright lights fade into the darkness. Rachel exits at her stop and buries her hands into her coat pockets as she walks the length of the platform to the stairs. Once at ground level, the black sky is oppressive. It seeps down into every crack and corner, swallowing warmth and joy. The lights from storefronts and apartments blink dimly against the night, giving the illusion of being much farther away.

Rachel hurries to her building's entrance, which is nestled between a mini mart and a nail salon. Her numb fingers fumble with the key before finally unlocking the door and pushing into the warmth of the landing. She checks the mailbox marked Louise Danforth. It's empty except for a coupon flyer and a postcard for a newly opened bank, both addressed to "Current Resident." She trudges up the three flights of stairs and slips out of her boots, leaving them dirty and dripping on the welcome mat.

Inside the apartment, the radiator hisses and clangs in the dark. Rachel flips on the only overhead light and begins to shed layers onto a large, worn desk that also serves as a vanity, a dining room table, a dresser, and a catch-all. Rachel found it in an alley along with most of her other belongings. Over the last few weeks, she's furnished the small studio by rescuing a chair for the desk, an oval mirror, a framed movie poster for *Drop Dead Gorgeous*, a wobbly bookshelf with a box of Westerns, an end table with several water stains, a braided rug, and a leather armchair with sides that were clearly used as a scratching post by the previous owner's cat.

Rachel bought her twin mattress, bedding, and towels brand new because she couldn't risk bed bugs. The rest she found at thrift shops and charity stores. The local dollar store has been her go-to for cleaning supplies and toiletries. Rachel had never lived on such a small budget prior to moving, but at twenty-nine, she is seasoned in ways that make her a quick study. She's lucky that her company doesn't require direct deposit but unlucky that the check cashing service down the street charges $10 per check. She tries not to get hung up on the necessary expenses. *What can we control in this situation?* Dr. Smada would ask.

Walking to the bathroom doorway, Rachel tosses the yellow knit into the laundry basket for a wash before donating it. She moves over to the bed and sits on the edge, peeling her jeans off and replacing them with a pair of leggings. She pauses there for a moment and watches alternating blue and red lights flash past her two windows. The city noise used to bother her, but she's comforted by it now. The sirens, loud conversations, and honking make the city feel alive. It's always there with her, a witness to her life.

The studio apartment itself is a shithole. Rachel is in a constant battle with roaches, and she's become accustomed to sharing the shower with centipedes. The windows are drafty, and the walls are thin. But the rent is cheap, and the landlord let her move in right away without a background check or even a security deposit. When she asked if she could pay cash, he looked at her, standing in the middle of the room with only a backpack and duffel bag to her name, and said, "No pets."

Rachel has grown to love this shithole because it's her shithole. The entire apartment would have fit in her mother's bedroom, but she prefers these confining walls to that sprawling country farmhouse. The family home was cavernous and labyrinthine. It spread over three levels, four if you counted the attic, and every room was stuffed full of memories. There were Rory's cartons of baseball cards stacked against a bedroom wall and every magazine he'd ever purchased piled in columns by topic: sports, video games, health, or girls. In the family room, Regina's trophies were displayed along an entire wall, framing the small television set. Once that real estate ran out, they were placed on tables, chairs, and the floor. A gold star for cheerleading sat on the loveseat while a woman spiking a volleyball leaned against an ottoman, propped up so she had a clear view of the TV.

You could wander for hours without running into another human being, even when Regina and Samuel moved in with the children after Samuel lost all their savings on a bad investment. Even when they brought Rory home from the hospital and hired a 24-hour nurse. The plaster walls absorbed all sounds of happiness, muting little giggles and silencing words of encouragement. That house was claustrophobic but empty. If you didn't keep busy and make your own noise, you'd begin to fixate on the beep of the heart monitor or the whispered arguments that haunted the silence.

In contrast, this shithole is cramped like a too-tight hug. It smells like curry, ginger, and turmeric from the neighbors below and is filled with the sounds of the neighbors above: muffled conversations, footsteps over creaky wooden floors, watch parties for American Horror Story, and halfhearted sex. Rachel seems to be the only one in the building with a 9-5 job so she's never run into anyone on the stairs, but when she watches strangers at the closest laundromat, she wonders if any of them are her neighbors. She makes a game of creating elaborate backstories for all of them. The man in torn jeans is a foreign prince who tries to look normal so he can find true love. The woman with the twin toddlers that cling to her legs never wanted to be a mother, but someone left two babies in a box in the basement laundry of her building, and she couldn't just leave them there. That's why she goes to the laundromat now; she can't risk finding another child.

Rachel flops onto her back and stares at the water spot on the ceiling. It looks like a face if you stare long enough. She rolls onto her side and props her head on her hand. Her spider plant, Charlotte, sits on the small table that functions as a bedside table and an end table for the armchair. "Welp, Charlotte," she sighs, "I almost fucked up royally today."

The only response is the rumble of the train rushing past a mere half block away. Rachel would prefer to adopt a cat so that there could be an actual reply, even if it's just a meow. Even without her landlord's pet ban, she knows a cat is impractical. It wouldn't travel well if she had to flee the city without notice, and she doesn't know anyone to leave it with. She could never live with herself if she left this hypothetical cat behind, knowing it would slowly starve to death. She couldn't go through that again. She couldn't handle another Pellet situation.

Rachel tenses as her mind is involuntarily flooded with memories of Pellet: His cage with the squeaky wheel, his fat cheeks when he stuffed them full of sunflower seeds, how shriveled and stiff his body looked after leaving him in Regina's care for a week. *A week!* The grief and the anger well up in Rachel until her breath catches in her throat. She flexes her hands in and out of fists, the familiar tingle of rage spreading like electricity through her palms.

"I've got to get out of here," she says, pushing herself out of bed.

Charlotte watches as Rachel pulls a gray hoodie over her head and smooths loose curls back into her ponytail.

"I know it's the weekend, and I know it breaks my rule, but I also know I'm going to lose my mind if I stay here right now."

Rachel slips on a pair of high top sneakers. "If you disapprove, just say so."

Charlotte doesn't respond.

"Cool."

Rachel grabs a black beanie from a desk drawer and heads toward the door, but she stops midway. She walks back to the desk and sifts through piles of junk mail until she finds a small faux-leather notebook, the kind they give away at trade shows. She writes *from somewhere in western Nebraska* on a free line and then tosses it back under a pile of unopened credit card offers for someone named Stacy Chatham.

Halfway to Pale Gael's, Rachel wishes she'd taken the time to bundle up even though it's only a block. The wind claws at her earlobes. She tightens the hoodie against her face, but it barely helps. She reaches the corner and pushes into the small dive bar. The bar is dimly lit by strands of white lights along the ceiling where they'll stay until the end of winter. It's the perfect place to be left alone since most weeknights there's only one bartender, and you only get service if you go to the bar to order.

Normally, Rachel would grab a beer from the self-serve beer fridge, leave three dollars on the bar, and slide into her booth in the back corner. The crimson vinyl is torn and the table wobbles a bit, but it's directly across from a wood burning stove that smells like amber and smoked bourbon. Tonight, her booth is taken. All of the booths are full, there are two bartenders, and 90s bubblegum pop plays in the background.

She takes a seat at the end of the bar, leaving several empty seats between her and the next patron. One of the bartenders finishes drying a pint glass and makes her way over. "Hi there," she says through a smile.

"Hi," Rachel says. "Pretty busy tonight."

"That's because it's a Friday night, and you're normally here on Tuesdays with the regulars."

Rachel frowns. She's never paid attention to the staff since her only interaction is dropping a few bills for them on the bar top. "You recognize me?"

The woman laughs and tosses the damp bar towel over her shoulder. She pushes the sleeves of her black cotton shirt halfway up her forearms and presses her palms against the edge of the bar. A long strand of dark hair falls forward. "Of course, Tuesday. Are ya gonna grab a beer from the cooler or can I getcha somethin' else?"

Rachel feels herself flush at the immediate intimacy in this woman's clipped accent. She hates being a human barometer, her eggshell skin blooming with every new emotion. The bartender's skin is beautiful, like chai tea with just a splash of milk and faint freckles scattered across her cheeks like a dash of cinnamon. "Umm . . . I might need a second."

"Alright, I'll check back in a bit. I'm Julie so just holler if ya need me."

Julie straightens and moves down the bar to make another round of Manhattans for an older couple at the opposite end. Rachel stares at herself in the mirror between rows of alcohol and confirms that splotchy red patches have spread across her cheeks and down her neck like a rash. *What the fuck is wrong with me?* She takes her phone out of her pocket and sees that there are two new emails. She drops the phone onto the bar and cups her face in her hands. Some days are like drowning, and the others are the break between waves. Even in the breaks, the threat of impending doom is ever present.

"Ready, Tuesday?"

Rachel looks up from her hands and points at a bottle on the bottom shelf. "Can I get a gin martini?"

Julie raises an eyebrow. "That's a little stronger than your beers. Rough day?"

"Something like that."

"Want it dirty?"

"Sure."

Julie adds a scoop of ice to a shaker and darts about to grab the other ingredients, jumping to the side from time to time to avoid colliding with her coworker. Rachel knows nothing about martinis except that they're strong. She has no idea what makes it dirty, and she can't remember what gin tastes like. She suspects it's the disgusting pine needle one. There's a TV on the wall showing a singing competition on mute. The closed captioning appears to be a solid 15 seconds behind.

"Here ya go. One dirty martini. Forgot to ask if ya like bleu cheese so I brought ya some of the stuffed olives on the side."

Rachel looks at the skewer of olives in the shot glass next to the martini and smiles. "Thanks, Julie. This looks great."

She swirls the skewer in the drink. It's cloudier than the ones her grandmother used to drink. She takes a sip and tastes the salt of the brine followed closely by the bitter juniper. It burns as she swallows, but she hides a grimace and nods approvingly. Julie gives a thumbs up and rushes off. Rachel takes a deep breath and then lifts the glass to her lips again.

* * *

One drink takes the edge off and that's where a rational Rachel would have stopped, but she's tired of the constant calculations and vigilant vetting, so she has a second. She makes a quick trip to the bathroom and then polishes off a third. The world slows, and she allows herself to float along the surface. What would be the harm in making friends if she never shares anything personal or traceable? Surely it's ok to talk about innocuous things such as hobbies or likes and dislikes. It would certainly make it easier to keep track of the details if some of them were true.

"Whatcha think of Fridays?"

Rachel looks around and notices that the booths are still full, but the seats at the bar have cleared. Julie is collecting empties and wiping up rings of condensation. Rachel concentrates on acting normal. "I don't love the music."

Julie laughs and tosses a handful of bottles into the trash. The loud clanking causes Rachel to jump. "Tuesdays are probably the right day for ya then," Julie smiles. "Ya should stop sittin' all by yourself in the back, though. Grab your own beers if ya want but consider this your seat from now on. I won't bite."

Rachel's instincts fight to the surface of her consciousness, trying to sober her before she gets too comfortable and puts herself in danger. Seemingly in response, the alcohol spreads from deep within her core out to every crevice, a thick, warm blanket. She gives in to its weight and allows her skin to fluctuate between tingling and numb.

"Done with this?" Julie asks, holding up the empty martini glass.

Rachel nods, but she grabs the olive skewer before it's taken away. She slips an olive off with her teeth and chews it slowly. It tastes like nothing.

"Probably a good idea," Julie says. "Guessing that's the closest thing to food you've had all day?"

"Good guess," Rachel says, chewing.

"Yeah, the barely-in-the-room look gave it away. I've gotta ask ya somethin', though."

Rachel sweeps a palm-up hand across her body, the universal *go ahead* sign.

"Why ya drinkin' cheap liquor thatcha can barely stomach? And I know ya asked for gin, but your face says ya wish you hadn't. Every time ya take a drink, I wait to see if your body's gonna reject it. Are ya a masochist or somethin'?"

Rachel considers the question. She does hate gin, but how does she explain her urge to drink it anyway? She studies Julie, so put together, confident with dark eyes behind thick lashes and perfectly manicured nails. Rachel glances down at her own nails, chewed nervously short. "I guess I'm just atoning for my sins."

"Oh, so this is some sort of self-flagellation then. Ya *are* a masochist."

"Not exactly," Rachel slurs. "I don't *enjoy* the pain, but it's necessary. Maybe if I punish myself, the universe won't look for revenge. Maybe karma will skip over me."

"Well, has the universe come for ya yet? Maybe you're in the clear," Julie says with a shrug.

Rachel shakes her head vigorously. "You have no idea the things I've done. There's no way I'm ok yet. I deserve whatever happens to me, but I guess I'm trying to keep a bit of control over what those bad things are."

Julie leans across the bar, close enough that Rachel can smell the oil she uses in her hair to make it so shiny. "I don't think that's how karma works. Maybe ya should stop focusin' on punishin' yourself and just be a good person. Put some good out there to counteract the bad."

"I'd have to discover the cure for cancer to break even."

"Oh, come on, it can't have been that bad," Julie says, laughing lightly.

Rachel smiles, playing into the joke, but nothing about her situation is funny. She wants to be a good person and improve the community around her, but she doesn't want her atonement to seem performative. And she can't exactly risk being out in the community doing good deeds that could be photographed and posted for the world to see, not while her life is still in danger.

Rachel fumbles through her purse for her wallet and realizes it's not there. She looks around her on the floor, sure that it must have fallen, but then she remembers that she never took it out of her coat pocket. "Shit, I forgot my wallet in my apartment. Can I go grab it real quick so I can pay you? I promise it won't take long."

"Oh, I know ya must live nearby," Julie says. "There's no way ya went outside in a sweatshirt and leggings unless you're not far from home."

Rachel tries to come up with an excuse, but her thoughts feel like thick sludge. She doesn't want this woman to know that she only lives a block away. Maybe she could say someone dropped her off? Before she can actually speak, Julie jumps back in "I know you're good for it. I'll see ya on Tuesday, neighbor."

She winks at Rachel and walks to the other end of the bar. Rachel lowers herself onto unsteady legs and grabs her phone from the bar top. Now there are five unread emails. She ducks outside into the cold and rushes back to her apartment. She realizes too late that she should have walked in the opposite direction and gone around the block just in case she's being watched, but it's so cold and all of a sudden, she's certain that she's going to vomit.

She makes it upstairs to the bathroom before throwing up in the sink. There's not much in her stomach to throw up, but her body doesn't care. The cramps roll their way up her body, wringing every bit of liquid out of her. They finally subside, but she hovers over the sink, breathing heavily and wiping the tears away from her eyes. She washes her hands and then grabs her contact case out of the medicine cabinet. She removes the contacts, watching her eyes turn from brown to blue. *My roots are starting to show,* she thinks before crawling into bed and passing out.

CHAPTER 3

"Let's sing a song," Grandma says, stringing random thoughts together along a wandering melody. She plunges her hands into the soapy dish water, grabs a plate, rinses it, and gives it to Rachel to dry. Rachel smiles, wanting to join in on the song but never knowing what the words will be. She contributes by moving her head back and forth as she dries each dish that's handed to her.

The singing shifts to humming. Grandma dries her hands and checks on the pie in the oven. She picks up a bunch of freshly cut flowers from the kitchen table and places them in a vase of water. She sits at the table and thumbs through a gardening magazine. All the while, she hums. Rachel sits across from her and waits to be acknowledged. Did Grandma forget she was here? The humming grows louder and louder. Her eyes fixate on Rachel. Her mouth stretches wide into the shape of a howl, but the only sound that comes out is the deafening hum.

* * *

Rachel shoots upright in bed and blinks against the bright morning light. Next to her pillow, her phone buzzes loudly with a call, likely a scam. She hits decline and sinks back into bed. Her head is cracking into a million pieces, and she can tell from the dry burn of her eyes that they're bloodshot. Now is not the time for a dead grandmother to show up.

Slowly rolling out of bed, Rachel stumbles to the kitchen and makes a pot of coffee. She stands at the windows with a hot mug between her hands and watches the people below. The sun is finally out today, and there's a slight break from the freezing temperatures with an expected high of 37 degrees. For February in Chicago, that might as well be beach weather. People are out in droves, walking their dogs and meeting friends for boozy brunch. Rachel swallows a gag at the thought of alcohol.

Through the pounding headache, she tries to remember exactly what she said last night. From what she can recall, it was rambling and embarrassing but safe. She probably sounded like she should be medicated, but she doesn't remember giving away anything that would reveal her true identity. Hell, she didn't even give a name, real or fake.

Rachel rinses out her mug and fills it with water from the tap. She shakes two Advil out of a bottle from the counter and tosses them back with a sip from the mug. The rest of the water is given to Charlotte. Rachel stretches, hands on her lower back where a knot has formed from sitting on a bar stool for hours. She notices the jut of her hip bones protruding more than they did last month. She remembers Regina's in the end, looking like the leather, wingback chair that sat in the living room, buried under trophies. Regina, who as a child, let the water run while she brushed her teeth because Rachel told her it was bad for the environment. No one was going to tell her what to do.

Rachel decides it's too nice of a day to stay inside. It's worth the risk to see the sunshine before it disappears for several more weeks. She pulls her hair into a messy bun and climbs into the shower. She lets the hot water run down her shoulders and back, turning her skin cardinal red. She stays in the shower until the steam makes it difficult to breathe and the mirror is so fogged over that condensation runs down like tears.

She towels off and pumps a handful of lotion from a large store brand bottle. Her dry skin absorbs it immediately. She reapplies over and over again until her skin feels greasy. Her jeans are still draped over the desk chair from the night before. She puts them on and grabs a sweater from a pile. After a quick sniff, she tugs it over her head and rubs a stick of deodorant under her arms. She puts on a pair of socks and redoes her bun, then she returns to the bathroom to put in her contacts. They sting against her tired eyes.

Dried, dressed, and disguised, Rachel walks over to the small entry closet that's deeper than it is wide. She squats down in front of a fireproof safe in the back corner that was clearly too heavy for the last tenants to bother taking with them. She couldn't believe her luck when she saw it sitting in the shadows, open with a slip of paper inside containing the combination. She twists the combination and opens it, taking a fifty-dollar bill from inside. She closes the safe and walks to the desk to find an envelope. She slides the money inside, licks it, seals it, and grabs a pen to scrawl *Julie* on the front. For a moment she reconsiders, but then she shoves the envelope into her pocket, scolding herself for being soft.

Rachel slides into her coat, grabs a small purse filled only with essentials, and slings it over her bundled body. She slips out the front door and laces winter boots up her ankles. She walks downstairs, pulling on her gloves as she goes. Fumbling to drop a large pair of sunglasses over her ears and onto her nose with her bulky fingers, Rachel steps out to the sunny sidewalk. It's immediately clear that while it's a beautiful day, free from clouds and wind, the terrain is still marked with the spoils of winter. The grassy parkways between the sidewalks and the streets have turned to mud. There are stretches of half melted snow peppered with cigarette butts, litter, and dog piss. The sun only exposes the ugliness more effectively.

Rachel walks to the end of the block and stops outside Pale Gael's. She checks her phone. 10:57 AM and two more unread emails. She puts her phone back in her purse and waits for the bar to open. A couple walks by, aggressively arguing about whether gluten intolerance is a real thing. Both seem to be on the losing end.

"Come on in," a man says, holding the door to the bar open for her.

Rachel walks in but stops just inside. "Here," she says, pulling the envelope from her pocket and thrusting it into his free hand. "Can you tell Julie this is the money I owe her for last night, plus tip?"

She turns and walks out the door before he has a chance to respond. Normally, she would agonize over whether it was rude to shove money at a stranger like that, but she knows she'll never see him again. There's no way she can go back there.

* * *

Three miles into her aimless walk, Rachel begins to feel the strain in her knees and briefly stops at an unfamiliar donut shop to buy a carb with the calories required to keep her from collapsing. She eats her pistachio old-fashioned slowly, studying the interiors of boutiques, pet shops, art studios, and fitness clubs from behind the safety of tempered glass storefronts. People flow past her, focused on their conversations with others or their phones if they're alone. Rachel moves with the flow of traffic, enjoying her anonymity. She can go entire days without making eye contact with another human.

Rachel pauses in front of a store, a children's boutique. There are tiny clothes on small mannequins in the window. Behind them, Rachel can see a table covered in toys. Books line a row of shelves along a wall opposite the checkout area. She puts the last bite of her donut in her mouth and examines the selection of toys. She wonders which ones Regina's kids would pick out if they were here on a visit, if things were different.

She never really got to know the kids well enough to learn their interests. She couldn't risk getting too close to anyone, even family. The house was a time bomb set to destroy them all, and Rachel knows she only escaped because she didn't let feelings get in the way. It allowed her to light the fuse and walk away. She swallows, wondering if she's even capable of feelings anymore, of anything beyond fear and residual anger.

At the corner, Rachel waits for the signal to change, watching the seconds count down across the adjacent crosswalk. The neighborhood is unfamiliar, but she can tell from the aesthetics that it's well beyond her price range. A woman in head-to-toe Chanel stops next to her, maintaining a phone conversation at full volume. "I know it's just preschool, but it's the foundation for the rest of her education. She's already learning French, Spanish, *and* Mandarin. Anyway, I'm going to have the nanny pick her up from ballet because it's supposed to snow this afternoon, and I just got a blowout. Check your schedule and let me know if you're free for facials tomorrow."

In Rachel's former life, a blowout meant you were stranded on the side of the road, but she's learned that here it means paying someone to wash and blow dry your hair. Facials are an attempt for people with disposable income to cling to their youth, despite the description she'd been given by gleeful college boys. The light changes and Rachel rushes across the intersection, desperate to put more distance between herself and that woman. She's disgusted by vulgar displays of new money, and then she's repulsed by herself for having thought the phrase *new money*, as if her mother's money was ever her money.

The street leads toward a park with a view of the lake and the clouds rolling in, dark and heavy with precipitation. Rachel wishes she could check the forecast throughout the day, but that would mean using apps with location sharing. She heads west, hoping to find a train line before the snow starts. After several blocks, she finds the elevated tracks and follows them to a stop. She taps her Ventra card at the turnstile and enters, but then she pauses at the foot of the stairs. Judging by the vanishing sunlight, she guesses she has little time to get home before the snowflakes appear, but she's pulled in the opposite direction. These days make for perfect museum days and it's been weeks since she's seen Beatrix. Rachel climbs the stairs leading to the Brown Line that will take her to the Loop.

At Adams & Wabash, Rachel exits the train and walks along the wooden platform, weaving around rusty metal beams to access the exit. She hurries down the stairs to the sidewalk and makes her way toward the oxidized bronze lions, their pale green a pop of color against an increasingly dreary background. As she clears the corner of a granite high rise, an older man wrapped in a thin blanket steps out from behind the building and stops directly in front of her.

"'Scuse me ma'am, but would ya happen to have a dollar or two so I can get somethin' to eat?"

Rachel freezes, unaccustomed to being so seen. She fixates on the deep crevices around his eyes and the scabs covering the exposed parts of his face. She feels a weight settle over her chest and struggles to pull air in. If she could just bring herself to move, she could grab a couple loose dollars out of her purse and he'd move on, but she's rooted in place. A cold tear spills out of her left eye and runs down her cheek.

"O-oh," the man stutters, "sorry to bother ya."

He moves past her, leaving behind the distinct smell of rot. Rachel wipes away the wetness on her cheek, mortified at her behavior. She leans against the edge of the building and draws in a long, shuddering breath. It comes out as a soft whimper. "Jesus Christ, get it together," she mutters, pushing off the building and propelling herself toward the crosswalk.

As she reaches the other side, she sees big, wet flakes beginning to fall but can't bring herself to move any faster. Rachel stomps up the stairs to the entrance of the Art Institute, letting each foot connect fully with each step. She bypasses the ticket line and walks up to a smiling docent, pulling her membership card out of her purse and handing it over to be scanned. It was the one splurge she allowed herself because it was vital. She approaches the Grand Staircase and lets her gaze sweep the panorama of opulence. Walking up the enormous marble stairs, hand lightly grazing the wooden banister, she feels like royalty. She walks straight to Gallery 223 in the European Art Before 1900 section of the museum.

Beata Beatrix glows, surrounded by a thick golden frame that seems to cast a halo of light around her red hair. Her eyes are closed as she peacefully accepts her death. On the left, the embodiment of love shines bright, while on the right, grief lurks in the shadows. Rachel is obsessed with the details: the poisonous poppy in Beatrix's lap, the white veil in the predella, the serene look on her face as she takes her last breath. *What can we control?*

Rachel could have chosen any city when she disappeared. She chose this city because of this museum and this painting. When her life was fully unraveling, she came across Beatrix in a book of art gifted to her by her grandmother. She recognized herself in Beatrix and took it as a sign. Rachel knew she needed to go wherever this painting was. She read the caption beneath the photo and set course immediately.

Rachel sits on a nearby bench, keeping the painting within view. She unlocks her phone and opens her email, clicking the oldest message.

Yesterday: *I know what you did. You can't hide forever.*

She moves on to the next one.

Yesterday: *How dare you! How could a person do that?*

And the next one.

Yesterday: *You think I'm bad but you're a monster.*

Rachel takes a shaky breath and skips to the most recent email.

2:44 PM: *You were a mistake.*

Rachel puts her phone next to her on the bench. She knows she'll have to read the other messages later, as painful as it is. These emails and their fury are an indication that her mother has no clue where she is. They're also clues to her mother's mental state and just how believable her mother's theories might sound if she went to the authorities. Rachel has been counting on the fact that her mother doesn't trust authority figures, especially ones that carry guns. As the anger in the emails builds, Rachel becomes less sure that she can continue to be so naive. But to think about what could happen, just how wrong it could all go, is too much agony to shoulder on her own.

She hears Dr. Smada's voice in her head again. *What can we control?* Every move. She can control everything she does moving forward and hope it's enough.

* * *

Rachel shivers inside a Michigan Ave. bus shelter, watching the snow fall through the glass. A couple huddles together on the other side, leaning against an ad for perfume. The 151 approaches, which will take an hour longer than any of the express buses, but Rachel can no longer tolerate the freezing cement beneath her feet.

She climbs aboard, taps her card against the reader, and heads to the back, choosing a seat in the far back corner, directly over one of the heaters. Her damp hair lays flat against her head, sending cold shivers down her neck. She pulls her coat tighter and stares at the big snowflakes outside the window. They flutter in the air until they smash against the glass, melting into each other to form watery veins.

Even though the bus is sloth-like in comparison to the train, Rachel prefers it. She enjoys the predictability of the computerized voice announcing each upcoming intersection, the sharp ding every time a stop is requested. She looks around her at the strangers scattered throughout the bus. Everyone studies their phones, oblivious to their surroundings, and Rachel feels herself start to relax. The anonymity allows for boredom, a respite from the anxiety.

The bus approaches a family, two men and two small girls. It stops and kneels to make the step up easier for the little ones. As it tilts lower, it emits a loud beeping sound, a reminder of the merits of the train. The beeping seems to grow in volume, taunting, filling Rachel with a familiar fury. The family steps on and the girls rush to the accordion-style middle section of the bus. One of the fathers lifts them up one by one onto the side-facing seats, stumbling as the floor rotates. The other father hands the girls their American Girl dolls before taking a seat in the row directly behind them, next to his partner. They sit together, holding hands and reviewing photos from the day.

Rachel's anger shifts to jealousy. The bus sways from stop to stop, in and out of traffic. The accordion twists, shifting the two giggling girls to face Rachel. They carry on a conversation between their dolls. The bus twists again and they're removed from view momentarily. Rachel leans against the frigid window, alone.

Storefronts blur behind the wet windows. The bus pauses at a red light and a bar on the corner catches Rachel's eye. She sits up straighter. It looks similar to Pale Gael's, dark and warm and Irish. Her chest tightens. She wonders if Julie will be working tonight. If visiting Beatrix is confession, speaking with Julie is an act of contrition. Rachel wants to chase that feeling, to wake up unburdened every morning. She's never been religious, but there was something almost spiritual about meeting Julie. She feels lighter. Redeemed.

The bus jerks forward and Rachel shifts in her seat. She looks away from the window, ignoring the bar as it glides past, the *look at me, look at me,* like a magnet pulling her toward the forbidden. She can't go back. She can't trust herself around someone who makes her want to be vulnerable. It isn't safe.

The fathers lift the girls down from their seats and guide them toward the back doors. They stand by the exit, the four of them balancing against each other, leaning on one another for support. The doors open and they're gone. Rachel watches them as the bus passes, letting the reality of her loneliness sink in. She lets a few tears spill over, silent so as not to draw attention. This new life will be monotonous and predictable. Every day will be the same, trapped in a self-created *Groundhog Day*, but if she sticks to the plan, she might come out of it alive.

Rachel feels a buzz against her thigh. She takes her phone out of her coat pocket and opens the newest email, bracing herself.

4:41 PM: *When I find you, you're dead*

CHAPTER 4

April's arrival brings a week of rain showers. Rachel hates rain but has come to view it as a renewing requirement after winter. Daily storms flood the streets, followed by loud blue street sweepers that push the excess water and trash into the sewers. Between showers, birds chirp in the trees and the city slowly peels back its layers to reveal something new. It feels like a fresh start.

Rachel eats a turkey sandwich in her cubicle and pretends that online shopping is the reason she can't peel herself away from her desk to eat lunch with her coworkers. Every time she hears movement behind her, she scrolls down the page, pausing occasionally to examine a pair of shorts or a strappy tank top. After the incident with Bangs, she'd managed to avoid her for an entire week and then, just in time, Bangs' husband cheated on her with a Pilates instructor. Or maybe it was yoga. Rachel had to piece together the story from bits of gossip whispered by others as they passed her cubicle.

Regardless of what happened, Bangs has been too busy crying or leaving to meet with her attorney to even notice Rachel. In fact, Rachel has mostly managed to stay under everyone's radar for months and has only added one new character trait to her notebook: deathly allergic to shellfish. It provided her with a free pass from attending the company's annual Year In Review party at Shaw's Crab House, and it was an easy lie to stick to since she's not the kind of person to bring fish into an office space.

Other office drama has provided Rachel with much needed camouflage. One of the designers with a bald head was fired after he had a relationship with one of the college interns. An editor, whose ample cleavage is always stuffed tightly into a small top, was diagnosed with some sort of cancer. Someone's daughter is pregnant at fifteen, and an admin quit unexpectedly, leaving behind weeks of meeting requests and travel bookings that she had completely ignored. The office has been a whirlwind of gossip, which allows Rachel to fade into the background.

It has also been months since her mother has emailed. Up until the very end of March, there were multiple messages sent every day, constant reminders that the family was ruined because of Rachel. As if Rachel could ever forget. The threats became increasingly hostile but also more disjointed. They oscillated between descriptive vitriol and incoherent ranting before disappearing entirely. Rachel concluded that her mother had finally lost her mind entirely or had given up on finding her. Either way, Rachel finally started to feel safe. Or maybe not *safe*, exactly. There were moments in every day when an uneasiness would descend upon her, but the full-on panic had mostly subsided. The anxiety that once felt like a second skin now feels more like a shadow, trailing behind her unseen.

Rachel gets to the end of the sandwich and tosses the last bit of crust in the trash. She closes the browser tab that displays summer's latest trends and returns to her stack of folders. She still can't believe that so much is done on paper at this company. She knows it could be completely digital, but some of the department heads have been around for a long time and prefer to see it "as it will appear on the page." Apparently no one has told them about e-books. Or audiobooks.

On Wednesdays the folders contain epigraphs. Rachel reviews them to ensure they're attributed to the right source and that the source isn't someone who's problematic. She also researches the quote in its original context. She's discovered that an alarming number of quotes actually detract from the point the author is trying to make with their writing.

"Happy Hump Day, Louise."

Rachel looks up and forces a smile at Plum Lips.

"Good catch on that Voltaire quote. Who knew it was actually his biographer?!"

Now Rachel's smile is genuine. She'd been proud of that one. It would have been a bad look for a feminist author to take another woman's words and attribute them to the better known man. "Thanks," Rachel says. "Just doing my job."

"Well, keep up the good work. And, Louise, get some sleep. You look terrible."

She gives the top of the cubicle wall her idiosyncratic tap and walks away. She's not wrong. As Rachel's stress levels have decreased during the day, her nightmares have increased exponentially. She dreams of backstabbing and betrayal. Sometimes she's on the run, but even if she drives through the night, she can't put enough distance between herself and whoever is after her. She moves through the day in a fog, maybe too tired from the nightmares to bother with anxiety. It's a wonder she's been able to keep up with her work.

Turning back to the page in front of her, Rachel reads an epigraph three times and still can't make sense of it. The words twist and jumble. Halfway through a sentence, it begins to dissolve before she can finish it. She folds her arms on her desk and buries her face in them. The darkness is a sedative. She allows herself a few deep breaths in the quiet, the world muffled through the barrier of her biceps. Then, slowly, she lifts her head and waits for her eyes to adjust to the brightness of her monitor. She types the entire quote into Google, letting the internet do most of her job for her.

Time ticks away slowly. Rachel looks back and forth between the large clock on the wall and the time displayed on her computer, never trusting just one source. Rachel works through the folders, but toward the bottom of the stack, she finally pries her gaze away from her monitor for a moment. She rubs her eyes, but the exhaustion is becoming too strong to fight. She needs a break. Rachel pushes out of her chair and grabs her purse, making her way out of the office. She steps into an empty elevator and leans against the back of it, waiting for the familiar ding. When the doors open on the vacant floor, a woman in a tailored skirt and blazer greets Rachel. "Hi there? Are you with ARC Consulting?"

Rachel leaps toward the control panel. "Sorry, wrong floor." She pushes the button for the lobby repeatedly until the doors close and the elevator car begins to move. The construction must be complete, which means she's lost her private bathroom. Rachel stares at her distorted reflection in the mirrored doors. She looks exactly how she feels, blurry around the edges.

The doors open in the lobby, and Rachel makes her way toward the revolving doors. She pushes outside and waits for a break in the traffic before jaywalking across the street to a coffee chain. The smell of coffee grounds and pastries greets her with a warm embrace. The line is short, but she's not the only professional in need of an afternoon pick-me-up.

When it's her turn to order, she asks for a double dirty chai, which always makes her feel like the main character of a cheesy chick flick. The barista writes her order on a cup and hands it to his coworker. He types the order into the register and looks up. "That'll be $5.67. Two shots at 3:30 PM, huh? Must be a rough day."

Rachel responds with heavy eyes and a small smile; she doesn't want to encourage conversation. She hands over cash and drops the change into the tip jar, shuffling down to the end of the bar. The sound of the espresso machine is soothing. She closes her eyes for just a second.

"Here you go!" The other barista nods at Rachel and slides the cup toward her. A perk to coming at off times is that you don't have to give them a name for the cup. Rachel heads back to the office, stealing sips as she goes. The warmth spreads through her chest, bringing her back from the brink.

She returns to her assigned epigraphs, trying to read over the loud thump of her caffeine-fueled heartbeat. In between edits, she looks up therapy practices close enough to work that she could go over her lunch hour. It's an expense she can barely afford, but she also can't afford to be so exhausted that she makes another Nebraska mistake. She has to find a fix for these sleepless nights. Luckily, there's an office one building over that has a whole team of therapists, each with their own specialties: addiction, depression, family conflict, grief, and trauma. Rachel settles on an older woman with short gray hair and eyeglasses with a vintage shape, the frames a brilliant red. Her profile says she helps clients explore past experiences in a safe space that allows them to rewrite their own narratives. *If only.* Rachel adds the therapist's contact information to her phone and returns to her work.

* * *

At five o'clock, Rachel locks her computer and gathers her things. She no longer waits for the office to clear. No one notices her, and the few staff members that might think to say goodnight if they saw her leaving don't spot her among the crowd. She rides a cramped elevator to the lobby and walks outside with her jacket in hand. The building's thermostat has been unpredictable, confused by the spring weather that can feel pleasant, sweltering, and chilly all in the same day, sometimes in the same moment. Today the air in the office was stiff and stagnant. Outside the revolving doors, Rachel allows the brisk breeze to sweep the thin layer of sweat off her skin and raise goosebumps on her arms before she slides into her thin fleece.

The commute home is especially noisy. A teenager blasts music from his phone, and a group of college students complain about midterms. Two women speaking in thick Russian accents shout a conversation across the aisle from each other. When she finally closes the apartment door behind her, Rachel stands motionless, preserving the moment of relative quiet for as long as possible.

Rachel drops her purse on the floor and sheds her jacket. She takes a half empty glass of water from the desk and walks over to Charlotte, slowly pouring it into her planter. She then grabs a crumpled tissue from the bedside table and wets it with the remaining moisture inside the glass. As she lovingly wipes the dust from Charlotte's leaves, she tells her about her day.

Somewhere in the building, a door slams and she hears laughter. Rachel looks up at the ceiling where she can hear more laughter. She turns back to Charlotte. "So, by 4:30 I felt like my heart was going to explode, but at least I didn't fall asleep at my desk, right?"

Charlotte responds by absorbing the excess water into her soil. Rachel is suddenly very aware of the burden in the silence, and the intensity of her loneliness. She reaches for her phone.

"Center for Growth and Healing, this is Donna. How can I help you today?"

"Um, yes, hi. I'd like to set up a time to speak to a therapist. Preferably someone who's available around the lunch hour."

"We can definitely help with that. If you feel comfortable, can you tell me if there's a specific reason you're reaching out today or if you have a particular goal in mind? We want to make sure we pair you with the right person for your needs."

Rachel sits on her bed and looks around the sparsely furnished room. "Well, I'm new to the city and I don't really know anyone. I mean, I don't have anyone to talk to about-" she hesitates. "See, I left a pretty messed up family situation and I guess it would just be nice to talk to someone about that. It's been causing me a lot of anxiety and . . . is there any chance Mary Faucett is taking new clients?"

"Let me take a look," Donna says.

Rachel hears typing in the background.

"Why yes, and she has a 1:00 PM on Thursdays opening up next week. Would that work?"

Rachel lets the breath she's been holding out. "Yes, that would be perfect."

"Great. Let me just get some basic information from you so we can get you on Mary's calendar. We'll start with your name and date of birth."

All of the air leaves the room. Of course they'll need her real name, the name on her insurance card and driver's license. They'll make copies. Does it go into some sort of database? Rachel can hear Donna's voice asking if she's still there, but it sounds distant, tinny. She looks down and sees that her phone has fallen to the floor. She slowly brings her hand down from beside her ear and stretches down to end the call.

So that's it then. She will never feel safe enough to get real help or have a meaningful conversation with an actual human being. Her guilt will continue to prompt nightmares, slowly whittling away at her sanity until she becomes her mother. Maybe the universe has been enacting its revenge all along.

Rachel walks to the kitchen and fills the glass with water. She twists off the cap of a Tylenol PM bottle and pulls two capsules from it. She pushes one into her mouth and washes it down with a gulp of water, then repeats with the second. Climbing into bed, she pulls the covers over her head to block out the light that finds its way into the apartment between the slats of cheap vinyl blinds. The noise on the street only amplifies the quiet inside. It intensifies and sharpens until the only sound Rachel hears is the ringing in her ears. And then, nothing.

* * *

Grandma hums a tune that sounds like a hybrid of all her favorite songs. She sits in her favorite crushed velvet chair and knits - knit knit knit purl. Her hands are delicate with paper thin skin that reveals a roadmap of veins beneath. Her fingers, twisted with arthritis, move the needles at a steady pace - knit knit knit knit knit knit. It looks painful, but she hums when she's happy, never when she's sad. She's always humming.

Rachel sits at her feet, mesmerized. "I promise to always take care of you, Grandma."

"Oh, Rach, you don't need to worry about me. Go live your life. Use that fancy degree."

The humming resumes - knit knit knit knit knit knit knit knit knit knit purl.

"Grandma, Mom's getting worse. She can't take care of you in this big house alone."

Humming - knit knit knit knit knit knit knit knit.

"I'll be just fine, sweetie. But you're right about your mother. You kids need to stick together and look after her when I'm gone."

"It's just me, though. Rory is engaged. Regina and Samuel just had another baby. They're moving on with their lives. I can't leave you."

"Just worry about your mother."

Humming - knit knit knit knit knit knit knit knit purl.

"She's never liked me."

Grandma stops humming and looks up from her knitting. "Oh Rach, your mother loves you. I'm the one who's never liked you."

* * *

Rachel wakes up disoriented. She sits up and blinks to moisten the contacts that are uncomfortable against her dry eyes. She's at the foot of the bed. *How long was I asleep?* Reaching over the edge of the mattress, she fumbles on the floor for her phone. 8:12 PM. She doesn't remember falling asleep and would have guessed that no more than five minutes had passed. Her arm is damp. She runs a finger across her cheek and finds it's wet with tears. The dreams have become so vivid, actual memories interwoven with imagined horror.

She pulls her sweater up over her nose and inhales deeply, hunting for the perfume that will remind her she was loved. The scent has dissipated and her grandmother's absence fills the room. Rachel is desperate for someone to talk to. Just one person. Someone who won't ask for proof of identity.

She wipes her face dry on her sleeve and pulls her hair half up. She walks to the desk and adds another layer of concealer under her eyes. It does little to hide the purple bags, two sad, matching bruises. She adds another layer and some powder to set it, then swipes a bit of pink gloss over her lips to add a distraction.

Rachel looks at herself in the mirror. *This is a dumb idea. This is a dumb idea. This is a dumb idea.* She practices a smile and remembers that she just woke up from a nap, stepping into the bathroom to gargle some mouthwash, practicing the smile again. She locks up and jogs down the stairs to the damp air of the street.

This is so dumb. This is so dumb. She walks down the block until the wooden sign for Pale Gael's is hovering above her head. Neon beer signs buzz behind the glass, beckoning Rachel inside, but she can't. Not yet. She steps back and leans against the brick of the building next door. *What are you doing?*

A man in scrubs crosses the intersection and steps through the door to the bar, disappearing from sight. Rachel urges herself to follow him, to catch the door before it swings closed, but her feet are stuck. Finally, she pushes away from the wall and walks past the bar, circling the block, working out the nervous energy. After three laps, she pauses in front of the bar. It's starting to rain and she shivers without her jacket.

This is a mistake. Go home. Just turn around. Rachel takes a step closer, silencing the inner monologue. She reaches for the door slowly, half expecting a response from that voice in her head. There's silence. She opens the door and steps through the doorway. Turns out there's something more embarrassing than talking to a plant, and that's talking to no one.

CHAPTER 5

The bar is warm, dry, and half empty. It's darker than it was last time; the strands of lights have been taken down from the ceiling and replaced with strands of soccer banners, each one marked with the logo of a national beer brand. The familiar weekday playlist of yacht rock emits from hidden speakers. Rachel walks straight to the beer cooler and pulls out a can of PBR.

"Tuesday!"

Rachel pivots and sees the bartender from the fateful martini night. It takes her a second to remember her name. Julie is waving her over to the bar stool at the end of the bar. Her hair is pulled back tonight and she's wearing a black tank top. There's a tattoo that stretches from her right shoulder to her elbow, a cascade of colorful flowers. Rachel walks to where she's being directed and climbs up onto the stool. A bus driver in his CTA uniform sits at the other end, relaxing at the end of a long shift.

"Ya know it's Wednesday, right?" Julie asks, taking the can from Rachel and pouring it into a chilled glass. "I don't normally work on Wednesdays, but I'm coverin' a shift. Is that why I haven't seen ya around? Ya switch to Wednesdays?"

Rachel takes a long drink from the glass and wipes her mouth with the back of her hand. "I haven't been at all for a while. Needed to take a break from drinking."

"Oh, thank god! I thought I scared ya away!"

Julie is leaning against the bar on folded arms, her breasts resting on top, threatening to spill out of the tight, low-cut top. Her mouth curls slightly into the beginning of a smile. She smells like rose water. Rachel looks away. "No, I uh . . . just needed a break. It had nothing to do with you."

Julie's lips pull back and reveal perfect, brilliantly white teeth. "That's a relief. Ya know we have pop, too, right? I can even make ya one of my world famous waters. The secret is I add a lemon wedge."

She gives a quick wink and Rachel feels her face flush. She knows this is just a bartender trick to get more tips, but it feels good to have someone recognize her and miss her when she's not around. For months she felt like she'd been listening to that old brag of her heart, except instead of Sylvia Plath's *I am I am I am*, it's been *Just blend Just blend Just blend*.

"So, Tuesday . . . or is it Wednesday now? Ugh, don't make me call ya Wednesday because all I'll be able to think 'bout is *The Addams Family*."

Rachel lets out a loud laugh and the sound nearly startles her. "Tuesdays generally work better for me."

"Or . . . " Julie leans closer, "ya could tell me your *actual* name."

Rachel fumbles for her glass and takes a drink. She holds the beer in her mouth, struggling to swallow. The glass feels slippery in her hand. The silence stretches out and Julie's brow furrows. "It's uh . . . Louise."

Julie grins. "Oh, I get your hesitation now. That's an old lady name."

"I guess it is."

Julie tilts her head. "It doesn't suit ya. No offense."

"None taken. I should thank you actually . . . I've always hated my name."

Rachel remembers her shaky hand the first time she wrote it. She still feels uneasy every time someone says her mother's name and queasy when she has to respond to it, but it's the only thing that makes sense. If her mother were attempting to track her down, the last thing she'd do is search for her own name.

"Do ya ever go by Lucy?" Julie asks, filling a small glass from one of the taps.

"No. Honestly, is that better than Louise?"

"Yes?" Julie lifts her eyebrows and scrunches her face. "Ok, maybe not. How 'bout just Lu?"

Rachel repeats it in her head. It's so abbreviated that it barely sounds like her mother at all. She smiles.

"Good, it's settled," Julie says, clinking her glass against Rachel's. "To Lu."

She grins and takes a drink. Rachel picks up her beer and finishes the rest of it. When she puts the empty glass down and looks up, Julie's eyes are fixated on her. Rachel holds her gaze until her face becomes unbearably warm and she pretends to feign interest in a police drama playing out silently on the TV. After a few seconds, it goes to commercial and she's forced to shift her focus back to Julie, who is still studying her face.

"Gonna make it there, Lu?"

"What do you mean?"

"You look like ya could nod off right here at the bar."

"Oh, that," Rachel says, turning the empty glass between her hands. "I haven't been sleeping well. I thought I was hiding it a little better than I am, apparently."

Julie returns to leaning across the bar. "You're tryin' too hard. You've got so much concealer on that you've created this reverse raccoon look. At some point, isn't it better to just let yourself look tired?"

It should sound like a barb, but it comes out of Julie's mouth soft and suggestive. Her eyes sparkle and Rachel feels equal parts nervous and elated. Rachel isn't sure how to react so she lets herself smile. It feels natural and easy. Julie slips the empty glass out of her hand. "Wanna talk 'bout it?"

The bus driver at the end of the bar lifts an empty bottle. "Excuse me, Miss, can I settle my tab now?"

Julie walks away and Rachel contemplates her question. Rachel came to the bar to talk. The emails have stopped and she has finally settled into a routine that feels predictable. And yet, the unknown is a giant spider climbing up her spine; one wrong move and it will sink its poisonous fangs into her neck.

"Sorry 'bout that," Julie says, returning. "I'm just sayin' that I'm here if ya need to talk to someone. I don't even charge."

Rachel picks up her glass and tips it toward Julie who waits to hear what she wants to drink. "I'll have whatever you're having."

Julie refills her own glass and then fills Rachel's with the same amber liquid. They cheers and sip in silence. There's an effortlessness to this interaction that surprises Rachel. She's never had a close friend and yet this woman, by all means a stranger, feels familiar in a way she hasn't experienced since she and Regina were children, before Regina abandoned her.

"I'm not sure where I'd even start," Rachel says, clearing her throat to hide the slight tremor in her voice.

Julie leans forward against the bar again and waits.

"My family is pretty messed up, so I left home and moved here. Lately, I've been having really bad nightmares about what I went through. It's a long story . . . "

Julie gives a slight nod of encouragement. Rachel hesitates. She feels like once she gets started it'll be hard to stop. She starts slowly, carefully choosing her words. "Ok, don't judge me right away because parts of this are going to sound like I had a life that would have been very different from the one I actually had."

Julie nods again and Rachel continues. "My parents both grew up super wealthy, like generations and generations of wealth. They met in college and got married when my mother got pregnant with my brother. A couple years later they had my sister and then a couple years after that, they had me. My father left us shortly after I was born, so I never knew him, but I guess it really messed up my mother. Or at least that's what my siblings say. I've never known her to be anything but unbalanced."

Rachel takes a long drink. She feels the story unraveling in front of her, drawn out by the interest on Julie's face. "So, my mother moved us into her childhood home, which was this enormous, crumbling, old farmhouse that sat empty for decades. My grandmother had moved out when she married for the third time, but then her fourth husband passed away right around the time we moved into the house. She left

Florida and came to live with us so she wouldn't be alone. It was just the five of us in the middle of nowhere, but things were relatively normal for a while. We had close friends and did well in school. We were involved in lots of sports and activities, my sister especially.

"My mother was always quirky, but as time went on, she started to come unglued. She got banned from our favorite coffee shop because she approached the owner and told him that she had figured out the store was just a front for drug trafficking. She stopped leaving the house unless it was an absolute necessity, and it never was since she could just send my grandmother. Then she decided that I was too impressionable for the public education system because that's how the government indoctrinates people. My brother and sister got to stay in school, but I was homeschooled from seventh grade on because she claimed I wasn't smart enough to recognize propaganda, and she didn't want a government zombie living in her house."

Julie's face twitches ever so slightly.

"I know, I know," Rachel says. "You're thinking that I'm some freaky homeschooled kid who doesn't believe in evolution, but my grandma taught science at the local high school for thirty years so the education I got was actually really good. My social life . . . not so much. I was incredibly lonely so Grandma used to make up excuses to take me into town with her so I could still interact with other people. It started out as trips to the library or to church, but my mother didn't want the library tracking our books and she didn't trust organized religion so that didn't last long. Grandma found other ways, though. I took a watercolor class one summer because she said she needed my help getting groceries, and my mother never noticed that we were always gone for three hours every Wednesday for two months."

Rachel smiles, looking at Julie's tattoo. It reminds her of her final art project, a painting of Grandma's flower garden. When Rachel showed it to her on the drive home, Grandma made up a song on the spot about how beautiful it was: *The petals look so soft and pastel, with my favorite flower the bluebell.* She was always doing that, making life into a musical.

"I can tell ya really love her," Julie says, reaching across the bar to give Rachel's hand a quick squeeze.

"Loved," Rachel corrects.

"I'm so sorry," Julie says, covering her mouth in embarrassment.

Rachel doesn't hear her. She still feels the warmth of Julie's skin on her skin and something small flickers in her chest. She waits for the wave of regret, but it doesn't come. There's a relief in speaking about the past, of removing its power by telling her side.

"Anyway," she continues, "my brother, and then my sister, left for college and things got worse. My mom blamed me for everything. If she wanted to plant flowers that day and it rained, that was my fault. And then when some creature ate her flowers, that was my fault too. She screamed at me constantly and forbade me from leaving the house. My mother controlled all of the family's finances; she even had my grandmother on an allowance. I had no way of making my own money so I was stuck.

"I eventually got out when I left for college, but only because Grandma insisted I go. I thought there was no way they'd admit me with just a GED, but Grandma helped me with the forms and edited a short story I'd written that I submitted as part of my applications. I got a full scholarship to study English Lit at a small liberal arts school out of state. I still can't believe it."

Rachel takes another drink. Julie glances around the bar to make sure no one needs her and then focuses back on Rachel. "Keep goin'. I'm super invested now."

Rachel can't help herself, and more of the story pours out. "Grandma moved enough money around for my flight there, and my scholarship covered room and board with a small stipend for personal expenses. I had everything I needed, but I couldn't afford to go home. And I couldn't ask for help because my mother would take it out on my grandmother; she was pissed because she saw college as the ultimate brainwashing. So I didn't see or talk to my grandmother at all during those four years. I couldn't even call or write because my mother policed the phone and the mail."

"God, that's rough," Julie says, shaking her head.

"It was and it wasn't," Rachel says with a shrug. "Of course, I missed Grandma every single day, but it also felt great to be away from all the drama. It was like taking a long vacation, but then I'd start to feel guilty, and sometimes I still feel guilty and-"

"You hafta look after yourself, though," Julie interrupts. "Ya can't put other people's needs before your own all the time. It's not selfish to do things for yourself."

"I guess," Rachel says, tapping her fingers against the side of her glass.

Julie leans closer. "Ok, I know this can't be the end of the story because last time ya were going on and on 'bout these terrible things you've supposedly done and there's no way that *this* is it. I totally wanna hear the rest, but I need ya to hit pause for one quick sec while I run to the bathroom."

Julie walks quickly to the other end of the bar and pushes her way through the swinging gate. She disappears into the women's restroom, a small space with two dirty stalls, one unstable pedestal sink, and a single flickering light bulb overhead. Rachel takes another drink of beer and waits. The creeping sensation starts to work its way back up her spine, but without the panic or fear that normally accompanies it. Now it's that shame she was waiting for, the kind that appears when you've overshared.

Rachel reaches over the bar and grabs a pen and a napkin. She scribbles quickly, trying to finish before Julie returns. *Sorry had to run.* She counts out bills from her purse and lays a stack on top of the napkin before rushing outside. This time, she remembers to walk around the block, just in case someone is watching.

As Rachel rounds the corner to walk the last stretch home, she notices something sitting by a dumpster across the street. She crosses and steps into the alley, confirming her suspicions. It's a small television, one of the old, bulky ones with the built in VCR. She lifts it, struggling under its obsolete weight. The cord keeps tripping her as she makes her way up the stairs and into her apartment. Inside, she lowers it to the ground across from the leather chair and plugs it in, pressing the power button while holding her breath.

The tube buzzes and the rounded screen slowly turns lighter and lighter shades of gray until there's loud static. Rachel turns down the volume and changes the channel. Flickers of images appear behind the snow. She walks to the closet to grab a wire hanger and then grabs a roll of foil from the kitchen. Rachel lowers herself to the floor and creates old fashioned bunny ears the way her Grandma once taught her. She attaches them to the back of the television set and works them back and forth until the picture clears.

Rachel slides across the floor and pulls herself up into the leather chair. She slings her legs over an arm and watches the fictional court-room drama unfold. The main character appears to be a middle-aged woman who has returned to practicing law after taking time off to raise children. Rachel recognizes some of the actors but isn't familiar with the show. This late at night, she knows it must be a rerun. But it's new to her, and she struggles to make sense of a plot where she's been dropped in the middle.

After a while, the actual dialogue fades and all Rachel can hear is the tone of the characters' voices. She curls into the chair and closes her eyes, letting the sounds of fictional lives blanket her. She drifts in and out of sleep, comforted by the feeling that there are others in the room with her.

At some point in the middle of the night, Rachel awakes with a start. An infomercial is showcasing some sort of kitchen appliance, and Rachel has no sense of what time it is. She pulls herself upright, grunt-ing at the aches and pains that have settled into the parts of her body that formed unnaturally around the arms of the chair. She lurches to-ward the bathroom; one foot has fallen asleep and wakes now with pins and needles. Rachel pries loose the contacts that have sealed themselves against her corneas and heads back to the living room.

She climbs into bed and yawns. Tonight felt like a release, like something close to therapy. Maybe an occasional trip to the bar could be good for her so long as she doesn't get too close to Julie. Rachel knows there's a balance, but she can't be sure that she didn't cross a line tonight; the alcohol and exhaustion make everything a little hazy.

She tells herself she'll decide in the morning, that she just needs a few hours of sleep to clear her head. Maybe opening up—just a little bit— to one person will be enough to squelch the loneliness and keep her sane. On the other hand, she may just have to make due with late night television. It can wait until morning. She just needs a little sleep.

CHAPTER 6

Thursday flies by in the way time does when you're apprehensive about something in the future. For Rachel, that thing is sleep. She's tired in her bones, but she dreads falling asleep each night. She keeps herself awake as long as possible, watching one show after another. She wakes up Friday morning groggy, but if there were nightmares, she doesn't remember them.

Work is a typical Friday. She sits down in her office chair, narrows the selection of photos for an author's bio on the inside of her book jacket, has lunch, crops a photo for an author's bio on the back of his book jacket, and then gathers her things to go home. It seems that mere minutes passed between each of those actions. Once she's on a northbound train, she blinks and the doors open at her stop.

She fights sleep as long as possible, but eventually she succumbs to it. She wakes up Saturday morning, another night of unremembered dreams. Their presence is there, though; exhaustion confesses to a night of tossing and turning. It seems like it's only a matter of time before the dreams push back into her consciousness and haunt her during the day.

The weekend is worse because time stands still. Without the distraction of work, Rachel finds herself trying to pass the time with things she hates. She spends a rainy day deep cleaning her apartment. When the weather clears, she goes for a long run. She cooks multiple dishes and freezes them in lunch-sized containers. She reads one of the westerns out loud to prevent distractions. She guesses the number of seconds that will pass between announcements of *doors closing* from the nearest Red Line platform, then counts the seconds to see how close she can get. When her mind starts to drift toward sleep, she pinches herself until the pain pushes away the fatigue. By the end of the weekend, her arms are covered with faint bruises, but mercifully there are no dreams.

Monday comes, and Rachel is relieved to be back at work. The nightmares have been absent for five nights, and Rachel finds that every task is easier than it was before. Press releases practically write themselves and she gets a head start on Tuesday's jacket design edits. On the train ride home, she notices that the sunset is more vivid and wonders if this is how life will be now. She eats homemade spaghetti and meatballs for dinner and solves a crossword from the puzzle book she bought for herself on the way to work that morning. She feels content as she relaxes into bed that night, saying goodnight to Charlotte before turning out the light.

* * *

Rory isn't answering his phone. On the fourth try, Rachel decides to leave a voicemail. She moves to the side of the tree opposite the grave site and whispers into her phone, "Where are you? You promised you'd be here. Mom made a big scene at the church, and now she's telling everyone that came to the cemetery that it's my fault Grandma is dead. Please, Rory, I can't do this alone."

Rachel hangs up and leans against the tree. The bark snags the tulle skirt of her black dress. She takes a shaky breath and walks back to the grave. She stands near a group of old women who are dabbing their eyes with crumpled tissues. A priest is reading from a bible, but it's impossible to hear him over the howling sound coming from Rachel's mother.

As the casket is lowered, Rachel turns and heads in the direction of her car. She walks past the same tree from earlier and hears someone call her name. A woman she vaguely recognizes from her grandmother's church is smoking a cigarette and waving her over. Rachel approaches, steeling herself in preparation for the sympathy and pity.

"You know it was supposed to rain today?" the woman asks, taking a long drag.

"No, I didn't pay attention to the weather," Rachel responds.

"It was supposed to rain all week, but today the sun is out and the flowers are blooming . . . I think it's your Grandma sending you a message from heaven. She loved you so much. You know, you kind of look like her . . . through the eyes."

"Thanks, I get that a lot. I just hope I can be half the woman she was. She was always happy no matter what was going on in her life."

"Oh, honey," the woman says with a frown, "your grandmother was miserable. You're the only thing that kept her going."

Rachel returns the frown. "You must be confused. Grandma was always optimistic. She was constantly singing or humming . . . I never saw her have a bad day."

"Oh, honey," the woman says again, "she drank herself to death."

Rachel's phone buzzes in her hand, and she uses it as an excuse to walk away. It's a text from Rory.

Sorry couldn't make it.
Had to fix some issues
with the caterer and florist.

Rachel's hands start to shake as she types a response.

Are you kidding me? You
missed Grandma's funeral
because you were busy
planning your wedding?

Regina wasn't there either!

Regina just had a baby!
And she doesn't live
around here. You do!

Look Rachel, no one had a relationship with Grandma like you did. She wouldn't care that Reg and I weren't there so long as you were.

You have no idea what I've been through! You two left me to take care of Grandma AND Mom, who hates me btw. It's been torture.

You chose to do that. No one made you a victim.

Seriously?! If not me then who? You know what? I hope your wedding sucks. I'll never find out though bc I won't be there!

Grow up, Rach.

Burn in hell.

* * *

Rachel wakes up with a jolt. Her hands are balled into tight, sweaty fists. Her grandmother's funeral has long been a blurred memory that she'd rather not revisit, but the nightmare was jarring in its precision. All these years, she'd been so focused on her texts with Rory that she'd forgotten about the conversation with the old woman. She remembers Grandma during those last days, malnourished and confused. But that could mean anything. Her grandmother would never leave her behind on purpose like that, not if she truly loved her.

She swings her legs over the side of the bed and lets them hang off the edge. Her chest is tight and her breathing is off, gulpy and frequent. She concentrates on slowing it, but the very act of trying to calm down seems to accelerate the attack. Weaving through the panic is profound rage. Even after all this time, even after Rory's accident, she still finds herself hating him. She reminds herself that deep down she loves him, but then she hates him for making her hate him.

She stumbles to the bathroom and presses her hands against the rim of the sink, leaning her forehead against the mirrored medicine cabinet. A few moments pass and then she's able to turn on the tap. Another moment passes, and she can run her clammy hands under the cool water. One more moment and she's able to splash some water on her face. A loose piece slips into place inside her, and she's in control again.

She takes her time walking back to bed, carefully sitting down and pulling her legs into a pretzel. She reaches for her phone to check the time. Her alarm is set to go off in five minutes, but she knows she isn't capable of obeying it. The energy required to shower and dress, let alone make it to the train and then act like a real person all day—that level of energy seems unattainable. Instead, she calls her supervisor's number and leaves a voicemail.

"Hi, this is Ra . . . "-she coughs quickly to cover the mistake-"this is Louise. I'm feeling under the weather today and won't be in. I got most of my jacket edits done yesterday, so hopefully this isn't too much of an inconvenience. Sorry. I'll probably be back tomorrow."

Rachel hangs up and throws the phone across the room. It hits the armchair and bounces onto the rug. *Fuuuuuuuuuck.* She buries her hands into her hair and rocks back and forth. Angry tears rush down her cheeks, but she makes no move to wipe them away. She shrinks as the room expands around her, the space bearing down on her, heavy and accusing. After all this time saying and hearing and writing her alias, and all it took was one bad memory to trip her up. Or . . . maybe she got so close to making an error because, subconsciously, she wants to be found.

"No no no no no," she moans, trying to center herself. It feels like there are two competing forces in her brain, each pulling her in an opposite direction. One argues she's trying her hardest and is just worn out from a terrible night's sleep. The other suggests she's self-sabotaging; retribution is inevitable, so might as well get it over with.

Rachel slides off the bed and onto the floor. She edges over to the spot on the rug where her phone landed. She opens her email and confirms that there are no new messages from her mother. There are hundreds of emails from her in total, but Rachel can't bring herself to delete them. They serve as a reminder of the danger she would face if her mother ever found her.

Rachel lays down on the rug with her knees pulled to her chest. Clutching her phone between her hands like a prayer, she closes her eyes and listens to the sounds around her. Two squirrels squabble in the tree outside her building. A bus honks a greeting to another bus. Reggaeton plays loudly on a car stereo and echoes between buildings. The neighbors upstairs turn on the morning news. It will be hours before one of them leaves, shouting a goodbye to the other and then jangling keys to lock the door behind them. Rachel focuses on the constant city sounds. She inhales the musty fibers of the rug that smells like it was stored in a cedar chest for decades. It's nostalgic and calming.

She feels herself drifting toward sleep, fights it for a moment, but then gives in, too exhausted to prevent the inevitable. She floats in the nothingness, punctuated by disjointed emotions. Sorrow and fury merge until they feel like something new, a fire that burns with an intensity so strong, it feels dangerous.

And then there's something different, something soft and good and feminine. At first it's just an energy balancing out her anger. It grows, spreading, demanding more space. The past fades into the background, and this new force pushes forward until nothing else exists. It could create life or destroy the world. It smells like rose water. Rachel feels this new emotion welling up and overtaking her. She struggles to breathe.

She's drowning. There is only this feeling, harder and louder, building into a throbbing heat.

Rachel wakes with a gasp, back to reality and the sun-drenched, braided rug. Her skin is damp with cold sweat and her heart is pounding. The feeling fades, but remnants of it pump through her body. Everything tingles. She looks down and sees that one of her hands is between her tightly squeezed thighs. She pulls it away with a shiver and notices that her fingers are stained red.

Oh no, what did I do? In the seconds between seeing the blood on her fingertips and realizing it's hers, Rachel loses an entire year. She rolls onto her back and starts to laugh. It's a slow giggle at first but grows until she's nearly shrieking. The tears come violently, this time spurred by relief rather than anger.

Rachel props herself up on her elbows and looks between her legs. She's bled through her underwear and the thin cotton of her pajama pants. Holding her smeared hand away from her body like an infection, she folds her legs under her and lifts herself onto her knees. Gingerly, she stands, swaying to find her balance.

Rachel walks to the bathroom and strips out of her clothes. She rinses her hand and then scrubs at her clothing with a bar of soap, rubbing the material between her fingers to loosen the dark fluid from the fibers. The center of each stain clears, but the outline is stubborn. She fills the sink with cold water and leaves both pieces to soak.

She twists the handle of the shower faucet to hot and then crouches to dig through the contents of the cabinet beneath the sink. The box of dark brown dye is buried in the back. She pulls on the plastic gloves, shakes the bottle, then squeezes it along her hair line. She follows the path of her middle part and then empties half of the bottle onto one side of her head and the other half onto the other side. Rachel massages the color into her scalp and then tucks the curls up into the shower cap. She stands in the middle of the shower, cupping her hands to pour water over her shoulders.

The temperature of the water and the pressure of it are consistent. After fifteen minutes of steady, hypnotic flow, the timer she forgot she set goes off. Rachel leans out of the shower to tap the stop button and pulls the shower cap from her head. She tips her head back under the spray and rinses and rinses and rinses. The monotony is a mantra. The questions and indecision run down the drain and all that's left is Tuesday.

* * *

Rachel hesitates outside the bar. She spots some of the regular Tuesday crowd through the window and reaches for the door. A man turns from behind the bar and hands a customer his change. Rachel freezes before backing away and turning to leave.

"Hey, Lu!" a voice shouts from behind her.

Rachel spins around as Julie crosses the street, jogging toward her.

"I'm glad I caught ya. I traded shifts with Ricky tonight."

"Why?" Rachel asks, trapped.

"So we can have dinner together. It's hard to talk when I'm workin' behind the bar."

Rachel takes a step back. "Um, I don't know . . . "

"Listen, you don't hafta talk 'bout your family if ya don't wanna. We can talk 'bout whatever ya want. And if ya don't wanna talk, I'll tell ya some crazy work stories."

A cool breeze picks up and Rachel pulls her jacket tighter around her body. It's a green utility jacket she found at a Village Thrift Outlet. She relaxes long enough to take in Julie fully. She's in black jeans and Chelsea boots with a white t-shirt and a black leather jacket. Her hair is down and curled at the ends. Without a bar between them, Rachel notices how long Julie's legs are, how her eyes look warm like spiced pecans. Rachel feels her cheeks glow pink, matching the dusk sky. "What did you have in mind?"

"Ever been to that diner over there?" Julie points across the street and one block down. "If ya eat meat, they've got great burgers, and if ya don't, there's a Greek salad that isn't half bad."

Rachel nods before she loses her nerve. They wait for a gap in traffic and then hurry across to the other side. The diner is long and brightly lit, with booths and counter service. There's a milkshake mixer behind the counter and a glass case of various pies. Orders are written on greasy slips of paper and clipped on a wire along the pass-through window to the kitchen.

Julie leads her to one of the booths. Rachel slides in opposite her and grabs a menu from behind the napkin holder, laying it out in front of her. "Any recommendations if I'm not hungry enough for a burger?"

Julie taps a spot on the menu with a fingernail polished a ballet pink. "The BLT is really good. We hafta get some cheese fries to share, though. You're not on one of those dairy-free diets are ya?"

"I'd starve to death if I were," Rachel chuckles, remembering all the times in the last month she's had a grilled cheese sandwich for dinner.

"Good woman," Julie replies with a smile. She motions over a waitress, who greets her with a tone of recognition.

"Hi Margie, I'll have the Italian Beef, a large order of cheese fries, and a Diet Coke."

"Sure thing, Julie. And you, young lady?"

Rachel looks up from the menu. "I'd like the BLT and an iced tea please."

Margie finishes scribbling their order, already walking back toward the pass-through window.

"Italian Beef, huh?" Rachel says, placing the menu back in its place. "That's not a burger."

"I rarely follow my own recommendations." Julie winks.

Rachel smiles nervously and looks around the diner. This crowd is more diverse than the bar. There's a family with small children seated in a booth, a group of college kids in another, and two men on a date at the far end, passing a milkshake back and forth across the table to take turns eating a spoonful at a time. At the counter, workers still in uniform celebrate the end of their shifts by eating greasy food in silence.

"So, Lu, tell me more 'bout yourself. I know your family's messed up, but what else makes ya such a delightful lil weirdo?"

"A weirdo?"

"I mean that in the best way possible. Ya have an old lady name and ya smell like a nursing home with that perfume ya wear. Ya act like you don't give a fuck 'bout anything while simultaneously caring a whole hell of a lot 'bout everything. It's like you're this mysterious enigma, and I'm dying to figure ya out."

Rachel blushes, feeling it travel from her cheeks to her neck.

"First question," Julie continues with a smirk. "Doin' anything with that English degree?"

Rachel rolls her eyes and laughs. "I'll have you know that I work for a small publishing company, so yes, I actually *do* use it."

"No offense intended. It's just that I also studied English Lit and well, ya know what I do for a livin'. Next question. Ya said you've only been in Chicago for a lil while, so what did ya do between college and movin' here? Unless ya came straight here? Oh god, you're not a child are ya?"

"That's more than one question."

Now Julie rolls her eyes and Rachel weighs her options. She can either lie about her age and risk a slip up later or she can be honest and . . . *and what? What could a person possibly find out with an age and a fake name?*

"I'll be thirty this year, but thank you for thinking I could be fresh out of college. As for the other question, that explanation would involve talking about my family, which *you* said I didn't have to do."

"Ok, ok," Julie says, hands up.

The food arrives and Rachel watches Julie pick up a French fry by the tip and dangle it over her open mouth, slowly lowering the cheese soaked end into her mouth. Rachel looks down at her double decker BLT, sliced into two triangles, and picks up one half. She can't remember the last time she treated herself to restaurant food. Probably not since Atlanta, just before she ditched her grandmother's car.

"Ya don't hafta answer anything ya don't wanna," Julie says, a hand in front of her mouth to block her chewing. "When's your birthday?"

Rachel shrugs.

"Really? That's off limits?"

"I'm a Virgo."

"Yeah, that makes a ton of sense. I'm a Scorpio."

"Explains all the black," Rachel says, nodding toward Julie before taking a bite.

"Fair. Where'd ya grow up?"

Rachel shrugs.

"Not even a state?"

Rachel shrugs and takes another bite.

"Wow," Julie says, "you're not gonna make this easy for me, are ya?"

Rachel shrugs again, this time with a full smile. They both turn their focus to their food, making brief eye contact between bites. Sharing the fries becomes an awkward dance as they try not to reach for the same one at the same time. Rachel embraces the normalcy.

After they finish eating, Margie returns to clear the dishes and drops the check in the middle of the table. Julie grabs it before Rachel even has a chance to reach for it.

"I want to pay for mine. How much is it?" Rachel says, unzipping her purse.

"Ok, but only if ya agree to my terms," Julie replies. "We're gonna start doin' this every week, but Wednesdays from now on. That's my day off and they have $5 burgers. Meet here at 6:00 next week and come hungry, ok?"

Julie waves the check in the air, holding it hostage. Rachel watches Julie waiting for an answer, perfectly shaped eyebrows raised. Rachel ignores the voice inside her head; she deserves a friend. "I'd like that."

"Great! Gimme your cell so I can text ya if somethin' comes up."

Julie lowers the check and grabs her phone from the pocket of her jacket.

"Um, ok," Rachel stumbles. "Let me just remind myself what it is."

She takes her phone out of her purse and scrolls through settings to her account information. She hears Julie laughing and looks up. "What?"

"Ok, lemme get this straight. Ya claim to have done somethin' terrible in your past, ya won't tell me your birthday or where ya grew up, and ya give out your number so infrequently that ya don't have it memorized?"

Rachel freezes. She's horrified that it's her loneliness that got her in the end, that she was too weak to last longer than a handful of months. She holds her breath as Julie leans over the table toward her and whispers, "Are ya an assassin?"

The laugh that comes out of Rachel is not her own but that of a confident person. She mimics it to stretch it out, giving herself time to hide the extent of her relief.

"You got me," she says, lifting her palms to either side of her face.

Julie grabs the phone out of Rachel's hand and texts herself. "There," she says, handing it back. "Now ya have my number and I have yours.

Rachel shoves it into her purse and grabs a few folded bills. She drops enough for a generous tip and slides out of the booth. Outside the diner, Julie grabs her into a tight hug. "I'll figure ya out yet, Lu."

Unsure what to do with her hands, Rachel clumsily pats Julie's back. Julie is taller by several inches and Rachel is desperately aware of how close her face is to Julie's breasts. They separate and Julie walks away with a quick wave over her shoulder. Rachel stands outside the diner and waits for Julie to disappear around the corner before walking in the direction of her apartment. On the way, she pulls her phone out of her purse and looks at the text message Julie sent herself. The screen is blank except for one kiss mark emoji. Something in Rachel stirs.

CHAPTER 7

Rachel keeps her phone on her desk so the screen is visible every time it lights with a text from Julie. They exchanged playful messages all weekend, harmless jokes and gifs. On Monday, Julie switches from calling their Wednesday plans a meetup to calling it a date. Rachel spends her entire lunch hour at her desk reading and rereading every text, searching for the thing she must have said that changed the tone, that shifted the tenor from innocuous to suggestive. There isn't one from what she can tell.

Then what is that voice in her head, the rustling in her chest, suggesting she wishes she had instigated it? Rachel has never been the one to lead, to steer a relationship in a certain direction; the confidence required for that is covetous. Over the years, she let others dictate every part of her life for her until she finally took a stand. And look where that got her. Alone in a strange city, reading texts from a woman who is more or less a stranger, wishing she were brave like Julie. Shit, she'd settle for being brave enough to admit to herself what she really wants.

Is that what she wants? It's been so long since Rachel felt anything but fear or rage, and neither of those were decisions. Fear is about survival, and rage has a way of exploding out of her without consent. The only real choice she's ever truly made may have been the decision to run, to vanish before anyone pieced together that it was her mess they were left to clean up.

Is *this* what she wants? Throughout the day, she sits in her cubicle, legs concealed beneath the desk, pressing her thighs together, tighter and tighter until there's a spark. She coaxes it into a primal ember, then extinguishes it before it catches. She suspects that ember could quickly turn to a flame that would burn hotter than her anger ever has. She envisions it sweeping across a field in a beautiful controlled line. Then it jumps a highway, burning beyond its intended parameters, destroying everything in its path.

Rachel does not like to be out of control. She tells herself she'll wait a day before responding to the most recent text, an invitation to pick a different activity if she doesn't want diner food again. The word *activity* trips her up but she really needs to get her work done. She manages to ignore her phone, now residing in the purse slung over her chair, and focuses on a press release for the zombie vampire friendship book, now ready for advance copies to be sent out into the world. At five o'clock, she congratulates herself and grabs her purse, heading for the elevators. She rides the train home, still refusing to look at her phone.

But once inside her apartment, she's tingling and it seems reckless *not* to look. There's a string of messages stretching from lunch through the late afternoon.

Today 1:09 PM
We could go for a walk
if the weather is nice or
get Chinese takeout and
hang at my place

Today 1:31 PM
But I don't want to rush
things or make you
feel uncomfortable

Today 2:58 PM
Oh god did I scare you
away? I swear we can do
whatever you want to do

Today 2:59 PM
And now I realize I
sound crazy. You're probs
busy at work and not just
sitting around waiting
for a text from me. But
if I did ruin everything,
just tell me and I'll
leave you alone

Today 5:47 PM
I'd love more of those
greasy cheese fries.

Rachel smiles as she reads through the exchange again. It puts her at ease to know she has the upper hand. She may not be as outwardly confident as Julie, but Rachel's power comes in her silence, in her perceived reticence. She feels her sense of control returning and breathes a little easier. In the shower that night, she turns the heat up on the water until her skin feels feverish, matching the burning she feels in her core. *Ok, you can keep this one thing.*

* * *

Tuesday is a mixture of book jackets and innuendo. Rachel walks the fine line between casual conversation and friendly flirting. She's careful not to seem too eager or desperate, although she is desperate. This friendship is the only connection she has, the only one she'll allow herself to have. It's the thing standing between survival and certain insanity.

And the nightmares! This new feeling has blocked them for the time being. Maybe it's the amount of space these texts now take up in her brain. Or the post-shower surrender as she lays her head on her pillow, no longer fighting sleep. Rachel doesn't ask why. Every night of dreamless sleep is a blessing, and Rachel is grateful for every second.

Wednesday morning Rachel sticks to her routine, keeping her nerves in check through familiar repetition. She sips a mug of coffee while making a peanut butter and jelly sandwich. She looks out the window and studies the people passing by to get a sense of today's weather forecast. She pairs a gray sweater with black jeans and ballet flats, skipping the socks and jacket. She grabs her umbrella on the way out the door, locks up, and speed walks to the train.

When she arrives at work, a stack of books are on her desk, advance copies with paper sticking out on the pages marked [insert epigraph here] or [dedication to come]. Rachel reads the inside of the book jacket, reminding herself of the book's contents, and then removes the first sheet of paper. The book is a memoir about the end of the author's marriage after she caught him cheating with her best friend. It implies she's planned an elaborate revenge plot.

The paper has a typed quote attributed to Lang Leav. A quick search reveals she's a poet and that the quote is one stanza of a four stanza poem.

In my own time
I will take back what's mine,
For I am not your friend.

Rachel likes it. She finds it clever. But after reading it again, it twists into a new meaning, a karmic warning reminding her who's really in control. Rachel shakes her head and tells herself, *That's ridiculous.* But as she researches Lang Leav and reads more of her poems, the feeling intensifies. It's like walking home alone at night, sensing that someone is following you, but you're too scared to look behind you to confirm it. Rachel becomes aware of her heartbeat, the pounding inside her ribs. Her pulse quickens and her breaths shorten. She knows what's coming and braces for it.

The attack hits and it's as if the walls to Rachel's cubicle have fallen to the ground. She can't stay at her desk so exposed. She stands slowly and makes her way to the bathroom on her floor, hoping her unsteady steps are only noticeable to her. Inside the bathroom, she heads to the first available stall and latches the door closed behind her. She sits on the toilet and rubs the spot just below her collarbones, just like Dr. Smada taught her. The stalls on either side of her are occupied, and with the morning coffee making its way through staff, Rachel knows she has little chance of privacy. She fiddles with the toilet paper dispenser, attempting to make enough noise to cover up a few audible exhalations.

"Everything alright over there?" asks a voice she doesn't recognize.

Rachel murmurs an affirmative sound and counts the hexagons of the tiled floor. She reaches behind her to flush and uses the noise to take in a deep, heaving breath. At the sink, she lets the cool water run over her hands, long after the soap has washed down the drain. The owner of the unrecognizable voice is still in her stall, playing the waiting game, as Rachel forces herself to open the door and walk out of the bathroom.

She takes it one step at a time back to her desk, feigning a yawn any time she needs to take another gulping breath. The screensaver was activated while she was away, and when she moves her mouse, Rachel realizes she didn't lock her screen. She hopes no one walking by noticed her deep dive into poetry that isn't relevant to her job.

If anyone saw her unlocked screen, they must not have cared. No one says a word to Rachel the rest of the day. She finishes her research for the revenge book and the rest of the stack, working through lunch for the distraction. By five, her pulse and breathing have returned to normal. The only sign of the earlier attack is a tightness in her chest and two minor pit stains. Even so, she lets the rest of the office rush out before her and enjoys the extra room in the empty elevator.

The evening air revives her. Rachel bypasses her usual Red Line stop for the return home and chooses one farther south, giving herself more time to adjust and better odds at snagging a seat. The longer she walks, the more ridiculous she feels for letting something so small affect her so strongly. On the train, she wedges into an open seat and allows the whooshing of the train to calm her further. By the time the train emerges from underground, moving to the elevated track, this morning's panic has been pushed to the past. Rachel is ready for her date, a word that causes the fluttering in her chest to return. But this time, it's accepted.

* * *

Rachel rounds the corner and approaches the diner. She left her apartment early to take an extra-long path to the diner, so it seems like she lives in a different direction. She walks inside, looks around, and takes a seat in the same booth as last time. Margie sets two waters down on the table and walks away. Rachel smooths the front of the forest green blouse she changed into when she got home and picks at the denim above her knees. She's always hated waiting. She's never sure what to do with herself in the space between one action and the next.

Julie rushes in and slides into the spot across from Rachel. "Sorry I'm late. I was runnin' some errands and my regular grocery store was outta poblano peppers, so I had to go to a different one and then the bus was runnin' late . . . anyway, I'm here now. Hope I didn't keep ya waitin' too long."

"No worries," Rachel responds. "I just got here myself."

Julie's hair is in a messy bun and she's wearing torn jeans and a black mock neck shirt, the short sleeves revealing half of the flowers on her right arm. Rachel is relieved to see the high neckline that will hinder her uncontrollable flushing. Margie glances over from the table she's clearing and asks if she should put an order of cheese fries in.

"You're the best, Margie," Julie says.

She takes a drink of water, her eyes watching Rachel across the top of the red plastic tumbler. Rachel rubs her neck and looks out the window, pretending to take interest in a group of pigeons fighting over what's left of a burger bun. *Just get her talking about herself.* "Poblanos, huh?"

"Yeah, I made this stupid New Year's resolution to cook at home more."

"That's great! How often were you cooking at home before?"

"Never."

Julie smiles and her eyes sparkle, like they hold a secret. Rachel laughs, and it unlocks something in her. She feels her body opening, her anxiety loosening its tight grip. Julie's smile spreads wider. "Why do ya think Margie knows me so well? I used to eat every meal here. That starts to catch up with ya when you're thirty-four, so I've been makin' some changes. What 'boutcha? Any fun hobbies or interests?"

Rachel stops to think. She can't exactly say that she's made a hobby of concealing her identity or avoiding people. She used to love going to a coffee shop near campus to drink bad-but-cheap coffee and work on her research papers. She used to dabble in poetry. But that was another lifetime. "I'm interested in art."

"Oh, yeah?" Now Julie is beaming. "Have ya been to the museums here? The Art Institute is incredible, of course, but I like MCA. Contemporary art can be so weird and I love it."

"Oh, you've made it clear you like weird things," Rachel says, a blush forming even though she's the one doing the teasing.

Julie snorts in the middle of taking a drink, covers her mouth with a hand, and forces a swallow. Laughing, she wipes at the corner of an eye with a knuckle, smearing her liner into a wispy cat eye. Rachel has the sudden urge to lean across the table and use her thumb to smear the other eye to match.

"Have ya been to either? We should go sometime," Julie says, moving her tumbler to the side to make room for the arrival of the cheese fries.

Rachel takes one of the two forks Margie leaves behind and spears a few fries. She cups a hand under the fork as she moves it toward her mouth, ready to catch any dripping cheese. They taste especially good after skipping lunch.

"I've haven't been to MCA yet," Rachel says between bites. "I actually have a membership to the Art Institute. I try to go monthly and love wandering around at my own pace, but it would be nice to go with a friend for a change."

Julie finishes chewing and then sets down her fork, grabbing a napkin from the dispenser at the end of the table. "'Bout that," she says, wiping the corners of her mouth. "Is that what this is?" She points back and forth between Rachel and herself. "Is this just a friendship to ya? I mean, if it is, that's fine; I just wanna know up front. I once pursued a woman for months only to find out she was straight. I'd rather not do that again."

Rachel blushes at the forwardness. She twirls the fork between her fingers and stares at a spot on the wall behind Julie's head. "I don't . . . I've never . . . " She struggles to find the words.

How can she explain that she's never been truly interested in anyone before? That sex never crossed her mind until college when everyone else was doing it. That she initially figured she was asexual or just too busy with other things to notice. That later, it was a mechanism for getting what she needed.

Julie jumps in, "I just wanna know one thing. Am I totally misreading this?"

"No," Rachel says softly, "you're not."

"Good," Julie sighs. "In my defense, ya haven't made that very clear. Half the time ya seem interested in me and the other half, ya seem scared. Have ya been with a woman before?"

"No."

"Just men, then."

"Only one, and he kind of ruined things for me."

"Oh, god," Julie gasps. "Did somethin' happen, wait, no . . . ya don't hafta say anything."

Rachel shakes her head. "I wasn't assaulted or anything if that's what you're asking." She remembers the late night phone calls. The promises, ultimately broken. "Turns out he was married," she continues. "Not that it matters. I wasn't actually interested in him. I know that now."

Margie returns to the table. "Anything else for you lovely ladies?"

Julie orders a cheeseburger, and Rachel says she'll have the same. She doesn't feel up to making an actual decision right now. Alone again, she looks back at Julie. Julie is watching her with a blank expression. Rachel swallows and licks her lips to wet them. "I know how it sounds. I hate being such a fucking cliché. Especially because now I know why I went after someone who was unavailable. I get why I pursued a relationship that was destined to fail. I wasn't being honest with myself, but I am now."

Julie leans back against the booth and crosses her arms. Rachel can feel her pulling away.

"Julie, listen," she pleads, stretching her arms across the table, trying to shorten the distance between them. "I don't know exactly what this is between you and me, but I promise it's not just some meaningless flirtation for me. I'm not just trying this out temporarily."

She holds her breath, hoping Julie understands, praying she hasn't blown it, whatever *it* is. Julie bites her bottom lip and bounces a knee under the table. After several agonizing seconds, she reaches across the table and places her arms on top of Rachel's, grasping her forearms just short of the bend in her elbow. She smiles. "Men are disappointin'."

Rachel lets out her breath and chuckles. She wraps her fingers around Julie's arms and smiles back. "I'm not saying you're wrong, but that might be a *bit* of a blanket statement."

Julie leans closer. "Oh, I stand by it."

* * *

Rachel holds the door open behind her, letting Julie follow her out into the night. There's finally enough humidity to capture some of the day's warmth after the sun sets. They stand under a street lamp, listening to the bits of jazz that can be heard every time someone walks in or out of the club next door. The neon lights and flashing bulbs of the club's sign cast a glow across their faces. Julie moves toward her.

"I'm sorry," Rachel says, taking a step back. "I want to . . . I really do. But some of the physical stuff might take me a little longer. I'm still working through parts of my past and I haven't fully processed everything yet."

"We all have baggage," Julie shrugs with a grin.

She moves closer again, this time holding Rachel's shoulders, gripping tightly so that Rachel can't move away as she leans down to whisper into her ear, "I'll show ya mine if ya show me yours."

Rachel stands frozen in place, scared to move, but also afraid of what will happen if she doesn't pull away. She realizes a second longer than it should have taken that Julie is referring to the baggage. She forces a laugh. Julie steps back and pulls up the calendar on her phone.

"Next week is Cinco de Mayo, which means I'll be workin' a lot. Can't beat the tips on drinking holidays. But the Saturday after is my one Saturday off in May. Wanna do somethin' that day? The weather's supposed to be beautiful."

"That sounds great. Where should I meet you?"

"How 'bout over by the beach at 11:00? We can walk along the lakefront path."

Rachel calculates quickly. She'll be able to wear a hat and sunglasses. The people along the path are usually on a bike or running so no one will be paying attention to her. "Sure. And sorry . . . I mean, thanks for-"

Julie waves a hand, dismissing both the apology and the thank you. "Don't worry 'bout it. You've obviously been through some shit. We'll take it slow." She reaches out and gives Rachel's arm a quick squeeze. "I'm that way." She points, indicating a perpendicular street to Rachel's. "Ya ok gettin' home on your own?"

Rachel feels some of the tension leave her body. Julie's back will be to her on the walk home so she doesn't have to worry about disclosing the location of her apartment. "Of course," she responds. "It's not far. I'll see you next Saturday." Rachel smiles and moves into the intersection, rushing to beat the blinking countdown.

Halfway across, Julie shouts at her, "Goodnight, weirdo!"

Rachel keeps walking, unable to turn around. She knows that if she turns, if she sees the expression that matches the half-teasing, half-flirting tone of Julie's voice, she won't make it to the other side of the street. She must resist. She must be careful. Chasing love now would mean grieving the loss of it later because love requires intimacy, and intimacy requires trust. That's not something Rachel can spare. The weight of her secrets must be carried alone.

CHAPTER 8

The lakefront path is busy. Summer has come early and half the city is celebrating outdoors. Rachel stands in the shade of a tree and watches people jog past her in either direction. A breeze carries the sound of teenagers playing a game of pick-up basketball on the courts and two dogs barking at each other from farther into the park. People of all ages are on the beach, soaking up the sun far from the incessantly frigid lake. Small children run up to the water's edge until it laps at their toes and they run screaming back to safety.

"Hey, Lu."

She hears the voice a split second before a hand touches the small of her back, giving her just enough notice to keep from jumping out of her skin. Even so, her body tenses.

"Sorry, did I scare ya?" Julie asks as Rachel turns around to face her.

Rachel forgets to respond. Julie is wearing a thin white tank top over a black bra and cut-off jean shorts, her long legs tapering down to black Converse. Her hair is down and wavy, blowing wildly in the wind. She pushes it to the side to prevent it from concealing her face. Her skin has already darkened into a deeper shade of brown. Rachel's skin, in comparison, looks like she's been bedridden for a year. She's glad she opted for jeans and a t-shirt.

"Ready?" Julie asks, walking to the edge of the trail and waiting for a break in the flow of runners.

Rachel pulls her baseball cap lower and follows Julie into the first gap, walking quickly beside her. Rachel stays in the dirt rut next to the paved path to give the runners plenty of breadth, which gives Julie an unneeded extra inch of height on her. Seagulls circle above beachgoers. A constant dinging sound can be heard from a cart, advertising paletas and other frozen treats. The warmth of the sun on Rachel's bare arms is soothing.

"I'll start," Julie says, removing a hair tie from her wrist to pull her hair back.

Rachel tenses. Nothing good ever starts this way.

"I'll tell ya 'bout my crazy family and then maybe you'll feel more comfortable tellin' me 'bout yours."

Rachel relaxes slightly. She wonders how much Julie will want to know, will expect to be told. Her instinct, as always, is to stick to the plan and reveal only the most benign details. But there's also a growing urge to tell her everything. The relief that would come from unburdening herself of everything is tantalizing.

"The short version is, I grew up in Iowa City. My dad taught finance courses at the university, and my mom worked at a Christian bookstore. I have a younger brother who played football and was high school valedictorian. Now he's a lawyer and married to a beautiful woman and they have three adorable boys. They go to church with my parents every Sunday . . . one big, happy family. And then there's me . . . the big disappointment."

"Just because you're gay?"

"Not just that. They hated that I was an English major and then they were *really* pissed when I dropped out 'cause . . . never mind, it doesn't matter why." Julie waves away whatever she had considered saying and continues. "My parents couldn't get over it so I left and moved here. A friend from high school let me crash on his couch for a month 'til I got settled. Mike hired me at Pale Gael's and I've been there ever since. It's good money."

"That's really brave, leaving everything to start over." Rachel hates the word brave, but it's the only one she can think of in the moment.

"Me?" Julie asks, hand flying to her chest. "I moved four hours away to a city where I knew someone. Ya came from who knows where to escape what you've hinted was a toxic environment. If either of us is brave, it's you."

Rachel shakes her head. "I'm almost thirty. You were so young! That's harder. And I *had* to leave. It's not like I made some courageous choice. It was the only choice."

Julie's hand settles over Rachel's. Rachel lets Julie's fingers slip between hers. It doesn't feel odd or strange. It feels like a return to something, a homecoming.

"Ya know," Julie says, "every hard choice takes courage."

"Ok, sure," Rachel says, laughing and rolling her eyes.

They walk next to each other, quiet. There's no tension, no urge to fill the silence with needless words. A voice behind them yells *on your left* and Julie steps into the dirt with Rachel, allowing a large group of men on bikes to whizz past them.

Julie shakes her head and steps back up onto the path. "They couldn't just go 'round without makin' us move? Or use the correct path? Ugh, I hate people."

"No, you don't," Rachel responds, smiling slightly.

Julie let's out a sigh that turns into a laugh. "You're right. I love people. Except *those* assholes." She swings their clasped hands up to point at the cluster of bikers, already disappearing ahead. "So, you've already got me figured out, huh?"

Rachel shrugs. She knows Julie is friendly and trusting, that she assumes the best in people. That's what Rachel needs right now, but what about later? Julie is understanding, but Rachel doubts that sunny disposition can handle the darker, twisted things in her past.

A man in short shorts and a bro tank flies past them on rollerblades. He's wearing wired, on-ear headphones, connected to a Walkman that is clipped to the waistband of his shorts. *Easy Lover* plays loud enough for them to hear the distinct voice of Phil Collins. A smile stretches across Rachel's face, wide and spontaneous like it was hiding there, waiting, all this time.

"So, are ya gonna tell me more 'bout your hard choices?" Julie's voice is soft, free of expectation. Rachel looks up at her and sees the real question all over her face. Her eyes ask – beg – Rachel to open up, to let her in, if only a little. Rachel looks down at the dirt beneath her feet and considers the cost. Some truths are more dangerous than others. "I just wanna know why-"

"Why I'm so emotionally stunted?"

"Not how I would phrase it," Julie laughs. "No, I wanna know why you're so afraid. Why ya feel so guilty for leaving."

Oh that's not why I feel guilty. Rachel knows she can never tell her the ending of the real story, but Julie's assumption just gave her an alternate ending.

"Ok," Rachel says with a long sigh. "Where did I leave off? College?"

Julie nods. Her grip tightens ever so slightly. If Rachel weren't so tuned in to even the smallest sensation, *thank you anxiety*, she probably wouldn't have noticed.

"Alright, so I graduated and subleased my room for the remainder of the month. I used that prorated rent money to buy a ticket home. I was desperate to see my grandmother again and I hoped that a four year break from me was enough to soften my mother. Maybe she wouldn't take me for granted anymore.

"I got into town and then walked the four miles out to the house. It looked the same as when I left. My grandmother's car was parked under a tree on the side of the house. Her flowers were blooming in the beds along the front, and the grass was tall in some places but had mostly gone to clover. I let myself in and it was the same dark, dusty home I remembered. But something was different.

"I found my grandmother in her bedroom, sitting in her favorite chair, knitting. I remember hugging her and I remember she was so happy to see me, but something was just . . . off. We talked and I told her all about college, about the books I'd read and all the research I did for my senior thesis. She seemed so proud and happy for me. She said all the right things, but . . . I don't know . . . I thought maybe I was just away for too long. Maybe nothing had changed except for me."

Rachel pauses. She takes a deep breath and lets it out, slow and controlled. She can still smell the musty carpet and the mildew around the window frames. She can hear the clacking of the knitting needles and the creaking joints of her grandmother's knees when she stood up from her chair and insisted on making Rachel something to eat. The soup slid, can-shaped into the pot, the metal spoon dragging across the bottom as Grandma stirred.

"My mother's hoarding had gotten worse and I was home for hours before I even saw my mother. She wandered around that place like a ghost and refused to speak to me. It was clear she wasn't capable of taking care of herself, let alone my 85 year old grandmother. I reclaimed some space in my old room and moved back in to look after my grandmother.

"Over the next few weeks, it became obvious that my grandmother was getting dementia, probably from neglect. My mother was in no condition to care for her . . . I'd catch her talking to herself. It was always some conspiracy bullshit or incoherent rant . . . the only time she sounded semi-normal was when one of my siblings called to check in."

Two kites hover above the tree line of the park, a butterfly and a shark. They dip down and float up, circling each other in a delicate dance. At this distance, there's no way of knowing if the strings are held by children or adults. Rachel can't remember ever having flown a kite as a child. She doesn't see the point as an adult.

Julie drops Rachel's hand to point out a side path that will take them through the park before reconnecting with the trail. "Did your siblings help out? Where were they in all this?" she asks.

"Busy. My sister moved to New York when she got married and then she started having kids. My brother was still pretty close by, but he was a personal trainer and used that as an excuse to be too busy to visit. Plus, he started dating someone pretty seriously and spent all his free time with her."

"God, I'd be so pissed," Julie says, shaking her head.

"Oh, I was! I gave my sister more of a pass because I couldn't imagine being home with, at the time, two kids in diapers, but neither of them ever acknowledged what a burden this was for me."

"Ya mentioned your grandma died. Is that why ya moved here?"

Up ahead, a family sits on a plaid blanket in the shade of a tree, eating sandwiches from a picnic basket. Two kites lay on the grass next to two children, a boy and a girl. Rachel fights against a rising emotion, something akin to the taste of bile. Happiness is a privilege and public displays of it feel egregious.

"Actually, no. I took care of her for years, and before she died, she made me promise to look after my mother. I thought it would be temporary. Obviously, I'd put in my time already, so I expected my siblings to step up. My brother could start checking in on her, or my sister and her husband could help us put her in a home. None of that happened, though. They just assumed I'd take care of things like I always had, and they went about their lives. I was completely left behind."

Julie snatches Rachel's hand again and laces their fingers together. "I can't imagine. Your mom was clearly sick and needed help. More help than ya were qualified to give. Seems totally irresponsible and cruel to put that on ya."

Rachel bites her lip to stifle a smile. Yes. That's the story she wants to tell. Julie needs to see that Rory and Regina were the true villains. Their sins were just as great, if not greater than Rachel's, and yet Rachel is the only one grappling with guilt. She curls her fingers around Julie's soft hand and lets their elbows bump together as they walk.

"It's so nice to hear someone say that," Rachel says, giving Julie's hand a squeeze. "It was incredibly lonely. I had no one to talk to. I was so secluded during my teenage years that I didn't really know anyone that lived nearby, and I didn't want to make new friends because . . . well, the whole thing was embarrassing. When I graduated college, I thought I'd move to New York like my sister and visit my grandma when I could. I assumed my brother would handle things since he lived nearby. I was supposed to get out. I wasn't supposed to end up living in my childhood bedroom, taking care of my crazy mother and putting my dreams on hold. I felt like I'd failed. I did fail."

Julie runs a thumb over the webbing between Rachel's thumb and forefinger. A shiver shoots up Rachel's arm, and she tries to keep it from jerking noticeably. Julie tugs her hand toward the shade of a tree. "Let's sit down for a bit. You're gettin' pink."

Rachel takes a moment to scan her skin, and while she doesn't see a change in color yet, she feels the tightness setting in. She knows that in twenty minutes, her arms and cheeks will have splashes of red that will look like a mild chemical burn. She watches as Julie lowers herself gracefully down to the ground and leans back onto her elbows, legs stretched out into the dappled sunlight. Rachel reaches into a back pocket of her jeans and drops a small tube of sunscreen onto the ground before bracing herself against the trunk of the tree and folding down next to Julie's knees. She smoothes the lotion over her exposed skin, knowing it's too late but needing something to do while she gathers her thoughts.

Julie taps her own nose to indicate that Rachel missed a spot. "Ya know," she says, "I don't think of ya as a failure. Ya did what ya had to. Life doesn't care 'bout your plans. In my experience, life loves to fuck up good plans."

Rachel nods. "I know. I had options, though. I could have left after Grandma died, and that would have forced someone else to step up. Instead, I waited until they *really* needed me and then I bailed."

"Ah," Julie says, sitting up, "so that's the source of your guilt. Obviously, I'm just an outsider who doesn't know anything, but I don't think ya owe them anything. We all have our breakin' points. Ya pressed pause on your life for years. Did you even have a job to getcha outta the house?"

"Not really. I did a little freelance editing online. I dabbled in photography and sold some photos. Nothing worth putting on a resume."

"That musta been hard. I can see why ya felt stuck."

Time moves backwards. Rachel remembers how lucky she felt to find a wealthy benefactor who would buy her photos. The interactions, faceless and transactional. The mental gymnastics to convince herself she was just selling art to a patron. The custom requests, each one more degrading than the last. The promise of escape if she would just meet him in person.

Julie's voice cuts through the static and Rachel snaps back to the present. "Ya got out so ya must have been successful eventually, right?"

"Um, not really," Rachel says, carefully choosing her words. "I had one client who paid a lot for some custom portraits, but I ended up using that money for Grandma's funeral. After she died, I just couldn't do it anymore. I didn't feel . . . inspired."

Julie pulls her legs to her chest and leans across her knees. She reaches over and grabs Rachel's hat, settling it on her own head. "Yeah, depression is a bitch."

Rachel shakes out her curls and starts to correct Julie but then pulls back. Why not let Julie rewrite the story? Depression certainly makes more sense than the blind rage that ensued, the fury that sits under her skin even now, adding to the sting of her sunburn.

"Yep. I was in a really bad place for a while and then my terrible luck spread to both of my siblings. They ended up moving back home and we were all cooped up in that big house together. Everyone was broken and miserable. And then I left."

Julie crosses her ankles and leans between her knees to push loose curls behind Rachel's ears. She grabs the sides of Rachel's sunglasses and pushes them up onto the top of her head. Stripped of her disguise, Rachel realizes just how vulnerable she's made herself. She presses a fingertip to the inner corner of each eye, dabbing at the wetness that should be there but isn't.

"Ever heard of 'caretaker fatigue'?" Julie asks, her hands just above Rachel's knees now.

"Is that what you're suffering from, dealing with my baggage all the time?" Rachel replies with a short, sarcastic laugh.

Julie tosses her head back in a full laugh and slides her hands up Rachel's legs to mid-thigh. "Ok, I see ya took the same Intro Psych class I did. Doesn't make me wrong 'boutcha, though."

Her hands slide further up, testing the waters. "I'm not your care-taker, though. You've taken care of yourself long enough; ya don't need me for that."

Rachel's breathing stops. Julie leans in further and stops inches from Rachel's face. There's a pause, a chance to pull away or signal that this is too fast, but Rachel lets the moment pass. Julie lips connect with hers, soft and firm. Questioning. Rachel answers the question, pressing into the kiss, then opening to it.

There is no fear now. The live wire that runs through her core quivers, quickening with each shared breath. There is no time for thinking. Actually, no decision to be made. The electricity courses through her body, strong and powerful, building into something new. Something uncontainable.

CHAPTER 9

Rachel stares at a quote on a dedication page, trying to summon the motivation to research it. Every title, every quote, every origin source . . . everything is that kiss. They'd walked back to their meeting point where Julie suggested grabbing lunch. Rachel wanted to spend all day with her but decided against it. Her emotions were too raw and she'd fallen into storytelling at too comfortable a pace. She didn't want to risk opening up too fast or revealing too much. She lied about needing to do some work and then, seeing the flash of disappointment in Julie's eyes, agreed to a Wednesday dinner date at Julie's apartment.

Rachel's phone vibrates in a desk drawer. After texts about tonight's menu and questions about wine preferences, Julie has finally provided her address. Rachel stares at the apartment number, the street name. Just six blocks from her own apartment. This feels like pinching a flame with dry fingers, hoping to not to be singed. And yet, that kiss. Rachel reminds herself of the silence from her mother and the unbearable alienation before Julie. How dangerous could it really be to get close to one person?

"Hi, sorry, I don't remember your name, but one of the editors asked if you're done with that yet?"

Rachel swivels and smiles back at a nervous intern. There have been rumors circulating that this particular intern is the nephew of the creative director. His expensive clothes and frequent tardiness have only strengthened the argument. But Rachel prefers him over the others. He may think he's better than her, but that means he doesn't bother to get to know her or to learn the business. Self-absorbed idiots serve a purpose.

"Just about. It got placed in the wrong bin so I didn't realize it still needed research. Come back in twenty minutes and I'll have it for you."

Rachel watches the intern shift his weight and dart his eyes behind her head, where she knows a large clock says there are twenty minutes left in the day. This one likes to sneak out early. "Check back in fifteen. I might be able to finish it up by then."

Rachel opens a new browser tab and quickly types in a portion of the quote. The results attribute it to Maya Angelou. She adjusts her search terms, learns that the quote is from an interview with Oprah, and skims multiple pages of dialogue to find the direct quote. With context, the quote isn't as romantic as it seems on the dedication page, but the surrounding context doesn't negate its meaning on its own. She places a checkmark next to the copy and closes the file. The intern approaches out of nowhere, hand extended toward the file. Rachel drops it into his hand and starts to gather her things. Her phone vibrates and her stomach clenches.

Just started the lasagna
rolls. Get your shit and
get over here!

Rachel smiles as she slings her bag over her shoulder, heavy with the weight of a bottle of wine. She tries to imagine the inside of Julie's apartment, wondering if it's dark like her wardrobe or colorful like her tattoo. The nerves return, wriggling deep and low. They intensify as the train doors close behind her and explode when the doors open at her stop. By the time Rachel gets down to street level, she has to shove her hands into her pockets to keep them from fluttering away. When she reaches Julie's building, Rachel stands on the front steps, leaning against the doorframe to steady herself. She breathes in the heat from the concrete pillared archway framing the wooden door. *It's just dinner.*

Her finger runs over the buttons of the buzzer, searching for 4S. She finds it and presses until a tinny, faraway beep is emitted. She holds her breath. The buzz in response is louder than she anticipated and Rachel jumps back, laughing nervously as she grips the brass door handle and pushes inside. The long entryway is lined with mailboxes on one side and faded art on the other. A worn green carpet creates a path to the stairs. Rachel steps to the side onto cool tile and locates the mailbox for 4S. *Shirvani/Williams.*

Julie hadn't mentioned a roommate and Rachel had never even considered the possibility. They've stayed away from last names so far (Rachel's doing) and seeing two options taped over a golden box feels like stumbling upon a secret. Rachel rushes to the stairs and climbs them two at a time to make up for the minute wasted at the mailboxes. By the fourth floor, her heart is in a vice and her hairline is damp. The door on the right is cracked open, the smell of garlic and tomato spilling into the hallway.

Rachel pushes inside and closes the door behind her, scanning the room for additional clues that she has entered the correct apartment. The entryway opens to a large living area with exposed brick along one wall, built-in shelves, and a sunny circle of bay windows. Potted plants cover every possible surface and the shelves are overflowing with layers of books, souvenirs, and framed photos. A large Moroccan area rug adds a splash of turquoise, orange, and pink to a room furnished with gray mid century furniture, a long tufted couch and a Danish lounge chair angled in a corner with a reading lamp. There's a soft, scratching tick, tick, tick coming from that corner.

"Welcome! Could ya flip the record over before ya join me?"

With the reassurance of Julie's voice, Rachel kicks off her shoes and pads across the creaking hardwood floor to the reading nook. She lifts the needle, flips the record, and lets the needle settle back down onto the vinyl. A familiar drum beat and guitar strumming is joined by the unmistakable sound of Stevie Nicks and Lindsey Buckingham's voices. Rachel would not have guessed Julie to be a Fleetwood Mac fan.

A crate of records sits under the small table holding the record player. Rachel flips through a few, a collection of 70s-80s rock, R&B, and funk. She straightens and turns to the bookshelves. Virginia Woolf, Alice Walker, Charlotte Perkins Gilman, bell hooks, Zora Neale Hurston, Mary Wollstonecraft. The next shelf down holds Mark Twain, Edgar Allen Poe, Walt Whitman, Henry David Thoreau, Frederick Douglass, Ernest Hemingway, James Baldwin, Kurt Vonnegut. The titles suggest several English Lit syllabi. Maybe a course on feminist authors.

Rachel walks down a hallway, passing a closed door, bathroom, closed door, then enters the kitchen. Julie is stirring something on the stovetop, a glass of red wine cupped in the other hand. She turns and beams, her hair pulled back in a messy bun and a black sundress nipping at her ankles.

"I brought more," Rachel says with a wheeze, pulling the bottle from her bag and placing it on the white granite countertop.

"Stairs getcha?" Julie laughs, dropping the wooden spoon to pull Rachel next to her.

"I don't know how you do that every day."

"Just used to it, I guess."

Rachel lets her hip rest against Julie's hip and looks into the pot. The pasta sauce bubbles, flinging bursts of spice into the air. It's warm in the kitchen, but a breeze blows in from a window at the opposite end of the room. Rachel studies the soft brown cabinets, the colorful tile backsplash that reminds her of the rug in the living room, the recessed lighting, the stainless steel appliances. "Is this a condo?"

A teak table and four chairs, clearly purchased as a set, are placed in the corner by the window. A cloth-lined basket of bread sits in the middle, surrounded by flickering votives. On the edge, two plates are stacked on each other and topped with napkins and two sets of silverware. An empty wine glass sits next to the table settings. Rachel grabs the glass and pours from an open bottle of wine next to Julie.

"What gave it away?"

"I guess I didn't realize bartending paid so well." Rachel sips from her glass, the smooth, rich pinot noir clearly superior to the red blend she brought with her.

"It doesn't," Julie says with a laugh. "This is my roommate, Camille's place. She's a CRN Anesthetist over at Weiss. Makes real good money, but works long hours. She rents the second bedroom to me for cheap and in exchange, I keep the place clean, make sure the plants don't die, and let her eat my leftovers. Oh, and I take care of her cat."

Julie points her wine glass at one of the kitchen chairs, where a fat cream-colored cat is curled. Rachel can't believe she didn't see it before. "His name is Biscuit because he kinda looks like the Pillsbury dough when you break the seam of the can. I shoulda warned ya we have a cat."

Rachel shakes her head and steps over to pet Biscuit. He purrs but doesn't move from his perfect circle. She buries her hand deeper into the thick, downy fur around his neck. "I love cats. I wish my landlord would allow them. It would be nice to have the company."

"Did ya have any pets growin' up?"

"No, my mother was allergic, or so she said. When my grandma died though, I decided to get a pet. I bought a hamster because I could keep him in my room . . . well, in my grandma's room. He made too much noise at night."

Rachel smiles to herself, feeling the wine spread throughout her body, and the vibrations of Biscuit's purrs replace the tremors from earlier nerves.

"What was his name?"

"Pellet."

"I love that! Take it ya didn't bring him with ya when ya moved here?"

Biscuit stiffens into a stretch and Rachel jerks her hand away from the tightening tendons of his shoulder. She inhales sharply and then brings the shaky wine glass to her lips, swallowing deeply. Her eyes close for a moment to savor the wine, but in the darkness, she sees Pellet, rigid with matted fur. She swallows again, pushing down the bitter hatred.

"Um, no, I didn't bring him because he died. I asked my sister to look after him for one fucking week and she starved him to death."

Rachel's cheeks burn, a combination of wine and rage. Julie's hand flies to her mouth to stifle a gasp, and Rachel feels embarrassment take over. She shouldn't have lost control like that. She shouldn't let Julie see her temper.

"What a fuckin' bitch," Julie says. "How hard can it be to keep a hamster alive for a week?"

Rachel relaxes a bit. "Sorry, it's been a while since it happened, but sometimes it still feels fresh."

"Don't apologize! Honestly, I like it when ya let your guard down like this."

Julie crosses the room to set a large bowl of salad on the table. She sets her wine glass down with it and runs her hands down Rachel's arms. "Ya know you can feel things in front of me, Lu. Ya don't hafta be so restrained all the time."

Rachel flinches. Is it possible that a person can be in survival mode for so long that they don't even recognize they're doing it? All this time spent deflecting and filtering . . . maybe it was more obvious than she realized. Maybe the safer play is to truly open up. To only hide the very worst of it and not overthink so much.

"See, you're doin' it right now," Julie says, tapping a coral acrylic between Rachel's brows. "I can see ya thinkin' in there. I can practically hear the gears whirring."

Rachel laughs lightly and steps to the side to let Julie set the table. Julie walks back to the oven, slides on a pink oven mitt that says *Wish me luck* above crossed fingers, and pulls out a casserole dish full of lasagna rolls. She grabs the sauce pan and returns to the table, setting the casserole dish on a trivet and spooning marinara over the top of the rolls. Rachel feels a growl rip across her stomach. She was too nervous to eat lunch and realizes now just how hungry she is and how tipsy she's already gotten off one glass of wine.

"Sit," Julie directs, scooping lasagna onto Rachel's plate and nodding toward the bread and salad. Rachel adds a pile of salad to her plate and then grabs a thick slice of flaky bread from the basket, dipping it into the excess sauce. She bites down and sighs. *Relax relax relax.* It's delicious.

They eat in silence, silverware clinking over the soft sounds of the record in the living room. Julie keeps their wine glasses full. The reds of the sauce and the wine mix in Rachel's mouth and she feels present. The little voice of warning is a dull, muffled echo behind all other thoughts.

Julie leans back in her chair, pulling a foot into her lap and swirling her wine. Swirl swirl sip swirl swirl sip. "Let's play a game," she says suddenly, eyes sparkling and lips stained. "It'll be like truth or dare, but just the truths."

Rachel is only slightly aware of a high pitched ringing in her head. She tilts her glass back and washes it further into the recesses. "Ok, me first," she says. "What's your biggest pet peeve?"

Julie tilts her head in thought. "Hmm . . . I guess 'cause it happens so often, I'd hafta say people who insist on drinking their beer outta a glass, but only if the glass is perfectly clear, without a single water spot. And then they don't tip."

"Yikes," Rachel snorts. "People do that?"

"More than ya would ever imagine."

A car horn reverberates down a brick alley and the absence of music is suddenly apparent. Julie holds up a finger, requesting a pause, and disappears down the hall. Rachel fetches the second bottle of wine from the counter and opens it. She splashes a bit into her empty glass and sips it. She's relieved to find that the first bottle has muted her taste buds. This bottle could be absolute swill and she'd never be able to tell.

Julie pads back into the room, harmonized male voices following her. "Ok," she says, "what's your answer?"

"When an automatic toilet doesn't flush and rather than hitting the little button that will make it flush, someone just leaves their mess behind."

"Ooo good one! Ya were ready with that!"

"I work with some gross people."

"Ok, well on that theme, what's the grossest thing you've ever done?" Julie asks, uncrossing and recrossing her legs. "Mine is probably the time I ate a cockroach at the bar on a dare."

Rachel squirms and shakes her head vigorously, trying to dislodge the image.

"I knooow," Julie moans, "but I made $500 off one of those jackasses that doesn't tip . . . he . . . you shoulda . . . " Julie's explanation turns incoherent through her laughter. The laughter is contagious and soon both of them are wiping tears from their eyes. "Go, go," Julie gasps, trying to catch her breath.

"Well . . . speaking of the bars and bathrooms, I knocked the toilet paper onto the floor one time, but picked it up and used it anyway."

"At *my* bar?" Julie shrieks.

Rachel nods, knowing that Julie is picturing that bathroom at Pale Gael's, the damp, dirty floors.

"Oh, girl," Julie giggles, wiping more frantically at her eyes now. "If you're gonna do things like that, I don't know if this is gonna work."

She points to her lips and then down to the crime site. Rachel's entire body erupts into goosebumps and a shiver rolls up from her toes, spreading a bright flush like wildfire. She's caught off guard by Julie's forwardness and tries to sputter a response, but it catches in her throat. Julie scoots her chair closer to Rachel's and extends a leg between them, letting her foot rest against the side of Rachel's thigh. She pours herself more wine.

"Ok, question," Rachel squeaks out. "Why did you drop out of college? Why did you leave Iowa?"

Julie sets the wine bottle down hard. "I don't know if that fits the lighthearted vibe of this party game."

"Are we not past that yet?" Rachel asks. She takes a nervous sip of her wine.

Julie looks down, turning her glass in her hands. Rachel reaches across her own waist and squeezes Julie's foot in her hand. "You show me yours and I'll show you mine?"

Julie chuckles. Her eyes fall back on Rachel's face, warm and open. "Ok, ok," she says, inserting a dramatic eye roll. "Ya got me there."

She lets out a long breath, her foot tapping between Rachel's hand and thigh, an unconscious distress signal. Rachel rubs her hand up and down Julie's foot. She recognizes this code but is surprised by the maternal feelings it elicits.

"Somethin' happened senior year. I was takin' this incredible class 'bout feminist literature. The professor was so knowledgeable and engaging . . . she never made ya feel like an imposter if ya hadn't heard of an author. She'd say that was just the patriarchy's doin', and that she was grateful we'd found our way to her class so we could relearn our history."

Julie pauses to take a drink and Rachel congratulates herself on correctly identifying the course for the top shelf books in the living room.

"Anyway, I really respected her so I started goin' to her office hours to discuss an idea I had for a thesis or to ask 'bout a concept I was still digesting. I don't know . . . after a while, we seemed like friends. We talked 'bout our personal lives, our goals in life. I felt like I could really talk to her. Like she saw me in a way my family didn't. Ya probably see where this is goin'."

Rachel does, but she keeps her face blank. She wants to be sure, to hear Julie say it in her own words, to be united in their mistakes.

"So long story short, Lily and I fell in love. It only became physical after the semester ended. I got a well-deserved B in the course so it didn't seem like anything unethical had happened. Word got out, though, and the Dean of the department disagreed. They launched a formal inquiry and Lily was fired."

Julie falls silent. She stares at her hands, at her wine, at nothing.

"Did you get in trouble? Did they expel you or something?" Rachel asks softly.

Julie shakes her head. "No, that's the thing. They said I was a victim and offered me free counseling. But I *knew* what I was doin'. If anything, *I* pursued *her*. I convinced her it was ok. Lu, she was married to a man and they had kids. I ruined her life, and when she tried to reach out to make sure I was ok, I ignored her calls."

Rachel feels a click as their sins align. Affairs? Abandoned loved ones? Rachel's guard dissolves as they enter this new territory of shared deceit.

"The Dean of Arts and Sciences told the Dean of Business, so my dad found out 'bout it over a game of golf. He was furious. I'd tarnished the family's reputation, and with a woman. It was too much. I left. I've never met my nephews. My brother sends me pictures of 'em and updates, but they don't know I exist. When I left, my parents erased me."

Julie stacks her plate on top of Rachel's and carries both to the sink. Rachel grabs the casserole dish and follows her. The sink fills with hot, soapy water as Julie places the leftovers into plastic containers and puts them in the fridge. Rachel sets the casserole dish in the sink and watches as Julie plunges her hands deep under the surface, scrubbing vigorously with a sponge.

"I know it sounds crazy," she says, over the running water. "I know I could just go back and force myself into their lives. I miss my brother and he'd defend me if I went back. He'd help me repair things. But I guess part of me is angry that he let 'em disown me to begin with. And I feel guilty for blowing the family up like that."

Rachel turns off the water and pulls Julie's hands from the bubbles. "You don't have to explain anger or guilt to me. I loved my siblings, but I also hated them for getting out. Then I made some mistakes, and they were forced to come back home. But rather than helping them, I left. I abandoned them like they abandoned me."

Julie pivots to face Rachel, her forehead clouding. "Whatcha mean? What mistakes?"

Rachel steps closer and wraps her arms around Julie's waist. "Let's save that for another day."

She leans into Julie's body and tilts her head up to kiss her. Their grape-stained mouths meet, hard. Rachel feels Julie's soapy hands on her hips, on the bare skin of her lower back, on the sides of her breasts.

They leave damp spots on Rachel's shirt like trail markers. Rachel's tongue is so numbed by the wine that she can't tell the difference between giving and receiving. She presses harder against Julie until she's overwhelmed by heat on heat.

The room shifts and Rachel grips the edge of the counter to steady herself. Julie pulls back and Rachel's mouth tingles with her absence.

"I think we've had too much to drink," Julie whispers.

"No, I'm fine . . . just a little dizzy."

Rachel stumbles forward, but Julie pins her back against the counter, keeping a cooling distance between them. "Trust me," she sighs, "I like where this is headed, but I don't want it to happen like this. We've been drinkin' and I got emotional. Let's just wait. I wanna be fully present."

Rachel's cheeks darken. She bites her bottom lip hard and feels nothing. Julie is right. She nods.

"Ok, good. I'm gonna finish cleaning up. Do ya wanna hang out for a bit or did I kill the mood?" Julie's smile gleams in the setting sun, filtered through the warm wooden blinds.

Rachel feels a muscle pulsating between her legs and knows she can't stay here. "I have to get up early for work tomorrow, so I should probably head home soon. Before it gets dark and I'm that drunk girl with a target on her back."

Julie nods. "Yeah there are all kinds of creeps out there. I work the late shift Saturday. Wanna hang out during the day?" Julie moves toward the hallway.

Rachel grabs her bag from the back of the kitchen chair and follows her. They pause at the front door. The record has ended, leaving only the soft scratch of the needle. "Saturday sounds good. Should we meet somewhere?"

"Red Line at 10:00? We can go to the Art Institute and then kick it at my place 'til I hafta go to work? Unless you'd rather we go to your place? I don't-"

"No, no," Rachel interrupts. "Your place is nicer. I like that plan."

"Ok," Julie says, planting a quick kiss on her forehead. "I'll see ya Saturday. Text me when ya get home."

Rachel gives a half smile and darts out the door before she can ruin the moment. The pulsating has grown into a painful throb, one that can't be trusted.

CHAPTER 10

Rachel rounds the corner and approaches the Red Line station. She smoothes the front of her shirt, retucking a bit of it into her linen pants. Julie is already inside the station, leaning near the stairs with her hands in the pockets of a black jumpsuit. She waves as Rachel taps her card against the reader and pushes through the turnstile. The motion makes her long hair sway back and forth over her shoulder.

"I'm so excited we're doin' this," Julie says as they climb the stairs. "I haven't been since they switched over the rotatin' exhibit in the modern wing. I've heard the photos in there now are stunning."

Rachel nods, despite having no idea what Julie is talking about. Rachel has never been to the modern wing. She wandered around the second floor a bit the first time she visited, just to get her bearings, but once she knew where *Beatrix* was located, that gallery had a gravitational pull too strong to let Rachel veer off course. A train pulls up, and a nearly empty car passes followed by a full car and a very full car. Julie tugs Rachel's arm and they run toward the empty car, stepping in just as the doors begin to close. They choose two seats facing out the western windows so the sun won't be in their eyes.

"That was lucky," Julie says, breathing heavily. "Wishin' I'd taken some time to grab a coffee on the way to meet ya, though. We had a barfer last night right at closin', so I ended up stayin' late to help with the cleanup. Then I took a long shower when I got home to scrub the memory of it from my body." She laughs and smooths a loose piece of hair back behind her ear. "How 'boutcha? How's work been? You've been quiet lately."

It's true. Rachel has been waiting longer than normal to respond to texts, agonizing over the perfect response. She's replayed the night at Julie's over and over in her head. Was she too forward, or did she finally find that fine line between authenticity and lethal oversharing? "Work's been fine. There's just this intern who gets on my nerves . . . nepotism and all that."

"God, I hate that shit."

"He's mostly harmless, but he has this real punchable face, and sometimes it's hard to look at him knowing everything in his life has been handed to him."

The train lurches around a curve, throwing them into each other. A strand of Julie's hair falls against Rachel's neck. She has the inexplicable urge to put it in her mouth.

"So, uh, I have good news about your need for coffee," she says, shifting in her seat. "I forgot to mention that a perk of being a member at the Art Institute is that I can get you in for free, *and* we get free coffee and tea in the Member's Lounge."

Rachel tries to remember the location of the lounge on the map so it won't be obvious she's never been. *It's somewhere on the lower level, right?* Julie throws an arm over Rachel's shoulders and gives her a half hug. "I knew there was somethin' I liked 'boutcha weirdo."

At each stop, crowds of people pile into the train car, taking the seats around them and eventually standing over them. Conversations mix and overlap, fading to an indecipherable background hum once the train moves underground. Rachel's shoulder jostles into Julie's side as the train sways. She feels the side of Julie's breast against her bicep and the length of Julie's arm along her back. She wishes they'd made plans to visit the Museum of Science and Industry instead so this moment would extend past the Loop.

Rachel reads the ads above the windows. There's the promise of family fun in the Dells and attractive friends laughing together, tall cans of the latest hard seltzer in hand. Northwestern is looking for research subjects for a sleep study. Down the aisle, two teenage girls giggle and point at something on one of their phones. This is the normalcy that

Rachel craves. This is what life could be like if she could only strike the right balance between easygoing and vigilant.

Monroe signs appear and Rachel follows Julie toward the doors, pushing past other passengers and dodging the assholes who try to get onto the train before others have gotten off. The air is still and humid, despite being underground. And the escalator is broken again. At the top of the stairs, Rachel rushes toward the exit, pretending to stretch so the fresh breeze can get to her damp armpits. Behind her, Julie fans herself wildly with her hands. The fresh air at street level is a gift.

At the museum entrance, Rachel feels a smile growing as they skip the long line and walk straight to the docent, membership card extended.

"Two?" the docent asks.

"Yes, two." Rachel beams.

She takes a building map, pretending to need it for the information about a new exhibit. She was right about the location of the lounge.

"Coffee, please!" Julie sings, stepping to the side to allow Rachel to lead the way. Rachel leads them down the stairs, thankful for well-placed signage. She flashes her membership card at the door of the lounge and glances around the room while she pretends to fumble at putting the card away. Julie has already spotted the coffee. "Want one?" She asks, already making her way over to the table.

"Uh, sure. Black, please."

Rachel sits on an orange couch and looks around. Bright sunlight pours into the lounge through floor to ceiling windows that face a courtyard, speckled with patio furniture. Soft jazz plays in the background, and books about art are scattered around the space. Julie sits next to her, handing her a paper cup of coffee. They sip together.

"This is the life," Julie sighs. "Coffee is pretty good, too. But then again, everything tastes better when it's free."

Rachel opens the map on her lap. "Where do you want to start?"

Julie runs a finger over the pamphlet. Rachel can feel the delicate pressure on her inner thigh and clenches.

"Can we focus on the modern wing today? It's my fave and I don't wanna be overly ambitious. I wanna save plenty of time to lounge at home before work. Take a break from bein' on my feet all day long."

Rachel nods, taking a long drink of coffee. She's relieved that the plan won't cause them to cross paths with the *Beatrix* painting. She wants to keep it for herself as long as possible so that it feels like it's hers. But also, Julie is smart, and that painting is basically a cipher for Rachel's errors.

Rachel sinks deeper into the couch and closes her eyes. The jazz trumpet, the taste of medium roast, the sunlight warming her face. It reminds her of days spent at coffee shops writing college papers. Those four glorious years when she was only responsible for herself. She remembers the advent of Facebook. How it allowed her to mend her relationship with Rory and Regina from afar. They would never understand how tough things were for her at home, but during her college years, they showed a genuine interest in her studies, in her life. She'd had hope that they could be close again, like when they were small children. But then she was right back inside her mother's trap and they did nothing to help her.

The acidity on her tongue brings with it the memory of the lingering smell of bile in Regina's bathroom. Rachel breathes deeply, feeling her face grow warm under the refracted sunlight. Warm and then hot, like being too close to the lapping flames of Rory's car. Where did things go wrong?

"Ready?"

Rachel's eyes flutter open. Julie is standing above her, reaching out for the empty coffee cup in her hand. Rachel hands it over and grunts into a standing position. She smoothes the front of her shirt again, tucking and untucking until it feels right, then follows Julie out of the lounge.

As they enter the modern wing, Rachel gazes down the long hall and out the wall of windows that showcase the Pritzker Pavilion in Millennium Park, framing it as a work of modern art. Rory and Regina would have loved to visit her here. She imagines them sitting together in the park, Regina's three small children running circles around them while they sip wine and nibble on fancy cheese. If only they had listened to her.

* * *

"Have ya heard of The Gap Band?" Julie is bent over the record player, exchanging one record for another. Rachel sips her smoothie, pulling a boba into her mouth and relishing the chore of chewing. It focuses her brain on one task at a time. Julie walks over and moves a plant so she can sit next to Rachel on the padded window box. She pulls her knees to her chest and grabs her plastic cup from the sill, using the straw to swirl frozen mango into the creamy white milk tea. "You'll probably recognize *You Dropped a Bomb on Me*, but *Outstanding* is better. It's sexy."

"Your taste in music surprises me," Rachel says, immediately wondering if that's insensitive.

"Which part? The oldies or the vinyl?" Julie laughs. "My parents are Iranian, but they left to come to the States before I was born and fully embraced the 'melting' part of the melting pot. They rejected everything from their culture and refused to tell us stories from their days in Iran. I grew up listenin' to contemporary Christian and country music, one day Amy Grant and the next day LeAnn Rimes. But we got invited to a lotta of dinner parties hosted by faculty, and that's where I discovered good music. Stuff that has real emotion and isn't secretly talkin' 'bout having a boner for Jesus."

Rachel snorts. "Yep, instead, it's just secretly talking about drug use."

"Oh, shit," Julie says, brow furrowed. "I shouldn't talk shit when I don't know your spiritual beliefs. I know ya talked about going to church with your Grandma-"

Rachel waves a hand, shaking her head. "No worries. If god exists, he/she/they haven't done me any favors. I don't need another toxic relationship in my life."

A breeze comes through the open window, cooling against the sunny side of Rachel's body. Her smoothie sweats as she grips it, a bead hitting the side of her hand, running down her wrist. She shivers. Leaning into the warmth of her crossed legs, she plots the course of this conversation. She just disclosed something personal. Will that lead to questions about how she grew up?

"Stop that."

Rachel raises her eyebrows at Julie, thrown off by the directive. Julie taps the side of her head.

"I see ya thinking. Ya don't hafta do that. Let's just talk. I wanna get to know ya. Really know ya. Not whatcha think I wanna see."

Rachel sucks in her bottom lip. She remembers Julie's admission earlier in the week and the relief that she was not alone. No one wants to confess to the innocent. She forces a smile and nods.

"Good," Julie says, "'cause last time ya made me air out my closet and then ya bailed. My brother and I have a strained relationship so I wanna hear 'bout your siblings. Misery loves company."

Rachel watches a boba travel up Julie's straw and into her mouth. She imagines it as part of an abacus, edible counting beads to keep the score. "You're right. It's only fair."

Rachel uncrosses her legs and gathers them next to her, pulling her feet to her hip. She settles against the frame of the window and takes a deep breath. A bee climbs the mesh window screen just above Julie's right shoulder.

"So, like I said, I had a love/hate relationship with my brother and sister. I was pissed that they left me to take care of my mother like that, but all of us ended up back in that house in the end. My sister started calling me regularly. She and her husband were fighting all the time, and she was thinking of leaving him. Then one day, she calls to tell me that all of their money is gone . . . like it completely disappeared. My brother-in-law lost it all and ran up huge credit card debt. He got fired for borrowing from petty cash to pay a credit card bill.

"They sold their home for barely more than they paid for it and moved in with us. It's not the way I wanted to get my sister back in my life, though. She was so angry and they weren't speaking to each other.

She focused on her kids and didn't really have time for anything or anyone else, including me."

"Ok, wait." Julie sets her drink down and rests her chin on her knees. "Ya said somethin' last time 'bout it being your fault that your siblings ended up back home. How was any of that your fault?"

"Well . . . "

The sunlight shifts, casting new shadows. Rachel considers telling the entire truth about Samuel. She weighs this against dropping one stone at a time and letting the ripples dissipate before dropping the next, giving things time to settle rather than risking overlap that could grow into a destructive wave. Julie tips her head, and Rachel knows the overthinking is probably stamped across her face. She'll have to adjust as she goes.

"The bad investment was me. My brother-in-law empathized with my situation, so he started buying my photography online. After a while, I figured out it was him, but I assumed my sister knew . . . then it became obvious that she didn't know, but I kept taking his money. I was desperate to get out of there."

Rachel stops. This alone is shameful enough without bringing in all of the details. She remembers the thrill of getting what she wanted. And then the shattering of control after the money was gone and he was around all the time, in her space. The debt owed. The smell of his cologne. The cost to keep the secret from her sister.

"Hey," Julie says softly, placing a hand on Rachel's knee. "Ya couldn't have known that he didn't have the money to spend, right? He's an adult who can make his own decisions." Julie lowers her legs and stands, walking over to flip the record.

Rachel feels the tightness in her jaw ease ever so slightly. She's halfway there. Now Rory. She leans against the screen and inhales deeply, hot metal and freshly cut grass. It fills her lungs, forcing out the scents of the past.

Julie returns, stretching onto her back, her head in Rachel's lap. Rachel focuses on the weight against her thighs, on the contrast of sun-soaked hair against shaded legs. She can feel the warmth through the linen. She grabs a strand of hair and twists it around her index finger. It glides between her fingers, soft and smooth. Regina's hair was like that when she first moved back home. Before it became brittle and broken.

"We don't hafta talk 'bout your family anymore today," Julie says, folding her hands over her stomach and closing her eyes. "Let's just celebrate that we're both strong women makin' it on our own. We don't need 'em."

Rachel feels a surge of energy in her chest. She had prepared herself to divulge more and now the adrenaline is trapped inside her, vibrating against bone. She massages Julie's scalp with her fingertips, keeping her hands busy to hide the slight shake. Julie moans and settles deeper into Rachel's lap. "What's your favorite color, Lu?"

"Um, green?"

Julie laughs, her head bobbing against Rachel's pelvis. "You sound unsure."

"I like to change my mind. Why, what's yours?"

"Black," Julie says, sweeping a hand down her body, offering the jumpsuit as proof. "Did ya know black can be either the absence of light or the complete absorption of it?"

Rachel nods. She remembers reading that in her art book and wonders why it didn't resonate at the time. She has often felt that life operates this way. All or nothing. Anxiety or apathy. Unconditional love or withheld affection. Truth or chaos.

"I like that," she says, smoothing wispy baby hair along Julie's hair-line, tucking loose strands behind her ears. "You never told me what you wanted to do with your English degree. I imagine you didn't think you'd end up bartending when you picked your major."

"Is that shade?" Julie asks through a grin. "No, you're right. Honestly, I never really had a plan. I just knew that I loved to read and the thought of discussin' books with other nerds was appealing. Even after I dropped out, I kept thinkin' I'd find my passion someday. I don't love bartending, but I'm good at it and it pays the bills. I thought 'bout gettin' a real estate license or a paralegal certificate . . . it just seems like every job requires a college degree, and I don't feel motivated to go back. I'm fine with sittin' back and seein' where life takes me."

Rachel makes a humming sound that signals she understands the sentiment, even though she has never felt at ease with waiting. Life has always been about following a plan or struggling to stay upright as the universe pushes her along an unknown path.

Julie stretches her arms up and then wraps them around Rachel's waist. "I'm tired. Wanna take a quick nap with me before I hafta get ready for work?"

"Sure," Rachel says, knowing full well she won't be able to sleep. She's never been much of a napper, and lately, she's been sleeping well at night so there's no need for an afternoon rest. But the thought of lying next to Julie is irresistible.

They slowly untangle themselves and walk to the bedroom. The walls are the same soft gray as the rest of the condo, but the rest of the room is distinctly Julie. The queen-sized bed sits on a metal frame, covered in white linens, broken up by black-and-white striped throw pillows and a gray throw. A bedside table on one side holds a black reading lamp and a stack of books at least ten high. The bedside table on the other side also has a stack of books that spills onto the floor where dozens more are scattered. Two framed charcoal sketches hang above the bed, each a nude woman standing confidently and unafraid. Rachel feels a twinge of something like jealousy.

"Did you do those?"

Julie pulls back the duvet and inner sheet, stopping to look up. "Those? No, I'm not artistic at all. They were done by someone I dated for a while. I found out she was cheatin' on me so I stole those from her place. Ya know, I never considered whether one of the women who posed for them could be the woman she slept with while we were supposed to be exclusive. Hmm."

She shrugs and crosses over to a white dresser next to the closet with long strides, unzipping her jumpsuit. It falls off her shoulders and then to the floor, leaving behind a black bra and matching thong. Rachel is startled by the flash of bare flesh, the smooth tan curves. Julie unhooks her bra, flings it on top of the dresser, and pulls on an oversized t-shirt from one of the dresser drawers. She turns to Rachel. "Wanna shirt?"

"Um, yes, that would be great." Rachel catches the tossed t-shirt and drapes it over her shoulder. She takes off her blouse, rushing to replace it with the t-shirt before removing her bra and stepping out of her pants. Julie discards the throw pillows and slides to the far side of the bed, her dark body contrasting against the white sheets. She holds the sheet up, waiting for Rachel.

Rachel lays down next to her, settling herself into Julie's arms, the softness of Julie's breasts against her spine. She is suddenly very conscious of every exposed bone in her body. She feels Julie's hand along her ribcage and Julie's hips cupping her tailbone. She must feel like a sack of wooden rulers.

"Just relax," Julie sighs into Rachel's neck, the warmth of her breath spreading up Rachel's hairline and across her collarbone.

Rachel closes her eyes and tries to melt into the warmth of Julie's embrace. It's difficult to relax. She recognizes again that her anxious preparedness has become second nature. It feels more natural to be tense than to be calm. Rachel urges her muscles to loosen and for her mind to slow. After much prompting, she begins to feel her body ease, an unraveling of emergency responses. Being comfortable feels uncomfortable.

But Julie's breath deepens, and her arm grows heavier against Rachel's side. *Just relax. Just relax.* A warmth spreads across Rachel's body. She remembers sitting in her grandmother's lap, listening to a story while she was rocked to sleep. So much has changed since those days. She is a harder, tougher person than that little girl was. But there is no room for shame as Rachel's eyelids close. The darkness floods over her, absorbing all light.

CHAPTER 11

Rachel agreed to attend tonight's event weeks ago. Back then, it felt like a good idea, a way to show Julie that she's serious and doesn't mind being seen in public with her. She circled the date on the calendar, a flimsy freebie from the Vietnamese restaurant down the street. The red circle around the date looks ominous now. In the white space next to it, she'd written, *book thing 7pm,* in the same red ink, smeared slightly by the side of her hand. Does it matter if a 7:00 PM event on June 6th is just one off from 666? Rachel has never believed in that brand of superstition but wonders now if she should take it more seriously.

Today 6:20 PM
*What's the dress code
for this?*

*Lu it's a book reading in
a coffee shop. I'm sure
whatever you wore to work
is fine. I'm in jeans and a
t-shirt if that helps*

*I just don't want to be
too dressy. Or too casual.
I don't want to stand out.*

Lu. You're overthinking this. Just come. You're not getting out of this

Rachel leaves her jeans and loafers on but changes out of her blouse, wet at the armpits with that particularly pungent, nervous sweat. She applies another layer of deodorant then carefully pulls on a sapphire-blue shirt with capped sleeves, trimmed with a ruffle and dotted with eyelets. The blue brings out her freckles, which have multiplied and intensified over the last few weeks. She applies a little mascara to her pale lashes and stares at herself in the mirror. She feels ridiculous, like she's trying too hard, but she needs to catch the next bus or she'll risk being late.

Rachel grabs a jacket on the way out the door just in case; she forgot to check the forecast before leaving work. She makes her way to the bus stop, keeping her pace brisk, but not so quick that she starts to sweat. Seated on the bus, she chews her bottom lip and bounces a knee, pushing the nervous energy out of her. Every public outing feels ripe with danger, like testing fate. Rachel takes a deep breath and reminds herself that they'll be surrounded by strangers. They'll blend. She focuses on her breath and counts the light poles as they pass.

The bus slows at a four-way stop, and Rachel notices a woman pushing a small wire cart down the sidewalk, loaded with groceries. She's dressed in dirty, billowing clothes and hunched over the cart, her hair wild in the wind. Rachel gasps and places a hand over her mouth, sliding back from the window but unable to look away. As the bus picks up speed and passes the woman, Rachel sees her face and realizes it's a stranger and not her mother.

Rachel lets out an incredulous laugh. Of course it's not her mother. Even if her mother discovered her hiding place, there's no way she'd make the trip herself. She never leaves the house, let alone the state. But still, the fear rushes through Rachel's veins. She feels exposed. If she weren't so close to the coffee shop, she'd get off the bus and head back home.

Rachel spots Julie outside Mean Beans before the bus reaches the end of the block. She's leaning against the brick facade, dressed in her characteristic head-to-toe black. Rachel hops off and practically jogs over, ready to be in Julie's self-assured presence.

"Hi," Julie says, kissing Rachel's cheek before pulling her into a tight hug. "Have I ever mentioned how sexy it is that you're always on time?"

Rachel laughs, her body softening into Julie's embrace. She pulls back and reads the white imprint on Julie's t-shirt. "Did you run a marathon?"

Julie glances down at her shirt then back up, a nervous look on her face. Rachel has never seen her nervous. "Ugh, you're gonna think I'm such a loser . . . "

She places her hands on the side of her face, squishing her features into an adorable mask to hide her embarrassment. Rachel smiles at her, delighted to see a small, humanizing crack in her confidence. "Ok, so sometimes I stalk my brother and his family online," she continues. "I found out he was runnin' a marathon in Ames and his family and friends had these t-shirts printed to support him. I don't know . . . I just liked thinkin' about a world where I was on the sidelines in a matching t-shirt, cheering him on, too. So I showed a picture to a local print shop and had this made. It makes me feel closer to him."

Rachel looks closer at the design. It's a bucket list of athletic accomplishments. About half of the list is checked off, *run a marathon* included. Next to the list is a picture of an actual bucket with small cartoonish people poking out of the top, cheering for him. "If anyone's a loser, it's the person that made this design," Rachel says, pointing to the image.

Julie pulls the shirt flat and looks down at it again. "Yeah, god I shouldn't even tell ya this, but I had this one added." She points to the character on the far right side of the bucket. "It's supposed to be me. I know it sounds insane, but this is all I have. I only get to be a part of their lives from a distance."

Rachel takes her hand. "You don't have to explain anything to me. I miss my brother and sister, too. Even after everything they did."

Julie nods and Rachel can see the confidence pouring back in, inflating her back to her larger than life self. She lets Julie pull her hand to lead her into the coffee shop. It's a large space with a long bar and storage cubes loaded with merchandise. The room is filled with mismatched furniture that spills into an adjacent room, which has been rearranged to accommodate more seating. A woman in a bulky, sack-like dress greets them as they step into the room. "Name?"

"Two for Julie Shirvani."

The woman flips a page over the top of her clipboard and runs a finger down the next sheet. "Great, found you," she says, marking a line across the page. She twists to the side and grabs two paperbacks from the table behind her. "Enjoy."

Rachel stares at the book in her hands: *More Coffee Please* by David Dixon. Between the title and author's name is an IV bag full of brown liquid. A label for Mean Beans' dark roast is affixed to the side of the bag. "Now I get why this reading is being hosted here," Rachel says, following Julie over to a green velvet couch along the far wall.

"Yeah, this guy writes these funny, short stories or essays or whatever, and this collection is inspired by people he observed while writin' in this coffee shop. My friend, Morgan, told me about 'im."

Morgan? Is that a man or a woman? Rachel feels her spine stiffen. She's embarrassed by her jealousy. Of course Julie has friends and a life outside this relationship, and Rachel knows her isolation from the rest of Julie's world is of her own making. She has actively resisted being pulled into the mix. She only agreed to tonight's event because she knew it would be just the two of them.

"Holy shit," Julie whispers, clutching Rachel's knee. "I know the author!" She nods toward the podium. An attractive thirty-something Black man stands next to the podium in a blazer over a floral tee. His beard is freshly trimmed and his hair is buzzed short, the lines crisp. He rests one hand casually on the side of the podium, gesturing excitedly with the other hand to a woman in a Mean Beans waist apron. When he laughs, his head tilts back so drastically he has to readjust the tortoise-shell glasses on his face.

"How do you know him?" Rachel asks.

"Well, I don't *know* know 'im, but he comes into the bar a lot. Weekdays durin' the day. He's always on his laptop in one of the booths. I thought he was just a functionin' alcoholic." Julie laughs, giddy. "Let's go say hi."

She tugs on Rachel's arm, but Rachel stays put. "Um, I don't want to bother him before his reading."

"Oh, come on," Julie says, pulling harder. "He won't care."

"But we'll lose our seats."

Julie is already standing. "Just leave your stuff. Let's go." She smiles and spins around to walk toward the front of the room with a strong stride, assured that Rachel is right behind her. Rachel rolls her eyes at the brazen certainty, but she stands and places her bag and book on the couch.

When she gets to the front, an introductory handshake is already turning into a hug. Julie pulls away and reaches an arm out toward Rachel. "David, this is my girlfriend, Lu."

"Hi," Rachel says, extending a hand. "Sorry to bother you before-"

"Nah, don't worry 'bout that," David interrupts. "I'm just as much a fan of Julie, here. She makes a mean whiskey neat." He winks and nudges her with an elbow.

Julie playfully punches his arm. "Rude! Ya just need somethin' to balance out all that coffee."

Rachel watches the two of them, the way they've fallen into a light banter like old friends. She feels like an awkward ostrich trying to fit in with swans. "So, David," she says, fighting the waver in her voice, "why are you spending so much time in a bar? I thought coffee shops were your thing."

His eyes light up, a chance to discuss his craft. "Oh, that was just for this one. I pick a different spot for each book. For the first one, *Lactose Tolerant*, I spent a lot of time in this ice cream shop on my block. Gained a lot of lbs. writin' that one." He rubs a hand over his stomach, clearly taut beneath his shirt.

"Wait," Julie says, "are ya sayin' your next book is about the people who come to Pale Gael's?"

David brings a finger to his lips in a shushing motion. "My deadline is comin' up so you're gonna see a lot of me in the next few weeks."

Julie presses her lips together and nods. "This is all so fascinatin' to me. I'm sure it's nothin' to Rachel. She works at a publishing company."

Rachel inhales quickly, caught off guard as the attention turns to her. "Oh yeah?" David asks. "Which one?"

She stutters and looks away. "Oh, I, uh, it's just a small set-up."

Julie leans closer to David and lowers her voice. "She won't even tell me. She's very secretive, this one."

David shakes his head. "Nah, I get it. You don't want strangers hittin' ya up all the time tryin' to get you to look at their bad poetry and shit. I respect that." He smiles and Rachel releases the breath she didn't know she was holding.

"You're from here, right?" Julie asks him, undeterred by the seats around them filling and the start time for the event quickly approaching.

"Yep, born and raised. Gresham. What about you?" he asks, pointing at both of them.

"Iowa," Julie says.

Rachel sees the woman with the clipboard approaching out of the corner of her eye. She feels the eyes of the other attendees on them. "Uh, yeah, same," she says, ignoring Julie's head tilt. "It was nice to meet you, but we should probably let you get started." She touches Julie's elbow, desperate to get back to their seats at the opposite end of the room.

"Cool, See ya around," David says, tipping his chin at Julie before stepping closer to talk to the woman with the clipboard.

Rachel pulls Julie toward the back. They squeeze together, hips touching, their spots narrower now that others have also chosen to sit on the couch. "Why didn't you tell me you're from Iowa?" Julie whispers, her mouth close enough that Rachel can feel each word, warm against her ear.

"Because I'm not." Rachel keeps her eyes glued on the front of the room.

"Wait . . . sooo you lied?" The S is a hiss that echoes in Rachel's ear.

"Uh, yeah." It comes out as a high-pitched squeak. Rachel feels a hot dampness spreading under her arms. She busies herself gathering their copies of David's book and putting them out of the way in her tote bag, attempting an air of distracted indifference.

A middle-aged woman greets the room and Julie twists forward, crossing her arms tightly across her stomach. The woman at the podium says she's from a local bookstore that works to support diverse voices, especially those who write through an intersectional lens, and that they're thrilled to host David in the very place that inspired his latest book. She continues on about the bookstore's efforts and mentions other upcoming events. Rachel feels her attention drift. She glances over at Julie, who's rubbing her lips together and staring straight ahead, a blank look on her face.

The room claps as David takes his place behind the podium and Rachel snaps her gaze back to the front of the room. David reads a passage from one of his stories, an overheard argument between a couple about caffeine levels in different types of coffee and which has more, blonde or dark roast. Rachel listens half-heartedly, laughing lightly on cue. Julie's body does not move. Rachel lifts an arm and settles it over Julie's shoulders to create more space on the crowded couch. Julie's body is stiff and unyielding. It does not react to the pressure of Rachel's arm or the laughter in the room.

David ends his reading and shifts to Q&A, moderated by the woman from the bookstore. The back and forth conversations sound like they're filtered through water, muddled behind the thumping pulse in Rachel's ears. She struggles to breathe, ashamed that the lie slipped out so easily, undeterred by the obvious consequences. She wipes at her nose, pretending the sudden sniffles are from the air conditioning and not an outpouring from her tear ducts.

David launches into one last reading, this time, a sad passage about an elderly man who sips his coffee alone each morning, staring at the same page of a newspaper. Rachel turns her head just enough to see Julie's face out of the corner of her eye. Julie is looking at her hands in her lap, her nails a bright, sunny yellow that pops against the black of her jeans.

The woman from the bookstore is talking again, inviting everyone to stay and have a glass of wine. The people on the other end of the couch stand and Rachel scoots over, pulling a knee onto the couch and twisting sideways to face Julie. "I'm sorry," she says, unsure what else to say, how to explain.

"Huh?" Julie looks at Rachel for the first time since the reading started. She blinks slowly, her eyes glassy and dead.

Rachel swallows. "For earlier. The Iowa thing. I just . . . uh-"

Julie lifts a hand to stop her. "It's whatever."

Rachel reaches over to touch Julie's arm. The inches between them feel like a deep chasm, opening and widening with each passing moment. Her hand feels warm against the coolness of Julie's arm. Julie lets out a long sigh. "Could ya get us some wine?"

Rachel nods, desperate to feel useful, needed. She walks to the entrance of the room where they checked in. A small table has been lined with plastic cups. The woman in the Mean Beans apron is pouring the wine, alternating between red and white. Rachel takes one of each, smiles at the woman, and turns back toward the couch. She pushes past a cluster of people, elbows out and eyes glued on the heavy pours within the thin, plastic cups. As she clears the group, she glances up. The couch is empty, abandoned.

Rachel freezes, the acidity of panic leaping from her stomach to her throat. She rotates slowly, searching the room. She spots Julie, staring at a piece of art on the gallery wall at the front of the room, behind the podium and table where David is now seated, signing copies of his book. Rachel approaches slowly, afraid that her sudden presence might startle Julie from her trance, causing her to sprint away, bounding out of the coffee shop like a deer into the woods.

"I wasn't sure which one you'd want so I got a red and a white . . . "

Julie reaches blindly for the cup closest to her. Rachel eases the Riesling into her hand then stands next to her, studying the drawing in front of them, gray lines on crisp white. A woman stands in warrior II, her feet planted firmly on the ground, legs and arms extended in opposite directions. She wears a crop-top and thong, but both are so sheer that she may as well be nude. Rachel leans closer. The woman's nipples press against the tight fabric of her top and there's visible stubble along the edges of the thong. "This reminds me of those nudes in your bedroom," Rachel says.

"Mmm hmm," Julie hums, taking a long drink of wine.

Rachel looks back and forth between Julie and the sketch. "She kind of looks like you."

Julie pulls the cup away from her lips. "She is."

"What?" Rachel spins toward Julie so quickly that she nearly spills her wine. "Did you pose for this? Did you know she was going to show it?"

"Nope and nope," Julie says, taking another drink. She turns her back to the drawing, shaking her head. "Sorry, this thing was distractin' me during the whole reading. It was my idea to come to this and I barely heard a word David said."

"Oh," Rachel starts, "I thought you were mad at me about the Michigan thing." She feels the tension in her shoulders begin to ease as Julie smiles.

"Nah, I mean, ya haven't told *me* where you're from so I'd be pretty surprised if ya told a complete stranger." Julie reaches down and intertwines her fingers with Rachel's.

Rachel takes a deep breath. "So, you're not mad that I lied?"

Julie tips her head to the side and looks down at Rachel, pursing her lips in thought. The tension creeps back into Rachel's shoulders.

"Look," Julie says, "I know there's shit you're not ready to tell me and that's fine. You've been through the ringer, and ya don't trust people. That's fine too, but ya hafta learn to trust me if this is gonna work. Lie all ya want to other people . . . just don't lie to me." She jerks a thumb toward the drawing behind them. "Don't be that bitch."

Rachel smiles as she lifts her cup to her lips. She squeezes Julie's hand, overwhelmed with appreciation. She swallows a mouthful of wine and considers whether to push her luck. "Not to sound ungrateful, but"-she watches Julie's face as she chooses her words-"why are you so patient with me?" Julie laughs, but Rachel continues, "I mean it! You say you're ok with a lot of things *now*, but this is my life . . . there will always be secrets. I worry that you won't be ok with this forever."

Julie's lips curl into a playful grin. She moves closer and wraps an arm around Rachel. "Ya know why my past relationships failed?"

"No, why?" Rachel asks, stepping closer. She can smell the wine on Julie's breath. She feels Julie's thumbnail as it runs along the edge of her bra.

"'Cause they always fell into one of two categories," Julie says softly, dropping her hand to Rachel's waist, tucking the thumb into the waistband of her jeans. "Either they were liars or they were boring. Maybe it's fucked up, but I like that there's so much I don't know 'boutcha. It keeps things interestin', right?"

Rachel leans in, simultaneously aware of and oblivious to the others in the room. "Sure," she says, in an exhale that leaves her chest hungry for the honeyed air from Julie's mouth.

"Are you bored?" Julie asks, raising her eyebrows as her lips part.

"Never."

Their noses bump together first and then their mouths connect. Julie's tongue is sweet against the earthy spice of Rachel's. Rachel shifts to press her body against Julie's, but her foot catches Julie's and she stumbles. Her tote bag slides off her shoulder to her elbow, nearly spilling the wine in her hand. Julie pulls back and looks around the room. "Maybe we should get outta here. Find a place a lil more private."

Rachel's face flushes as she nods. Julie throws back the rest of her wine, and Rachel mimics her, but slower, grimacing against the astringency. Julie smacks her lips and squints. "This is truly terrible wine," she says, wiping the corners of her mouth with a knuckle.

"At least it was free," Rachel says, placing her empty cup inside Julie's.

"Free for *you*," Julie says, nudging Rachel playfully. "I paid for these tickets."

She takes Rachel's hand and leads her toward the exit, tossing the empty cups in the trash. As they start to step out of the room, Rachel pauses. "Wait, don't you want to have David sign our books?"

Julie looks back over her shoulder and shrugs. "I'm sure I'll see 'im at the bar. I'll take the books with me to work and get 'em signed there." She tugs Rachel toward the door. "Besides, I'd rather make out with ya on my couch."

Warmth spreads up Rachel's body, rippling across her skin and exploding out of her body in a loud laugh. She steps outside with Julie into the bright heat, drawn toward the bus stop that will lead them to seclusion.

CHAPTER 12

Rachel hears a knocking on the top of her cubicle wall. She looks up from her open folder of book jacket edits and sees Plum Lips staring down at her. "Hey Louise, got a minute to chat in my office?"

Rachel feels sweat form at the nape of her neck and trickle down the same damp, salty path formed during this morning's commute. "Uh, sure. Do I need to bring anything?"

"Nope."

Plum Lips pushes away from the cubicle wall and strides toward her office. Rachel stands and follows, trying to keep up on wobbly knees. P.L. holds the door to her office open and motions toward an open chair. The other chairs are covered in stacks of folders and boxes of advance reader copies. She closes the door behind her as Rachel sits down and then rounds the desk to sit in the position of power, an upholstered executive chair.

"So. Louise. I want to talk about a change I've noticed in you."

Rachel frowns. "A change?" Had she become careless? Sure, she'd been a little distracted by texts from Julie, but had her work really suffered enough to be called out like this?

"Yes, you seem . . . happier."

Rachel can't help but recoil in surprise.

"Your work has always been solid," P.L. continues, "but lately it's been excellent and you really seem to be finding your voice. Honestly, you used to just blend in, but your notes have been top notch lately, and you seem to be getting more comfortable with your coworkers. I see real potential."

"Well, thank you," Rachel says slowly, waiting for the catch. "I really enjoy my work."

"It shows! And that's why we want to promote you to Associate Editor. You'll read submissions from unpublished authors, vetted through agents, of course, and find ones that seem promising. You'll do the first round of edits and get the author to sign off on them before it goes to a Copy Editor for a real thorough look. Interested?"

Rachel nods, unable to find the words.

"Great! We'll email you some paperwork to sign and information about the pay raise, and we'll have you start after the holiday. Are you doing anything exciting this weekend for the 4th?"

"Um, I'm not sure. I'm going to brunch with a friend. Does that count?"

"Of course it does! God, I miss brunch with my girlfriends. Kids really put a damper on all your fun plans. I'll be at a baseball tournament all weekend, but have a mimosa for me."

"Sure thing," Rachel says, standing with P.L., feeling just the tiniest bit guilty for not knowing her name.

P.L. walks her to the door, removing a few books from a box on the floor. She hands the empty box to Rachel. "Just take the next couple days to finish up any outstanding work and pack up your things because we'll move you to a spot by Editor Row. It's still a cubicle, but it's closer to the windows."

"Ok. Thank you," Rachel says, a genuine smile spreading across her face. She steps out of the office and heads back toward her space.

"And Louise," PL calls after her, "congrats."

Rachel collapses into her office chair and stares at her screen saver. She lets out a long breath and places a hand over her chest, the painful thumping a sign that the panic is setting in. Getting a promotion isn't exactly keeping a low profile.

Rachel opens a desk drawer and pulls her phone from her purse. She checks her email. Nothing but spam. *See, it's ok to be happy.* If a normal person were after her, sure, they could stop emailing to make it seem safe to come out into the open. But this was Rachel's mother, full of conspiracies and rage. There's no way she'd be able to just quit like that. Something must have happened. Rachel is sure of it now.

Mr. Khaki rounds the corner of the cubicle bank and walks directly over to Rachel's cube. He leans over the wall and whispers, "Hey congratulations. We can't wait to have you on our team. Let me know if you need any help finishing up your projects, and I'll lend you an intern."

He smiles before rushing off, back to Editor Row. Rachel feels herself start to relax. What if her coworkers are just nice, normal people and being friendly would actually help her to blend in? Rachel realizes just how many names she's going to have to learn in order to pull that off. A slow itch spreads across her arms, triggering goosebumps along the way. She opens the last text from Julie and starts typing.

You'll never guess what just happened.

You finally burned the place to the ground, good for you

Actually the opposite haha. I got promoted!

Lu that's amazing! I'm so proud of you! Honestly it's about time

I don't know about that, but it feels strange to have something positive happen for once.

Is that my cue to act upset that I'm not a positive in your life

You already know you're the best thing to happen to me in a really long time. Maybe ever. You're the reason I'm sleeping at night and doing a good job at work. I owe so much of this to you, Julie.

Nah this is all you. You just needed to open up a bit and see that the whole world isn't out to get you

Rachel's thumbs hover over the keypad. She knows the entire universe isn't actually conspiring against her, but having one person in it who wants you dead makes you question everything around you. It makes you question yourself.

It's hard for me to open up. You know that. But I'm trying. I want to fit in here. I promise.

Practice makes perfect. Oh shit you're gonna have to learn a lot of people's names

Rachel snorts. She starts to swivel to see if anyone noticed but then realizes she doesn't care who may have heard. She takes a steady breath, sedated by the mutual understanding necessary for an inside joke.

* * *

"Hey, Lu, over here!"

Rachel spots Julie at a table toward the back of the restaurant's patio and maneuvers over. A woman with a large bun of braids is seated across from Julie, sipping a mimosa. Julie pulls out the chair next to hers, indicating Rachel's seat assignment.

"I hope ya don't mind, but I invited my roommate, Camille. She finally has a day off and she's awake during the daytime, so I had to take the opportunity to introduce the two of ya."

Rachel greets Camille, forcing a welcoming smile. She didn't realize they'd be extending their circle so soon. The safety of their bubble feels threatened, but the excitement of the promotion has given her new confidence. She sits down and extends a hand across the table.

"Thanks for letting me tag along," Camille says. "I don't know the last time I hung with your girl here. Or anyone really. I was starting to feel like a goddamn vampire. It feels so good to wear something that isn't scrubs."

Camille's neon orange crop top, which clings to her substantial curves, stands out against her deep espresso skin and Julie's typical black and white wardrobe. She smiles with her whole face and shakes Rachel's hand enthusiastically. Rachel likes her immediately.

"Oh, it's not a problem at all," Rachel says. "Happy to meet a friend of Julie's."

"So, ya hafta break the tie," Julie says. "Are ya team mimosa or team Bloody Mary."

Rachel looks at both of their drinks, wavering between sweet and savory. A waiter approaches and sets a cup of coffee in front of her. "Here you go," he says. "Can I get you anything else to drink? The mimosa flavor of the week is mango or we've got a special wasabi Bloody Mary."

"Ooo, I'll have the mango mimosa. Thanks!"

He walks away and Rachel reaches for the coffee, grateful that Julie knew to order it before she'd even arrived. She squeezes Julie's bare knee under the table, feeling emboldened.

"Woohoo, team mimosa," Camille whoops, cheersing no one before drinking the last of her drink.

Julie places her hand over Rachel's and nudges her arm. "We're not just celebratin' Camille's return to the world, but also Lu's promotion. Associate Editor! Congrats, babe, ya earned it."

Rachel freezes as Julie leans over and gives her a quick kiss. This level of public affection and the pet name are new, and, as always, her body's response is to shut down. She resists, offering a half smile.

"You two are so fucking adorbs," Camille says, resting her chin in her hand and looking at them wistfully.

The waiter reappears with a mimosa for Rachel and a refill for Camille. "Can I get you ladies something to eat?"

Julie orders huevos rancheros, Camille asks for key lime pie pancakes, and Rachel realizes she hasn't even looked at the menu. Hurried, she finds the specials and skims them. The crab cake benedict sounds incredible, but Louise can't have shellfish so Rachel orders the traditional benedict.

"I can't believe how beautiful it is today," Julie says, leaning against the back of her chair.

"It really is," Rachel says, meaning it.

The sun is out, the humidity is reasonable, and every so often, a gust of wind provides relief from the heat. Rachel notices that their table is one of the few tables with an umbrella over it, and since she's the only one at the table who sunburns, she knows it was chosen for her. Julie's thoughtfulness and attention to detail shakes something loose in Rachel's chest, and she feels the tension release its grip.

They exchange crazy work stories and tales of the Red Line. Camille tells them about a cute new ER doctor and her quest to learn his relationship status. They talk about upcoming street festivals, which ones have the right vibe and which ones are too crowded with bros. The food arrives with another round of drinks, and they shift to talking about weekend plans.

"It's back to work for me tomorrow night," Camille sighs, "but I'm going to make the most of my one day of freedom. I'm meeting some friends at the beach after this and then we're doing a little shopping and then there's a movie in the park tonight. Paige's friend James might be there so I'm gonna see if he's as cute as she claims he is. Don't wait up for me." She laughs and signals to the waiter for another mimosa, raising an eyebrow at Rachel's empty glass.

"Oh no, I'm fine," Rachel says. She knows she's already reached her limit.

"Oh right, you're a tiny bitch," Camille says, holding up two fingers for the waiter. "I'll drink yours and save this man another trip. What are you two lovebirds up to this weekend?"

"This one is finally stayin' over," Julie says, reaching over to squeeze Rachel's shoulder.

"Well okaaay then," Camille teases. "I guess I'll keep my earbuds in when I get home tonight."

Rachel's body erupts in a hot flush. When she agreed to spend the day with Julie and end the evening binge watching *Parks & Rec*, Julie's invitation to sleep over had made perfect sense. They'd already napped together and it was safer to stay there than walk home alone late at night. Now the invitation seems loaded with innuendo. Rachel twitches her foot under the table, frantically looking for a way to change the subject.

"Camille, do your box braids get heavy when they're in a bun like that? Like do you notice if they're off center?"

Julie bursts into laughter. "I told ya she's my little weirdo."

Rachel's cheeks burn, and she regrets the second mimosa. The question just slipped out, but maybe it was offensive?

"Damn, sis," Camille says with raised eyebrows. "It's definitely a weird question, but you're, like, the only white girl I've met on the North Side who can recognize box braids." She turns to Julie. "This one can come to the cookout."

The two laugh together, but Rachel's chest tightens. What cookout? And who will she have to meet there? Julie called her a weirdo; what has she been saying about her to other people? A sound like crashing waves fills Rachel's ears, and she grips the side of her chair for balance. Camille stands and excuses herself to the bathroom.

"Hey, what's wrong?" Julie whispers. "Ya just disappeared on me."

Rachel takes a breath and forces a dry swallow. "You know I just get nervous around crowds. I like Camille, but I don't know if I'm ready to meet anyone else just yet."

A frown clouds Julie's face for a moment, but then her mouth stretches into a wide smile and her eyes sparkle. "Lu, ya know the cookout thing is just an expression, right? I can't believe ya know what box braids are, but you've never heard of bein' invited to the proverbial cookout!"

Rachel sinks deeper into her chair and leans her head back, closing her eyes. *Why am I such an idiot?* Her pulse slows and the panic subsides. She feels Julie's hand rubbing her forearm and focuses on the steady back and forth.

"When Camille gets back, we'll ask for the check and get outta here," Julie says tenderly. "I know she's gotta get to her beach day anyway."

Rachel tries her best to act normal when Camille returns. She goes through the motions of asking what she owes and tossing cash on top of the community pile. She stands when the others stand and returns Camille's embrace, agreeing that it was nice to have finally met. The weight of her fear gradually lifts, replaced by a returning excitement to spend time with Julie. The two of them round a corner onto a residential street.

"Look," Julie says, stopping and turning Rachel by the shoulders to face her. "I know ya get anxious and don't trust people, but I want us to work out, and that means incorporatin' ya into my life. All of it."

Rachel bites her bottom lip and nods. She feels tears building behind her eyelids, but blinks aggressively to keep them at bay.

"What are ya so afraid of?"

Rachel waits until she's sure her voice won't wobble. "My mother blames me for everything that happened with my family. I knew she would . . . that's why I left. She's threatened to kill me."

"She's threatened ya? How? She doesn't know where ya are, right? And seems like ya don't even know your phone number so how would she?"

Rachel swallows. "She sent me lots of emails. Said she knows what I did and that I should die . . . stuff like that."

"What?" Julie's head snaps back. "Who sends a death threat in writin'?" Rachel shrugs, but Julie jumps back in before Rachel can attempt an explanation. "Wait, she's this mad just 'cause your siblings had to move back home? No offense, but doesn't she like them more?"

"That but also . . . " Rachel pauses. She should stop here. But Julie's eyes are eager and Rachel needs her to understand. She can't lose her now. "My brother and sister are dead."

"Fuck, Lu! I didn't know! But I get it now, I mean I don't get it, but . . . shit." She grabs Rachel into a tight embrace, pulling Rachel's head to her chest. She kisses the top of Rachel's head and rests her chin there, her breath tickling Rachel's scalp.

Rachel soaks up the sympathy, allowing herself to be reassured that this is not the end of their relationship, that Julie may have the capacity to comprehend it all someday. Rachel steps back and lets out a nervous laugh. "So, what now?"

Julie looks down the street, calculating her plans for the rest of the day. "If ya feel up for it, I'd still like to go to that feminist bookstore that hosted the readin' last month, and then we can just chill the rest of the day. Thoughts?"

Rachel nods.

"And ya know ya don't hafta spend the night if ya don't feel comfortable."

"It's ok," Rachel says. She slips her hand into Julie's and turns in the direction of the bookstore.

"Awesome," Julie says, leading the way. "Bookstore and then home."

Rachel smiles. *Yes, home.*

* * *

"Ya asleep?"

A hand touches the middle of Rachel's back. She blinks and sits up on the couch, scanning the room to get her bearings. "Not anymore."

"Sorry, I didn't mean to wake ya up," Julie says. "Ya were so quiet that I couldn't tell if ya were really into this episode or asleep. Wanna get ready for bed?"

The clock shows 11:56 PM and the room is dark except for the flickering TV. Biscuit sleeps on the coffee table, smiling in the glow of an artificial sunbeam. Rachel's hand fumbles along the floor for her tote bag. She grunts into a standing position and follows Julie down the hall to the bedroom.

"Ya can change in here while I go use the bathroom. Unless ya hafta go right now . . . "

Rachel shakes her head and closes the door behind her. She takes a navy tank top and floral cotton shorts out of her bag and changes, staring at the nude sketches on the wall. These women are stunning in their authenticity, in their unapologetic existence. Rachel feels more exposed as the voyeur than they appear to be as the subjects.

Grabbing her toiletry bag, Rachel opens the door and pads down the hallway. The bathroom door is open, and Julie is brushing her teeth, face red from removing her makeup. Without eyeliner, she looks younger, but fatigued. Rachel runs her toothbrush under the tap and stands next to Julie, comparing their freckles in the mirror. Julie spits into the sink, rinses, and returns her toothbrush to the medicine cabinet. She kisses Rachel's cheek and pulls the door closed as she exits the bathroom.

Alone, Rachel fingers through the contents of her toiletry bag. She removes her facewash and moisturizer, balancing them on the edge of the sink. She fumbles through her nightly routine, trying to remember what was happening in that *Parks & Rec* episode when she dozed off. Her brain is too foggy to recall.

Rachel gathers her things and flips off the bathroom light, following the scent of Julie's night cream down the hall. In the doorway of the bedroom, she freezes. Julie is sitting cross legged in bed, propped up by pillows, reading in nothing but black underwear. There are large, rounded glasses on her face and a hardback book in her lap.

"Oh, hey," Julie says, glancing up. "I read at night 'cause it helps me sleep, but let me just finish this chapter, and I'll turn off the lamp."

Rachel feels bolted to the doorway, the gears in her sleepy brain fire back up, sparks flying. She should feel more comfortable seeing another woman's breasts, for fuck's sake she has breasts too, but this is unexpected. And these are not like her own small breasts, high on her chest, no competition with gravity. Julie's breasts are large swells, parting across her sternum in an upside down V. They look like heavy dew drops dripping from the edge of a leaf, crescendoing down into upturned brown nipples.

"Can I help ya with somethin'?" Julie asks, a playful smile spreading across her face.

"I'm sorry . . . I . . . uh . . . I promise I'm trying to be a normal person . . . I'm really trying . . . "

Julie closes her book and waves Rachel over. Rachel sits next to her, one leg dangling off the edge of the bed for an easier escape. She focuses on Julie's eyes behind the glasses, even as Julie scoots closer. Even as Julie's hands are on her hands. Even as her hands are guided to Julie's breasts.

"Tell me to stop if you're uncomfortable, but Lu . . . " Julie leans closer. "Don't overthink it."

What would a normal person do? Rachel isn't sure, but suddenly she doesn't care. Julie's words are the permission slip her brain needs. She crawls into Julie's lap and kisses her forcefully. She runs a thumb over a nipple, feeling it stiffen. She moves her mouth down to the nipple and tickles it with her tongue. Julie pulls Rachel's tank top up over her head and kisses her neck, starting behind her ear and working down to her clavicle. Rachel touches her fingertips to the wet triangle of Julie's thong, pressing into the warmth.

Cupping Rachel's ass in her hands, Julie flips Rachel onto her back, her curls spilling over the foot of the mattress. "You first," Julie says as she tugs at Rachel's shorts.

Rachel looks down the length of her abdomen, noting that the spaces between her ribs have filled in over the last month, happiness clinging to the bone.

"By the way," Julie says, positioning herself between Rachel's legs, "your eyes look better blue."

As Julie kisses her way to Rachel's pelvis, Rachel's brain clicks. She had originally planned to sleep in her contacts, getting up in the middle of the night to wet her eyes with saline solution, but in her tired stupor, she'd gone through the motions without thinking. *Do I bail? What if she tells someone? What if . . .*

A gasp escapes her as Julie's mouth connects with soft flesh. A thick nerve inside her vibrates like a cello string and with each lick of Julie's tongue, a hot euphoria reverberates through her body. *What if . . .* Julie's lips tighten. *What if . . .* Julie alternates between sucking and licking. *What if . . .* Rachel's hips arch and a trapped moan cascades out of her.

There is only this.

CHAPTER 13

The door to the hotel suite is propped open by the swing bar, the sounds of sports highlights spilling out. Rachel knocks as she pushes it open. Rory stands in front of a full length mirror in a full tuxedo, cursing at the lilac tie that hangs too short on his chest.

"Here, let me," Rachel says, crossing the room to undo his attempt at a Windsor knot.

"Thanks, Rach. You know I've never been comfortable with this formal stuff. Ashley wouldn't agree to marry me in my sweats though."

Rachel smiles up at him. She pulls the wide end of the tie lower, then loops and tucks the silk, reminded of Rory's junior prom when she first watched a YouTube video to teach herself how to tie a tie. She has always enjoyed these small moments together and feels herself welling with pride. Rory, who turned his love of sports into a career and used his success to urge Rachel to pursue her dreams. Rory, who found a CrossFit coach to marry and when announcing the engagement, reassured Rachel that she'd find her other half someday. Even when he was absent, these little things felt protective. She tightens the knot and reconsiders her decision.

"You're not wearing that to the wedding, right?" Rory says with a chuckle, looking down at her t-shirt, jeans, and sneakers.

Rachel adjusts his collar and sighs. "Rory, I told you I'm not going to the wedding. I love you, but things aren't fixed between us. I know I'll get stuck dealing with Mom, and I just can't do that again."

"Seriously?" Rory asks, taking a step back, his voice a deep gravel. "You can't just get over yourself for one day?"

"*One* day?"

Rachel balls her hands into fists and feels the anger pulsating inside them. "Every day is your fucking day! I'm the one who made all the sacrifices so you and Regina could go about your lives. Hell, Regina and her whole family just moved back in, but they're of no help."

"Whatever," Rory says, moving closer to the mirror to straighten his perfectly-centered tie. "You love playing the victim. You moved in with Mom because you didn't know what else to do. That makes you an indecisive crybaby, not a martyr."

Rachel's mouth goes dry. The tingling in her palms is painful now. Rory turns to her. "Where is Mom anyway?"

"I told you I can't be in charge of her today, and Regina's getting her hair done. You'll have to pick Mom up on the way to the church."

"What the fuck, Rachel! The guys are going to be here in 15 minutes so we can take wedding party photos before we go to the church and I need her here for those. I don't have time for this shit."

Rachel shrugs, refusing to engage. Rory grabs his wallet and car keys from the bedside table with a huff. He spins around and marches over to the dresser, yanking his phone off a charger that's plugged into the outlet next to the TV. On his way to the door, he stops and spins back around. "Can you at least wait for the guys to get here and let them know what's up?"

He leaves without waiting for an answer. Rachel looks at her watch and then drops onto the bed, picking up the remote to find something more palatable to watch. She eventually settles on a reality show, hoping the "unscripted" drama will reassure her that everyone's family is crazy. Through the windows of the far wall, Rachel hears the revving engine of Rory's red Corvette followed by screeching wheels. She rolls her eyes and increases the volume of the TV.

Down the hall, a collection of male voices moves toward the propped door, a thundering announcement of testosterone. Five men in tuxedos enter the room, practically falling over themselves as they backslap and arm-punch each other. Rachel clears her throat.

"Oh shit, hey." The one in the lead extends an arm to hold the others back.

Rachel recognizes him from Rory's high school graduation. "Hey guys," she says, changing the channel back to ESPN. "Rory had to run a quick errand, but he'll be right back."

"And who are you?" a voice from the back of the group asks.

"I'm Rory's sister, Rachel."

"Rory has another sister? I thought it was just Regina," the high school classmate says.

Nice. Rachel forces a tightlipped smile and tips her head sweetly. "Excuse me, fellas."

Rachel steps into the ensuite bathroom and slides the pocket door closed. On the other side of the frosted glass panel, the conversation she interrupted picks back up. She leans against the vanity and stares at her reflection in the mirror. The light from the exposed bulbs casts a soft blue hue that creates rings of light around her pupils. As she takes deep, gulping breaths, the circles of light flare.

Fuck you, Rory.

Rachel closes her eyes and the floor opens up beneath her. She drops down and when her eyes open, she's in the driver's seat of her Grandma's car. She's headed back home, almost there now. The final stop light is up ahead in the distance, but there's a line of cars stretching back, farther than normal. She can see that the light is green. She eases to a stop behind the car in front of her. There are lights flashing up ahead. And smoke.

The line moves forward slightly. Rachel can see that there's a cop directing traffic. An ambulance is on the shoulder. The cars inch forward again. A semi-truck is pulled over on the opposite shoulder. A cop is talking to the driver and taking notes. The driver is bent over in a slight squat, hands on his knees. He's crying.

Rachel rolls forward a few feet. There's a red car ahead of the ambulance. They're loading someone into the back of the ambulance. She puts her car in park and gropes blindly for the door handle, unable to take her eyes off the red car. She's outside her car now. Her feet are heavy anchors, dragging along the asphalt. The smoke is black and thick. It churns out of the crumpled Corvette.

"Ma'am, stay back! Ma'am!"

Flames shoot out of the roof, lapping at the sky. The heat is oppressive, but Rachel moves closer. Someone grabs her arm. They're dragging her away. The ambulance lurches onto the road, sirens screaming.

* * *

The cicadas are screaming. Rachel is screaming.

"Lu, babe, what's wrong?"

Rachel's eyes fly open. "I . . . I . . . oh that noise."

Daylight streams through Julie's window and splashes across the bed. Biscuit is curled up in the sun by Rachel's feet. She grabs her crumpled pajamas off the floor and jabs her limbs in them, desperate to be unexposed.

Julie rubs her eyes and yawns. "Yeah, those assholes are crazy loud this mornin'. Were ya havin' a bad dream?"

"Yes," Rachel mumbles, grabbing a hair tie from the table next to her and pulling her curls into a loose ponytail. She jumps up and hurries out of the room. The hallway is dawn gray, but a light beam cuts through the cracked bathroom door. Rachel tiptoes over and peers through the slit into an empty bathroom. She pushes into it and closes the door behind her. *Why was the light on?* She leans against the sink, pulling breaths deep into her body, holding them in place as long as possible before releasing them in a rush. Her reflection stares back. *Fuck you, Rory.*

Rachel stumbles back and crashes into the towel bar. She grimaces and reaches a hand behind her to rub the shoulder that took the brunt of the hit. *I can't be in this bathroom.* She pees as quickly as she can and rinses her hands briefly before bolting back to Julie's room.

Julie is tugging a threadbare shirt over her head when Rachel enters the room and collapses back into bed. She drapes an arm over her eyes to block out the sun and blows air out between her lips.

"Wanna talk 'bout it?" Julie asks. "Let me rephrase. Ya should really talk 'bout it."

She sits next to Rachel and traces the outline of a flower on Rachel's shorts. "I thought ya weren't havin' nightmares anymore."

"I thought so too."

"And . . . ?"

Rachel drops her arm to her waist and studies Julie's face. That same yearning is there. *I've already made it this far.*

"That one was my brother's car wreck. It happened on his wedding day and only because I made him leave the hotel to pick up my mother. I was still mad that he skipped my Grandma's funeral so I refused to go to his wedding. Anyway, he was rushing to pick her up and get back in time for pictures when he ran a red light. A truck hit him."

"That's terrible! So that's how he died?"

"Actually, it hit the back passenger side and spun him around. He wasn't wearing a seatbelt and was projected from the car. He was alive when they took him to the hospital but unconscious. He never woke up from the coma."

"I'm so sorry, Lu," Julie whispers, giving Rachel's leg a squeeze.

"The doctors said it was likely he'd never wake up, and that if he did . . . well, he would never be the same. Of course, my mother, being the nut that she is, couldn't let him go. After several months in the hospital, she paid to have him moved to the house and hired a 24-hour nurse. I loved my brother, but . . . I don't know. We basically brought a dead body home with us."

Julie looks toward the door and sniffs the air. She excuses herself and a minute later, returns with two mugs of coffee. She waits for Rachel to sit up and then hands one to her and motions in the direction of the kitchen. "I'm so glad that thing has an automatic setting. I don't mean to be insensitive. Ya just told me this awful story and here I am talkin' 'bout coffee."

Rachel takes a tentative sip. "It's ok," she says. "I could use some caffeine to get through this." She takes another sip then rests the mug on her knee. The warmth is comforting and then it's uncomfortable. It starts to burn, but Rachel holds the mug in place, biting the inside of her cheek against the pain. Julie is saying something.

"Sorry, what?" Rachel asks, bringing the mug back to her lips.

"I was askin' if ya feel guilty 'cause your brother was rushin' and ran a red light. 'Cause that's not your fault. Your brother made that decision."

"Well, he didn't mean to run the light," Rachel says, before she can stop herself.

"What?"

The words start tumbling out. "The car had a ton of damage, but they were able to save enough of the front to take a look at the engine and everything under the hood. Apparently some mice got in there and chewed on some wires, including the brake lines. Which is weird because he drove that car all the time, including the day before for the rehearsal dinner."

Shut up shut up shut up. You sound insane.

"They said it was highly unusual, but not unheard of . . . a freak accident."

Julie shakes a puzzled look off her face and hums sympathetically. "What a strange set of circumstances. I'm sure that only makes it harder to process, right?"

Rachel nods. "It does. And I keep coming back to the fact that he shouldn't have been in the car to begin with. They were taking a limo from the hotel to the church, and if he hadn't driven his car until the day after the wedding . . . I don't know . . . maybe there would have been more damage by then and it wouldn't start or something."

"Ohhh, the 'what if' game," Julie says through a tender smile. "I'm sorry ya had such a terrible dream. I can't even imagine what you've been through, and I honestly don't know what to say. Can I make ya breakfast?"

Rachel laughs and nods, happy to have the subject changed. She drinks her coffee at the kitchen table and watches as Julie cooks strips of bacon on a griddle and then cracks eggs into the grease. Julie reaches inside a cabinet for a loaf of bread. Her shirt lifts just enough to graze the bottom of her ass, exposing the curve where each cheek meets thigh. There's a hole near her hip and Rachel can see the string of her thong.

"Well, good morning," Julie says, drawing it out in a sing-song voice.

Camille shuffles into the kitchen in sweats, her hair wrapped in a colorful, satin scarf. She makes a beeline for the coffee maker and fills a mug, then snatches a piece of toast from the toaster.

"Fun night?" Julie asks with a knowing look.

"I am too old to be hangin' at the club."

"The club? How'd you end up there?"

Camille shrugs and heads toward the hall. She stops, walks backwards, and grabs a piece of bacon from a paper towel-covered plate.

"I thought ya were gonna stop eatin' meat," Julie says.

Camille is already halfway down the hall as she shouts back, "Girl, bye!"

Julie walks to the table with a plate in each hand, her coffee mug balanced on top of her toast. Rachel cuts open a yolk and dips her toast in the runny yellow. She chews and watches Julie watching her. Julie takes a bite of bacon and tilts her head to the side, continuing to stare at Rachel.

"What?"

"I'm sorry," Julie groans, "but I hafta know the rest of the story. What happened to your sister?"

Rachel sets her toast down and reaches for a napkin. She makes a scene of wiping every bit of egg goo and every crumb from her fingers. She chews slowly and then takes a drink of coffee to wash it down. *Just get it over with.*

"Eating disorder. She struggled with bulimia in high school, but we thought she was past that. Then my brother had his accident, and it must have triggered something in her. She told us it was something else making her sick, but it looked the same as the last time. I think she was just too embarrassed to admit it or ask for help. She wasted away and then her kidneys failed."

"Oh, her poor kids!" Julie sighs. "How old were they?"

"Let's see . . . they would have been five, three, and two. A boy and two girls."

"Wow." Julie shakes her head. "But wait, how could her eating disorder be your fault? How could ya possibly blame yourself?"

Rachel takes another bite and a sip of coffee. "When she moved back home, I thought she'd help me with my mother, but she and her husband were fighting constantly, and she was so busy with the kids . . . and then my brother was in his old room with that nurse. When Pellet died, I was pretty cruel about it. I should have seen how much she was struggling with everything. I should have been more kind."

Biscuit waddles into the room, enticed by the smell of food. He brushes up against Julie's legs, meowing and begging. She shushes him and attempts to shoo him away with a harmless swat.

"Anyway," Rachel continues, "she died on a Monday, and my brother died that Wednesday before we could even bury her. I left as soon as he died. I didn't even stay for their funerals. I had to get away from there."

"Is there any comfort knowin' they went together?" Julie asks, reaching across the table to touch Rachel's free hand.

"Not really."

They finish eating in silence. Julie puts their dishes in the sink, but when Rachel approaches to help wash them, Julie waves her away saying to leave them for later. They go back to the bedroom so Julie can slip into a pair of shorts and brush her hair into a ponytail. Rachel sits on the foot of the bed and waits for instructions.

"Have ya tried therapy?" Julie asks. "That's a lot to process on your own."

"I found a therapist after I moved back home. After my brother's accident I even checked myself into a treatment program, but it didn't help. I learned some coping skills, but I also picked up some unhelpful shit. My therapist basically validated my anger and said I should put myself first for once. Look where that got me."

"But it gotcha to me," Julie says, drawing it out and doing a dramatic twirl.

Rachel chuckles, "Oh, but *I'm* the weirdo?"

Julie crosses the room and sits next to her on the bed. "Seriously, though, these dreams sound rough and ya shouldn't hafta carry all of the past by yourself. I'm always here to listen, but I'm not a professional. Which means I can't prescribe the good stuff. Just think 'bout it." She taps her temple and stands back up. "I hafta pee, but meet me in the living room for more *Parks & Rec*?"

Rachel smiles in affirmation and Julie steps forward to kiss her forehead. "Oh, and we should get somethin' to strip that brown outta your hair. Blue eyes, pale skin, freckles . . . I'm guessing there might be some red in there?"

Rachel tenses. "But my mother . . . I don't-"

Julie dismisses the train of thought with a waving hand. "Chicago's a big city. Even if someone figured out you're here, how could they possibly track ya down?" She pulls Rachel to her feet and guides her down the hallway. "See ya in a sec." She slaps Rachel's right buttcheek and winks at her before disappearing into the bathroom.

Rachel snickers to herself as she settles comfortably on the couch and searches for the remote. Julie might be right. It's been seven months since she left home, and there's no indication that her mother has any clue where she's hiding. Maybe she can let her old life die with Rory and Regina. She twirls a curl around her finger, nostalgic for her red hair.

CHAPTER 14

Rachel tacks the last photo on the wall of her new cubicle, then pushes her chair back to admire her work. It was Julie's idea to make Rachel's new space more personable. Rachel spent the weekend exploring the city, snapping photos, and then printing them at FedEx. There are photos of the downtown skyline taken from a beach, a mural painted under a viaduct, and the giraffes at Lincoln Park Zoo. And there's a picture of Julie leaning against a brick wall with an ice cream cone, smiling like they have a shared secret.

"Getting settled?" Plum Lips asks.

"Yep, thanks Tamara," Rachel responds, thankful that the paperwork she'd needed to complete for her promotion was sent in an email with an identifying signature.

"Great! I have to say, I almost didn't recognize you with the new hair color. It looks so good! I wish I could pull off red."

Rachel touches a hand to her curls and smiles. She'd resisted Julie's advice at first, but after she finally relented, it seemed ridiculous that she'd ever been so nervous. It felt entirely possible to stay vigilant while also looking like her true self. When she saw her reflection after the hair treatment, it was like being reacquainted with an old friend. And just like that, Rachel settled into a level of comfort she hadn't felt since college. Once she did it, it was easy, like walking through an open door.

"Well, let me know if you need anything," Tamara says. "Jim will schedule some training with you this week, but in the meantime, feel free to dive into those."

Tamara points to a neat stack of manuscripts sitting in a tray labeled INBOX. Rachel grabs one off the top and spends the morning reading a teenage love story, circling the word *horny* after she notices a trend. It seems to be the only way the author knows how to describe being sexually aroused. *Aroused.* Rachel adds it to a list she's curating of alternative options.

While eating a peanut butter and jelly sandwich at her desk, manuscript in the opposite hand, a new voice interrupts her reading. "My best advice is to get out of here for lunch. Go for a walk. Give those eyes a break."

A tall, sandy-haired man in navy slacks and a tucked-in company polo takes a seat on a filing cabinet in the corner of her cubicle. He looks to be a few days away from a full beard and is wearing white sneakers without socks. Rachel takes note, shifting in her itchy blazer.

"Hi, I'm Jim," he says, extending a hand. "I'm technically your new boss, but we're a team on Editor Row, so don't be afraid to drop by my office if you ever have any questions or concerns."

"I appreciate that," Rachel says, letting him pump her hand twice.

"Now, go get some fresh air and finish that sandwich outside. Just drop by when you're back, and we'll go over a few things. I know I'm supposed to do formal training all week, but you've got this, right? There's really not much to it."

"Uh, ok, sure."

"Sweet. See you later."

He saunters away, hands stuffed casually in his pockets. Rachel sits straighter to look over her cubicle wall and out the window. It *is* a beautiful day, and she doesn't want her new boss to think she can't follow instructions. Rachel puts a sticky note on the edge of the manuscript page to hold her place and gathers her things. She takes her phone out on the way to the elevator and texts Julie.

Got a compliment on my hair. New boss seems cool.

Rachel walks to the park and sits cross-legged on the edge of a short wall that forms the boundary of a floral garden. She takes a baseball cap from her bag and places it on her head, pulling it low to the tops of her sunglasses. She munches on chips from a Ziploc bag and observes the groups of tourists as they walk slowly, always looking up, stopping suddenly to take a picture, which causes a bottleneck in the flow of traffic. She wishes she'd brought the manuscript even though she's been instructed to take a break; there's nothing like reading outside when the weather is so pleasant.

Rachel grabs her sandwich from her bag and takes a bite. The peanut butter sticks to the roof of her mouth and she reaches for her bottle of water, a freebie imprinted with the publishing company's logo. She's careful to keep her hand over the logo as she drinks, then turns it toward the flowers when she sets it back down. Across the sidewalk, a woman poses for a photo, instructing her partner on the height that the camera should be held. She pretends to look off into the distance, but her eyes lock on Rachel. Rachel's muscles seize and she sits motionless, the sandwich up to her mouth.

As the couple moves on, she takes a long breath and gathers her food back into her bag. Next time, she'll choose a less popular spot.

* * *

Rachel walks into Jim's office with a notepad, a pen, and the horny teens. "Is this still an ok time?"

He looks up from his computer and waves her in. "Of course! Have a seat."

Rachel sits across from him and is surprised when he gets up and comes around the desk to sit next to her. He crosses an ankle over his other knee and leans back, hands clasped behind his head.

"Alright, you're going to learn pretty quickly that this is a game of numbers. You're getting the drafts from the agents we've worked with in the past and have an established trust. Just look for big things like plot holes or major inconsistencies. Don't worry about the little details; one of the Copyeditors will take care of those. After you get the hang of things, we might try you out on some drafts that are less likely to be a sure thing. Those usually require more work on the first round of edits, or you might decide it's a dud and move on."

Rachel nods along, rubbing her lips together in concentration. When Jim pauses she jumps in. "Wait, so I get to reject people?"

"Woah tiger, slow down," he chuckles, flashing a sparkling smile. "For now, assume everything we give you is headed to the bestseller list and just needs a little tweaking. We'll see how you do over the next few months and talk about it then."

Rachel flushes and bobs her head up and down, trying to erase the misstep. Jim leans forward and reaches for the manuscript on her lap.

"Let's see how you're doing so far," he says, flipping through the pages, looking for her red ink. "Ok you're going to need to go a little faster, but this is solid work. Jesus, how many times does he use the word horny?"

"Um, so far I've found thirteen."

"Oof, yeah we'll need to fix that . . . keep circling those. These other notes are good, but a lot of them are things we'll deal with at the next review level, so don't let those slow you down. Good though. Real good! Alright, get back to it champ."

Jim taps Rachel's knee with the manuscript before handing it back to her. They stand and shift back and forth, both trying to get around each other, but moving in the same direction at the same time in an awkward dance. Jim stops moving and holds his hands up, palms out in surrender. Rachel ducks out and returns to her cubicle. She takes her phone out of her desk drawer.

Let me know how training
goes at some point

Rachel considers telling Julie more but hesitates. Is Jim just a really friendly guy, or is he giving off a slightly creepy frat guy vibe?

*I think I'll be really good
at this*

She drops her phone back into the drawer and finds her place in the manuscript. She'll wait until she sees Julie later in the week to tell her all about Jim. Specifically, she'll wait until after they've had sex, which Julie claims is the best time to talk about people behind their backs. She says shit talking is the modern day post-coitous cigarette.

Rachel reads, letting herself become immersed in the world of teenage love triangles and shifting sexual preferences. She's fully absorbed when the sound of Jim's voice startles her. "Oops didn't mean to sneak up on you, but it's after 5:00, so you should head out. I know I said to read faster, but I meant in the future. It's your first day. Go home."

Rachel looks down at the manuscript, assessing her progress. "Thanks, but my girlfriend works late tonight, so I don't have anywhere else to be. I really want to finish this so I can start on something new tomorrow."

"Suit yourself. Girlfriend, huh?"

Rachel nods, as much for her own benefit as his. This isn't the first time she's thought of Julie as her girlfriend, but it's the first time she's said it out loud. It feels foreign in her mouth, but satisfying once it's floating in the air.

"That her?" Jim asks, pointing to the photo tacked to the gray fabric of her cubicle.

Rachel glances over her shoulder and smiles. "It is."

"Nice catch!" Jim says with a slight pout. "Well, don't stay too late. I'll see you tomorrow. Good job today."

He points finger guns at her as he backs away, then spins around and rushes toward the exit. Wide-eyed, Rachel turns back to the manuscript on her desk. She reads two more chapters, trying to do a better job of skimming, but now she's invested in the story. She rubs at her dry eyes and finishes another chapter. The words start to blur. She blinks hard and then closes her eyes, tilting her head against the back of her chair. She just needs to rest her eyes for a couple minutes.

* * *

Rachel shifts the duffel bag to her other shoulder and jogs up the stairs toward her Grandma's bedroom. She needs to unpack but wants to check on Pellet first. Turning the corner, she finds Regina pacing the hallway, blocking her path.

"Regina, what's wrong now?"

Regina's eyes are wild and flashing red. "I know! I know he's hiding something."

"This again? No one is having an affair. You both just have your hands full with the kids and it's been an adjustment moving back home . . . and Rory."

Regina's eyes widen. She snaps her head back and forth. "No, no, no . . . I know something is going on. It's been going on for months. He's always texting someone, and sometimes I'll wake up in the middle of the night, and he's not there. When I confront him, he has some lame excuse like he went for a walk. A walk! Out here! At night! And where did all our money go?"

"Ok ok," Rachel says, grabbing Regina by the shoulders. "You're under a lot of stress and I think you're just reading into things. Samuel *loves* you!"

Regina closes her eyes and takes a deep breath. "Maybe you're right. The kids have been running me ragged."

Rachel smiles and gives Regina's shoulders a compassionate squeeze, but the guilt sits heavy in her stomach. She despises her arrangement with Samuel and hates herself for what this is doing to her sister, but she just needs a little bit more time . . . a little bit more money.

Regina gently wipes at her damp cheeks and laughs softly. "Look at me, I'm a mess. Wait, where are you going?"

She frowns and points at Rachel's duffle. Rachel looks down at the bag and then back at her, puzzled. "What are you talking about? I told you I was going to that retreat for a week. I just got back."

"Huh?"

Rachel's heart drops. She drops her bag and pushes past Regina to her grandmother's room. Something putrid assaults her nostrils as soon as she opens the door, and it increases in intensity as she approaches Pellet's cage. Rachel knows what she's about to see will haunt her, but she can't stop herself. Pellet is curled in a back corner of his cage, a dried, shriveled version of himself. His jaw begins to wiggle. Rachel pinches her nose closed and leans closer to the stench. Small, gelatinous maggots come spilling out. A wail claws its way up Rachel's throat as she stumbles back. She cups both hands over her mouth to trap the sound and screams into her palms.

Rachel hears Regina humming down the hall. The rush of tears streaming down her cheeks turn blistering hot. Her blood is lead in her veins. She sets her jaw and steps out into the hall, following the sound of the hum to Regina's room. "Regina!" Rachel shouts. "How could you?"

Regina's hand pauses, mid lipstick application. "Shh, keep your voice down. The baby is asleep in her crib."

She turns back to the mirror on her vanity. Rachel speaks through gritted teeth. "You let Pellet die. I asked you to feed him once a day while I was gone, but you couldn't do this one favor for me. I can't even be gone for a week without you fucking things up."

"Gone? Where'd you go?" Regina asks, reaching for a tube of mascara.

"Jesus Christ, Reg, you're so self-involved."

"Look, I've been so busy with the kids and this shit with Samuel. I honestly don't remember you asking me to feed him, and I didn't realize you went somewhere."

Regina's lashes thicken with each swipe. She sweeps blush over her cheeks in long strokes. A high-pitched ringing builds in Rachel's ears.

"You know what, Reg," she says slowly, "maybe Samuel *is* having an affair. I mean, I wouldn't blame him. All you care about is your kids, and you don't have time for anyone else."

"What? But I . . . " Regina's eyes well.

"And you still haven't lost the baby weight so you know . . . I get it."

Regina's face drops and she whips her head back to center, studying herself in the vanity. She pinches a bit of extra skin beneath her chin. Rachel backs out of the room, closing the door behind her and leans against it. She imagines Regina on the other side, studying every stretch mark and slight imperfection. Rachel smiles.

* * *

Rachel snaps forward in her chair, triggering the motion sensor fluorescents above her and down the row of adjacent cubicles. She wipes drool from the corner of her mouth with the back of her hand. It's dark outside the windows and the office is eerily silent, a sign that it's been empty for hours. Rachel picks her phone up from the desk. 11:49 PM blinks to 11:50 PM as she stares at the screen.

Rachel squints and blinks repeatedly, trying to rehydrate her arid eyes. She yawns loudly, shuffling the manuscript pages into a neat pile and gathering her purse. She trudges to the elevator then stumbles into the lobby, nodding at the night security guard as she enters the revolving door. The air is still warm, but a cool breeze blows in from the lake. Rachel stands tall, widening her shoulders, and walks to the Red Line like it's normal to be heading home at midnight, like she's ready for someone to try some shit.

She takes a seat in the mostly empty car and chews on the inside of her mouth to cut through the thick groggy feeling. The train sways, a gentle rocking sensation, lulling when combined with the warm, summer air trapped in the car. Rachel sits up straighter. She takes her phone out and pulls up the latest conversation.

Done with work?

She breathes deeply, waiting on a response from Julie. The acidic smell of urine stings her nostrils. She takes another breath.

*Just locked up. Need to
wipe down the bar and
then I'll head home.
Why are you awake?
Bad dream?*

*Just left work. On the train.
Can I meet you at your
place?*

*Girl it's midnight! Don't
they know hazing is illegal?
Camille is working so just
buzz when you get here.
Be safe*

Always. Thanks.

Rachel taps a hand against her knee and hums the Empire carpet
jingle on repeat. It's the first song that comes to mind, and she clings
to it with her small amount of remaining willpower. The door chimes
at her stop, and she leaps to her feet just in time to dash through the
doors as they're closing. She jogs across the platform and down the
stairs, urging her body toward the pillow-top mattress and cool sheets
awaiting her at Julie's.

The building comes into view. She climbs the concrete steps and taps
the buzzer, leaning against the door frame until the lock clicks beneath
the deafening drone. She shuffles down the long hallway toward the
staircase. Four flights of stairs await. She sighs and lifts herself onto the
first one, gripping the banister tightly. After one flight, she looks up to
see Julie waiting on the landing in a robe, hand stretched toward her.
"Come on, sleepyhead."

Rachel allows herself to be tugged upward, following Julie into the
apartment and down the hall to the bedroom. Julie undresses her and

pulls her into bed. "I already set an alarm. It's early enough that you should have time to run home to get ready for work."

Rachel murmurs a thank you and wiggles closer to Julie, resting her head on the corner of Julie's pillow, facing her. Julie pushes a curl behind Rachel's ear. "Why'd they make ya work so late?"

"They didn't," Rachel whispers, eyes closing. "I was reading and I fell asleep at some point. I'm not sure how long I was out."

"Well that's quite the nap. I can't believe you're still so tired."

Rachel pulls Julie's arm over her waist, smiling as the warmth of Julie's hand soaks into her lower back. "I guess I never really woke up."

Rachel hears Julie responding, but it sounds like waves in the distance. The ceiling fan blades produce a soft whirring noise, the metal chain of the pull tapping gently against the light cover. The air conditioning clicks on, flooding the room with cold air and another layer of white noise. Rachel tugs the comforter up from her hip to her shoulder and sinks below the depths of the steady ambient sound.

CHAPTER 15

There's a light rapping at the door. Rachel pretends not to hear it. Her phone lights up, a text from Samuel. She knows what it says without looking. She walks to the door and opens it. "What do you want?"

Samuel pushes into the room. He's in a white, cotton V-neck and navy boxer briefs. "You know this would be easier if you would just leave the door unlocked."

Rachel folds her arms over the front of herself, self-conscious of her matching tank top and shorts set with the childish cartoon print. The smiling bunnies seemed cute when she purchased them, but she can feel Samuel's forty-year-old judgment. She tips her chin up at him. "Should I keep the door unlocked while we fuck, too?"

Samuel rolls his eyes but grins. "Don't start with the attitude. I tried to break this off when your nudes practically landed me in bankruptcy court, but someone just can't get enough."

He slides his hands down Rachel's shoulders to her elbows, pulling her arms apart and away from her chest. His hands are curiously smooth, softened by expensive lotions and male privilege. Rachel shudders, playing it off as a chill.

Samuel tucks his thumbs in the waistband of her shorts and tugs. "If you're cold, kiddo, let's get you warmed up."

Rachel shrinks under his presumptuous gaze and condescending tone. He pulls her against him, pushing his tobacco tongue forcefully into her mouth. Rachel feels powerful and commanding through text, but when he's right in front of her, she relents. She lets him take control and practically invites him to destroy her sense of agency. She hates herself for it.

Samuel guides her to the bed and drops her to the mattress. He pulls her pajamas off and then drops his underwear, leaving his shirt on as he climbs on top of her. He slides into her, and she notices that his shirt smells like Regina tonight. The smell makes Rachel's jaw clench, wondering if he slept with Regina before visiting her tonight, but she knows he wouldn't be here if he could get this from Regina. She probably tried to cuddle before he snuck out.

The headboard thunks lightly against the plaster wall. Samuel keeps his eyes closed and never notices whether or not Rachel reciprocates so she lies there, still, letting it happen, pinned against the rocks by the crashing waves of his storm. She stares at the peeling paint on the ceiling. She makes a to-do list in her head. She calculates the remaining sum of money she needs in order to finish her project, her ticket out. If only Samuel would lend it to her in one lump sum instead of making her earn it, week after week.

The sound of the creaking bed frame gives way to a familiar grunt, a clear indication that the end is near. Rachel throws in a soft moan; might as well sell it. Samuel flops onto his back beside her, damp and panting. Rachel feels his sweat on her skin, his fluid between her legs. No one prepared her for the mess of sex. Its vile intrusiveness.

Samuel rolls onto his side and allows his eyes to roam over Rachel's exposed body. She feels crushed beneath the weight of her own held breath. Finally, he lifts his head to look her in the eyes. "Sorry I brought up the photos. I know you hate talking about them. But you have to admit, I'd still be in New York if I hadn't given you all that money. Or if my credit card info wasn't stolen from your website."

Rachel presses a hand to his chest, pushing to scoot herself away from him. She pulls the sheet up over her chest. "I didn't force you to spend all your money," she says, playing with the edge of the sheet, "or to steal from your company. You're here because *you* fucked up."

"Mmm, I love that dirty mouth," Samuel says, leaning toward her. Rachel turns her face away from him and moves a hand between them to block his advances. His face darkens. "Fuck you, Rachel. *You* pursued *me*! Every time I try to break this off, you pull me back in. I'm sick of this innocent little girl act."

Rachel can feel the tension in his body, that temper that threatens to snap her in half. She forces herself to look at him, to offer a small smile. "You're right. I'm sorry."

He stares at her for a moment, but then his face changes, a smug smile spreading across it. "You kill me, kiddo. I'll slide the money under your door tomorrow." He kisses her cheek and rolls out of bed, unlocking the door and peeking out before disappearing into the dark hall. Rachel lies frozen in place.

If her math is correct, she still has months of this ahead. The shame destroys a piece of her each time, but she persists. The only way out is money, but it needs to be consistent and it can't keep coming from Samuel. She has to make her project work. There has to be a faster way, a way to force a bigger payout. She knows what she has to do, but it feels risky. If she pushes him too far, who knows what he's capable of.

Rachel rolls her head toward the open door; Samuel didn't close it behind him. Rachel stares at the terrible noise that penetrates her room from the darkness. That beep. The unending beep of the monitor echoes its way up the stairs from the floor below. Rachel places a pillow over her face and screams.

* * *

A tinkling chime emits from Julie's phone on the nightstand. Rachel reaches over her and turns off the alarm. She hovers over Julie's s-shaped body, listening to the soft whistling sound she makes when she exhales. Biscuit scratches at the closed door. Rachel moves slowly, slipping out of bed and into her clothes in the early morning gray. A groan comes from the bed and she freezes. "Mornin', babe. Did I set the alarm early enough?"

Rachel smiles. "Too early. I think you overestimated the amount of time it takes for me to get ready by about an hour."

Julie sits up, stretching her arms up over her head. "Figured I'd err on the side of caution. Wanna get ready for work and then meet me at Uptown Coffee for a quick bite before ya head out?" She leans over, slumping face-first onto Rachel's pillow. "I just need a sec."

"Sure. I'll feed Biscuit and see you in a bit."

"Thanks, babe." Julie waves blindly in Rachel's general direction. Rachel opens the door to loudly meowed commands. She follows Biscuit to the kitchen, dumps a can of food into his bowl, and leaves the condo, easing the door closed with a muted click.

On the walk to her apartment, Rachel sniffs at a sour smell in the air. It doesn't take her long to find the source. The odor emits from her own body, in the crannies where the damp stress sweat lingers. She quickens her pace, eager to shower. She can taste the sleep on her breath and something darker beneath it. There's acid and the biting black pepper of nicotine.

Rachel climbs the stairs to her apartment two at a time. While she waits for the shower to warm, she brushes her teeth until her gums are raw. She steps in the shower and gives her skin an identical scrubbing. Her phone buzzes on the edge of the sink.

I'm up! I'm up!

Rachel throws a shirt-dress on over leggings and slips her feet into a pair of sandals, remembering Jim's casual attire. She pulls her hair back into a high ponytail and covers her face with tinted moisturizer, patting fingertips of blush along the apples of her cheeks and her hairline for color. She examines herself in the mirror. She looks tired, but not so much that it'll draw attention at work.

Locking the door behind her, Rachel slings her bag across her body and heads back in the direction of the coffee shop. Julie is waiting by the entrance in sweats and slippers. "Don't judge me," she warns with a grin.

They order and claim a small, round table on the patio with a swirling rose in the metal and matching chairs. Rachel can feel the pattern pressing through her leggings, imprinting into the flesh of thighs.

"Lu, I really think ya should see someone. It's not normal to fall asleep at your desk." Julie licks excess cream cheese from the edge of her bagel and takes a bite.

Rachel spins a coffee cup between her hands and shifts in her seat. "I know, but it's probably just temporary. I was sleeping well for a while, and I'm sure I just dredged shit up by telling you all these stories from my past."

"Oh, so now it's *my* fault?"

"No, I-"

"I'm kiddin'," Julie says, swatting the air. "You're probably right, but it doesn't seem healthy to ignore it either. If you keep suppressin' these memories, they might pop up in unexpected ways."

"Ok, Dr. Julie," Rachel says with a laugh. She takes a bite of a glazed donut. The sugar is sticky, and she runs her tongue along her teeth to loosen it.

Julie smiles at a small child that runs by on the sidewalk, stuffed animal in hand. She turns back to Rachel and sighs. "That's exactly my point. I don't know what I'm talkin' 'bout. Ya need a professional to give ya some guidance. I know ya had a bad experience with therapy before, but maybe ya just need to find someone else thatcha can feel comfortable with."

Rachel shrugs and sets the donut down, sucking the glaze from her fingers. A small sparrow hops closer, looking for discarded crumbs. The leaves on a neighboring elm tree rustle above them in the breeze. Rachel tilts her face up to the morning sky.

"Ok, ya clearly don't wanna talk 'bout this right now," Julie says. "But promise me you'll consider it. I think if ya work through this shit and make sense of what happened, you'll figure out how it affects your current anxiety."

"Who's anxious?" Rachel asks, smiling into the sun.

Julie picks up her bagel for another bite. "Ya know what I mean, babe. I just think that if ya can get to a place where these memories aren't so devastating, you'll sleep better and be happier. Just think whatcha could do on a full night's sleep!"

Rachel's head falls back down. She blows air between her lips.

"I'm serious!" Julie says, leaning closer to Rachel over the table. "You went to college on a full scholarship because of an essay ya wrote. Why dontcha start journalin' or write a blog or somethin'?"

"I tried to write a book once, actually. A Memoir." Rachel takes a drink of coffee from the bottom half of the paper cup. It's already gone cold.

"And?"

"Uh, it didn't work out. My brother-in-law lent me some of the money from their home sale as a sort of advance so I could buy all this fancy writing software so I could self-publish. There were so many additional costs. Editing, design, cover art and then I had to create a website to market the book . . . it wasn't going to be cheap. I poured my heart into that first draft and then I couldn't do it. I didn't want to put such a huge part of myself out there for others to dissect. The day I told him, I checked myself into that treatment program . . . the therapy thing I told you about."

"I guess it would be weird to share so many personal things with the world, but I bet it was so good." Julie sighs. "Did ya have to pay back the advance?"

"I'd already spent most of it. My brother-in-law was pissed. I've never seen him so angry, and that man has a temper." Rachel remembers the vein protruding from his forehead when she told him the money was gone, the taste of metal in her mouth when he showed her just how much worse it could get.

"Cool, another angry dude." Julie rolls her eyes. "Is that who ya were arguin' with in your sleep last night?"

"What?" Rachel asks. It comes out high-pitched, sharp. She takes another bite of her donut, feigning a level of indifference. The sugar churns in her stomach.

Julie brushes at the poppy seeds that have fallen into her lap. "Yeah, I couldn't make out any real words, but it sounded like ya were havin' a heated conversation with someone. I just assumed it was a man." She winks and takes another bite.

Rachel laughs nervously. She stuffs the rest of the donut into her coffee cup, wiping her fingers on a corner of the napkin. She walks across the patio to a trashcan and tosses everything in, pausing a moment to take a deep breath before returning to the table. She braces herself against the back of the metal chair while Julie finishes her bagel.

"Hey, it's ok if I sleep at my own place for a while right?" Rachel asks, stretching to busy her limbs. "I'd just feel more comfortable in my own bed until I get these nightmares under control again."

"Ya know that's fine with me," Julie says, pushing back from the table. She stands and links an arm through Rachel's. "When am I gonna get to see this place where ya sleep when you're not at my place, though?"

"Oh, my place is small and gross. You don't want to spend any time there. Trust me."

Julie shrugs and leads them toward the train station. "I'm sure it's fine. Dontcha think it's a *lil* weird that we're sleepin' together, but there's still so much I don't know 'boutcha? Like where ya live?"

Rachel trips on an uneven strip of concrete and stumbles forward. Julie grabs her forearm just in time to prevent a fall. "Woah, girl. Ok, ok, that's still off limits. You don't hafta be so dramatic."

Rachel matches Julie's light-hearted laugh as best she can and re-adjusts the bag on her shoulder. They enter the crowded train station and Julie pulls them into a corner out of the way. "If ya wanna stop by the bar after work, I'll be there every night this week. Most weeknights are slow so we can get cheese fries from across the street and watch terrible TV. I'll pour ya somethin' extra strong that might help ya sleep."

Rachel nods. "I like that plan. Thanks."

"Of course, babe." Julie kisses her on the lips then spins her around, smacking both buttcheeks to propel her toward the stairs. "Have a good day!"

Rachel looks over her shoulder as she climbs the stairs to the train platform. Julie is still in the corner, waving, and Rachel feels her heart squeeze. When Rachel was allowed to attend elementary school, her grandmother would put her on the bus in the mornings and then wave until the bus was out of sight. The memory burns in her chest. She remembers returning home after school and finding her grandmother dancing to a record in the living room, martini in hand. Maybe she *was* a drunk, but Rachel understands the need to cope in that household. She pushes her way onto the packed train, tired but smiling.

* * *

The clanking sound of a deadbolt jolts Rachel awake. She lifts her forehead from the surface of the bar, sticky from years of spilled drinks. It's dark, but she can make out the shape of two martini glasses in front of her, empty. A shape moves through the shadows, backlit by streetlights. "I told ya those were too strong for ya," Julie says, spinning Rachel's bar stool to face her. "But someone wouldn't listen."

She drapes her arms over Rachel's shoulders and leans in, rubbing their noses together. It tickles. "Wanna come home with me? Ya can grab a change of clothes this time."

Rachel hesitates. Julie's hands are at the back of her head, deep in her curls. Julie's nails lightly scratch her scalp. A cool tingle spreads down her neck, raising goosebumps along her arms. "I really think it's best if I sleep in my own bed for a while."

"Ok," Julie says, dropping her hands to Rachel's thighs. "I just worry 'boutcha gettin' home since ya won't let me walk ya." Her hands slide up Rachel's thighs to her waist. They grip the waistband of Rachel's leggings. "Plus, I like wakin' up next to ya." Julie's mouth closes over Rachel's, lifting her from the groggy, bleary-eyed depths of alcohol-induced sleep.

Rachel scoots to the edge of the bar stool, lifting slightly so her leggings and underwear can slip to the floor, dragging her sandals with them. She slips her hands inside Julie's shirt and fumbles with the hooks of her bra. Julie pulls away. "This one is tricky," she says, tossing her shirt on the bar and unhooking her bra, letting it fall onto Rachel's clothes on the floor. She steps back toward Rachel.

Rachel wraps her legs around Julie, removing any space between them, forcing the heat from their bodies to combine. Their mouths connect again, tongues circling each other. The bitterness of hops competing with briny olive juice. Rachel presses herself against Julie's breasts, yearning to be closer, closer.

Time slips by, a tempest of searching fingers and hungry mouths. In the aftermath of gasping breaths, Rachel pulls her dress and shoes back on and tosses everything else in her bag. She watches Julie adjust her breasts back into her bra, the colorful flowers on her arm twisting, muted in the dark. They smile at each other, and Rachel knows she's made it awkward by insisting on going home alone. She fixates on the heavy feeling of her eyelids, reassuring herself that this plan will work. She's finally found the right tonic for dreamless sleep.

CHAPTER 16

Rachel tips the blender and pours a smoothie into a glass tumbler, handing it to Regina. "Try to keep it down this time."

Regina's hand tremors as she lifts the glass to her lips and takes a sip. "I don't know what's wrong with me, Rach. I know everyone thinks this is like high school, but it's not. Sure, I started drinking these smoothies to lose weight, but I don't want to be sick all the time. I have zero energy to take care of the kids and . . . " her face contorts and she begins to sob. "What's wrong with me?"

Rachel runs a hand over Regina's back. "I don't know, but if you tell a doctor that you started dieting and now you throw up every day . . . with your history? They'll commit you."

"I can't go back there," Regina says through bleary eyes. "I can't leave my babies."

"Then let me keep helping you. These smoothies have so many vitamins and minerals that you have to be absorbing something before you throw it up." Rachel takes the blender to the sink and begins to rinse it out. The sound of the running water helps to drown out the sound of Rory's vitals monitor. Rachel sometimes takes three long showers a day, trying to silence the tell-tale heart. She sets the blender on a drying rack and walks to the living room.

Regina is slumped in a chair, staring out the window. Her cheekbones bulge out of her face, and her collarbones form deep trenches. She's all sharp angles and sallow skin. Rachel backs out of the room and climbs the stairs to the second floor. The monitor beeps loudly. The curtains are drawn and the room is cold. Regina is standing over

Rory, silently crying. The nurse is asleep in a glider, a magazine splayed across her chest. "What happened to us?" Regina whispers over Rory's oxygen tube.

Everything is baggy on her now. She wears drawstring pants so she can cinch them tightly over her jutting hips bones. Her hair has thinned and through the brittle strands, every vertebrae of her neck is visible. She turns, locking eyes with Rachel, then fades to shadow.

* * *

The August air is thick and muggy. Rachel kicks at the bed sheet that wrapped itself around her leg while she was sleeping. She misses air conditioning and waking up to the smell of rose water-scented skin. The oscillating fan whirs, but underneath the white noise is a sharp beep. It grows louder and louder and then stops with a shudder. Metal bangs against metal, the sound of dumpsters attaching to the garbage truck. A new beeping signals that the dumpster is being lifted up to empty its contents into the truck.

Rachel rushes to the bathroom and turns on the shower. She drops her underwear to the floor and steps into the cold water, immersing her face in the icy stream. As she showers, she tries to formulate a plan for the morning, a way to pass time while she waits for Julie to get her nails done. Rachel pictures the contents of her refrigerator and settles on grocery shopping. Maybe there's something stronger than Tylenol PM that she can purchase because the current sleep routine isn't working.

That night at Pale Gael's turned into every night, downing drinks and watching late night television, trying to clear her mind of memories. At closing, Julie locks up and turns out the lights. They fool around behind the bar, taking turns on the counter, propped up on elbows, toes curled over the edge. Julie always offers to walk her home, and Rachel always refuses, stumbling the long way around the block to her front door. Tingling with the dopamine from alcohol and sex, Rachel consistently feels like she's on the verge of a good night's sleep. And every night, her past catches up with her.

Rachel slides a thin cotton dress over her head and pulls her wet curls into a ponytail. She grabs her purse and digs for her sunglasses while slipping on sandals at the door. Walking to the store is like being boiled alive. The temperature on the sign outside a bank reads 94 degrees, and the humidity traps the heat against her skin. Her dress is damp and glued to her body by the time she reaches the grocery store.

Walking through the automatic doors, Rachel is met with a blast of frigid air conditioning that makes her shiver. She takes her time wandering the aisles, absorbing the cold air in her pores. Her basket fills with prepared meals, frozen dinners, and easy snacks; nothing that takes much energy since she doesn't have any to spare. She looks for sales and store brands. Despite the salary increase that came with her promotion, she still feels compelled to save every penny possible and has felt a certain delight watching the safe fill at a faster rate.

These days, when she's counting the accumulated money, she dreams less of using it to go back on the run and more about moving in with Julie and playing house, referring to Biscuit as a friend's cat that they co-parent, lying in bed one morning and deciding they should get their own place. And that's when Rachel would surprise Julie by having a down payment saved so they could buy a place together. In these fantasies, Rachel doesn't dwell on the details, like how to get approved for a home loan without providing a real name, or what she would do if someone discovered her and she had to escape. She focuses on the positives, hoping to dream them into existence.

"Excuse me, miss!"

Rachel's attention snaps back to the line for self-checkout. An attendant is waving her over to an open kiosk. She fumbles through the checkout process, then hoists two large tote bags up onto her shoulders and shuffles out onto the steamy asphalt parking lot. Muscle memory guides her home, beads of sweat forming and cascading down her body in choreographed repetition. At the door to her building, Rachel sets down the bags and jiggles her key in the lock.

"Well hello there, stranger."

Rachel leaves her keys dangling and turns to face Julie. She blinks repeatedly, sure this must be a mirage. Maybe she fell asleep or has heatstroke.

Julie pulls her into a sweaty hug. "I was just 'bout to text ya to letcha know that I'm done. How crazy is it that I've been gettin' my nails done next door to ya this whole time?"

"Wow, crazy," Rachel murmurs.

"Need help with your bags?"

"Oh no, I've got it," Rachel says, turning the key and lifting the totes. "Let me just run these upstairs and then I'll come right back down." She slips inside and lets the door slam behind her before Julie can respond. She puts the groceries away and takes a water bottle from the freezer, pressing it to her forehead and neck. The shocking cold lifts a bit of the cerebral fog. She rushes back downstairs, anxious to leave the area, as if this would erase her location from Julie's mind.

"Danforth, huh?"

"What?" Rachel asks, reeling. How does Julie know her mother's maiden name?

Julie taps a dark orchid nail against the glass of the front door. "It's on your mailbox."

"Oh, right. Welp, now you know my last name. Let's go." Rachel grabs Julie's hand and yanks her toward the crosswalk.

"Woah, woah," Julie says, resisting. "Where are we goin'?"

Rachel doesn't care where they go. She just wants them as far away from this corner as possible. She wants to go back in time and ask Julie where she gets her nails done. She wants to be a smarter person who would have thought to use the alley exit rather than the front entry. "It's so hot today. Can we just hang out at your place and order in or something?"

On the other side of the intersection, Julie drops Rachel's hand and plants her feet. "Lu, I've been workin' every day for, like, forever, and I wanna do somethin' other than lounge 'round at home. Let's *do* somethin'!"

Rachel squares off against her. She hadn't anticipated push back. "But it's so hot . . . "

"Ok, so let's go see a movie. It'll be cool in there. We can get popcorn and ICEEs. We'll pick somethin' dumb so ya don't hafta concentrate." Julie counts off her arguments on her fingers.

"Fiiine," Rachel grunts. "Can I also get a coffee?"

"Let's take care of the coffee right now before ya fall asleep on the train," Julie says, pointing in the direction of Uptown Coffee.

Rachel nods and follows her down the street and inside. Rachel orders a double-dirty, iced chai for herself and an extra-hot dark roast for Julie. Julie does not subscribe to different coffee preparations for different seasons and sips her steaming coffee as soon as it's handed to her, fumbling for her debit card with her free hand.

They head to the train and manage to find a train car with open seating. Rachel leans back into the air conditioning along the windows. "Thanks for this," she says, lifting her drink. "I didn't sleep well last night."

"Ya clearly haven't been sleepin' well for weeks," Julie responds. "You've been a zombie lately, but ya already know what I'm thinkin' so I'm not gonna say it."

"I know, I know, and I'm considering it. I'm going to try some over-the-counter sleep aids first and see if that helps. If not, I promise I'll find a psychiatrist." Rachel has no intention of seeing anyone. She did pick up some store brand Tylenol PM that's currently sitting in her purse, but that's the extent of her plans. Julie doesn't need to know that, though. Rachel wonders why it took her this long to just lie about it.

Julie slings an arm around Rachel and kisses her on the cheek. "I'm so glad to hear that. I know ya get tired of me botherin' ya 'bout it, but I nag 'cause I care."

"Ok, ok," Rachel says, squirming. "Get your hot lips away from me. I'm already so sweaty that I might slip right off this seat onto the floor."

Julie laughs and removes her arm. They drink their coffees in silence until the speakers announce that their stop is next. When Julie stands to head to the doors, Rachel follows. She holds her nearly empty drink in one hand and grips a metal support pole in the other. Rachel struggles to keep her balance as the train jerks back and forth through the tunnel. She stares at her reflection in the window of the door, the lights of the tunnel flashing past. Her eyes look sunken and her skin thin, the web of capillaries clearly visible. The lights on the train flicker, and for a moment, Regina's face reflects back.

Rachel sucks in a breath and backs up into the passenger standing behind her. "Sorry. I'm sorry." She moves closer to the door and squints at the window. Her eyes squint back and then the doors open. She shakes her head and follows Julie out of the train and up the stairs. At street level, the sky has darkened, compressing the humidity into something combustible.

"Let's get to the theater before it starts rainin'," Julie says, taking off in a jog.

Rachel trails behind, struggling to filter oxygen out of the thick, wet air. She prays the rain is heavy enough to provide respite from the heat. Somewhere far in the distance, thunder rumbles. They push through the revolving door and take a second to catch their breath, discarding their coffee cups in a wastebasket. On the escalator to the theater lobby, Rachel turns around and wraps her arms around Julie's neck, bending slightly to kiss her.

"Well, look who woke up. I thought my lips were too hot for ya." Julie smirks.

They walk to the "Now Showing" digital screen, and Julie points to a rom-com sequel. "That's sure to suck. Ya up for it?"

Rachel doesn't care what they see, but she knows that this is Julie's favorite kind of movie—terrible. For hours after it's over, she'll interrupt conversations with sentences that start with, *Oh my god, what 'bout that scene where...*

"Sure," Rachel smiles. "You get the tickets and I'll get the snacks?"

Rachel orders an ICEE for each of them, Coke for Julie and blue raspberry for herself. The cashier places them next to a large bucket of popcorn, a box of Junior Mints, and a bag of Reese's Pieces. Rachel pays and begins to calculate how she'll carry everything when Julie steps up beside her. Julie takes the bucket of popcorn and holds up the Reese's Pieces. "These go in the popcorn, right?"

Rachel smiles at her. "Yes, dear. I know what you like."

They find their seats and then take turns watching their belongings while the other uses the restroom. Something about this perfectly normal action solidifies their status as a fully adult relationship in Rachel's head. After endless previews, the movie opens in a woman's apartment as she prepares for a date. Names of actors and actresses flash across the screen, and Rachel studies Julie's reactions to discern if she's expected to know any of them. Julie turns to her and smiles. "Ya know I love ya, right?"

Rachel nods, surprising herself. "I love you, too."

Rachel stares at the screen, replaying the moment over and over to the soundtrack of a movie that, in the end, is a complete blur. She doesn't notice the sappy dialogue or unresolved plot lines. Her attention is focused on the placement of Julie's hand, high on her thigh, the light massage that comes dangerously close and then retreats. As the end credits roll, Julie leads Rachel toward a side door with an illuminated emergency exit sign. A dimly lit stairwell is on the other side.

Julie lifts Rachel's dress to her waist and presses her against the door. Rachel wraps a leg around Julie's hip, tilting her pelvis up. Their hands tug each other closer. Their mouths find each other, tongues greedy. The salt from the popcorn mixes with the salt on their skin. Julie pins Rachel's arms above her head with one hand; the other slips beneath Rachel's lace underwear.

A crack of lightning slices across the sky, splitting open nimbus clouds and spilling heavy rain on the sizzling pavement below. An echoing boom of thunder follows, reverberating through the stairwell. Rachel and Julie gasp simultaneously and collapse into each other. They take a few gulping breaths to gather themselves and then jog down the stairs to the street exit. They burst through the door and shriek as they find themselves caught in the storm.

Rachel points out an awning and they run to it, huddling together while Julie requests a Lyft. The combination of cool rain and warm air causes cold sweats, goosebumps rippling up clammy arms. Julie announces that their ride is two minutes away and pulls Rachel closer.

"Can I stay with you tonight?" Rachel asks through a shiver.

"I would love that, babe," Julie says. She pushes a wet curl out of Rachel's eyes and tips her chin up.

Rachel kisses her like it's the last time and does not startle at the next bolt of lighting. On the car ride home, Rachel turns Julie's hand palm-side up and writes I Love You with her index finger, replacing the word Love with a heart. Julie leans over and whispers, "Me too," punctuating each word with a squeeze of Rachel's hand.

The exchange is light and youthful but reassuring in its certainty. To Rachel, it feels like finding a key in her pocket that she thought had gone missing years ago. She delights in this second chance, an opportunity to relive her younger years the way they should have been, full of flirtation and discovery and longing so strong it feels like careening on the edge of a cliff.

When the car pulls up outside the condo, they exit from the same side, staying near each other, touching constantly. They fall into bed and Rachel scoots over to Julie's side, pressing herself into the mold of Julie's back. She tucks an arm under Julie's breasts and synchronizes her breaths to the rise and fall of Julie's chest.

"Hey, Lu?"

Rachel pushes Julie's hair aside and nuzzles into her neck. "Yes?"

"I don't tell people I love 'em . . . not like that. Not so quick."

"Okaaay . . . " Rachel lifts herself up slightly so that she can see the side of Julie's face.

"I just feel somethin' different with ya. I really admire everything you've done."

"Admire?" Rachel's brow furrows. She runs down the list of stressors in her life, curious what anyone could possibly envy.

Julie rolls onto her back and smiles up at Rachel, burying a hand in Rachel's curls. "Yeah, admire," she says. "Ya left an incredibly toxic environment and I know ya feel guilty 'bout that, but ya made the decision, even though it was tough. You've been strugglin' with those nightmares, and yet, ya get up every morning and do such a good job at work thatcha got a promotion. You're a survivor, and I'm super attracted to that."

Rachel smiles back at her tentatively. "So, you're still ok with the secrets? With there being things I can't tell you . . . maybe ever?"

"Ok, maybe this says more about me than it does you . . . " Julie pauses, her eyes shining in the light that sneaks in from the edge of the curtains, " . . . but all of it kinda turns me on. I can't imagine how hard it must be to carry those horrible memories with ya. You're the strongest person I've ever met. And I understand that part of stayin' strong and safe means keepin' things from everyone, includin' me. I'm just happy you've told me as much as ya have." Julie groans and rolls back over onto her side. "God, I should probably see a therapist, too."

Rachel settles back down next to Julie and breathes in the calming rose water. She pushes one of her legs between Julie's, wanting so badly to be even closer to her, to be so entwined that they're essentially one body.

"Lu, just don't-"

"Lie. I know," Rachel murmurs. She says it earnestly, like a promise. It's as much for her own benefit as for Julie's, but what exactly is a lie? Do omissions and half-truths count?

A silence falls over the room. Rachel sighs and closes her eyes. She takes herself back to the theater, to that moment. *Love.* She doesn't care if sleep brings nightmares, or secrets exposed. The past can do what it wants with her. She is loved.

CHAPTER 17

Rachel creeps down the stairs and stands on the bottom step, listening. She moves forward and peaks over the banister, down to the bottom floor, and notices the missing shoes by the front door. Samuel and the kids must have left already, headed into town to finish making arrangements. Rachel moves down the hall. A loud shout travels up the stairway, and she freezes. It happens again, and she recognizes it as her mother screaming at the TV. She resumes her walk to Rory's room.

Rory's heart rate is a jumping blip on a machine. His blood pressure, pulse rate, oxygen levels, and temperature are represented by colorful numbers, almost cheerful. The ventilator pushes and pulls oxygen in and out of his body with a rushing sound like static on an unused television channel. Rachel understands how someone could become accustomed to that noise, like waves coming to shore. What she does not understand is how someone could stand being in this room day in and day out with that piercing beep of his heart. There's a neatly made daybed against the wall where her mother insists the nurse sleep. *What kind of person takes a job like this?*

The nurse has just stepped away to make herself some lunch. She eats each meal at a set time every day, following a strict schedule as ordered. *Can she hear the beeping from downstairs? Maybe.* Rachel turns a dial a few clicks to the left. The volume decreases, and she feels the tension leave her shoulders. She waits a few minutes to see if the quiet will bring the nurse. It doesn't.

Rory's eyes are closed. His face looks thinner, and there are scars from the shattered safety glass. Rachel pulls her cardigan tighter and sits in the chair next to him. "I'm sorry about Regina. They're going to wait to bury her until after Christmas. Strange to think about her being in cold storage until then, but this room you're in is basically an ice box, so you know better than I do."

Rachel sits with him, holding his cold and lifeless hand. "Are you in there, Rory? Can you even hear me?" She scans his body, looking for any sign of change. "You're never coming back are you?" She sighs. "This isn't a way to live. You're not even living . . . not really." She leans closer. "You can just let go. If you want. You don't have to stay like this. If you can hear me, just let go."

Rachel waits, half expecting a response. The only answer is the beeping, still so loud despite the lowered volume. And then the beeping turns to a solid tone. Rachel's heart begins to race. *Can the nurse still hear the monitor? Surely there's an alarm that will bring her running?* The screen of the monitor goes blank. The room is silent. Rachel looks to the doorway and back to Rory. She backs toward the hallway, numb. Her lips move, but no sound comes out. *How much time has passed? Too much.*

She runs from the room and up the stairs to her bedroom. A half packed suitcase sits on the bed. Rachel packs a few more clothes from the closet and spins around, looking for essentials. She takes Grandma's perfume from the top of the dresser and the art book from her bedside table and adds them to the duffle bag before zipping it closed. Her purse is slung across the back of her desk chair. She grabs it in one hand and the duffle in the other, rushing out of the room.

Rachel descends the stairs two at a time. She pulls her coat from a hook in the foyer and puts it on, shoving her feet into her winter boots. A floorboard creaks and she looks up. The nurse is walking to the stairs from the kitchen. In her hand is a plate with a sandwich and baby carrots. She smiles at Rachel and begins to climb the stairs two at a time.

Rachel's chest tightens. She laces her boots tightly, slowed by her fumbling hands. She snags Grandma's car keys from the catch-all on the entryway table and opens the front door. Behind her, the sound of a plate shattering echoes down the stairway. The snow crunches under her boots as she trudges to the car.

* * *

Rachel snaps awake, throwing the blankets off and scrambling against the wall behind her pillow. Julie stands next to the bed with a coffee mug in each hand. "At least ya didn't scream this time," she says, placing a mug on the bedside table for Rachel. "Did I wake ya up?"

"I don't know," Rachel says, pulling her knees to her chest. "If you did, thank you."

Julie sits on the edge of the bed, a black silk robe tied loosely around her waist. She sips her coffee and stares at a stack of books on the floor. She sighs, and Rachel braces herself for a lecture. "I had plans to get up and make breakfast, but that thunderstorm gave me a lil bit of a headache. How do ya feel 'bout breakfast on a patio somewhere? Maybe that new place we read 'bout? Supposed to be cooler today, so it might be nice to be outside."

"That sounds perfect," Rachel says, reaching for her mug. "I don't have a change of clothes, though."

Julie slowly walks to her dresser and opens a drawer. "You're smaller than me, but I'm sure I can find somethin' for ya to borrow. Here." She tosses a romper with a drawstring waist onto the bed and moves to the window. She resumes her coffee drinking, watching the birds on the power line and rubbing her temple with her free hand.

Rachel dresses, trying to stay silent so as not to exacerbate Julie's headache. Biscuit pushes the open door another inch ajar and squeezes into the room, meowing loudly to be fed.

"Ugh, can ya take care of that," Julie grumbles. "I just need a minute for this Excedrin to kick in."

Rachel scoops Biscuit up and pulls the door closed behind them. She puts him in front of his food dish in the kitchen and fills it with dry kibble. He gobbles it while Rachel sits at the table and watches him absentmindedly. She closes her eyes and lets her head bob, floating in the darkness. A fly lands on the IV tube coming out of Rory's left hand.

Rachel jumps to her feet, blinking away the image.

"Ready," Julie calls from the hall.

Rachel grabs her purse from the bedroom and slips on her sandals before following Julie out onto the landing. Julie locks the door, dressed all in black with large sunglasses over her eyes. As they walk down the sidewalk, Julie is quiet. Rachel looks down at her feet, unsure what to say. *Is it really a headache, or is she mad at me? Did I do something wrong? I thought last night was so magical, and now it seems like . . .*

"Look out!"

Rachel looks up to see a car barreling toward her in the intersection. She moves in slow motion, urging her body back to the safety of the curb where Julie stands. The side mirror clips her elbow and sends her reeling. She falls to the ground, scraping the palms of her hands and landing hard on her knees. She hears a pop.

"Oh my god, Lu!" Julie screams, running into the intersection to help her up. "Are ya ok?"

Rachel brushes the dirt and pebbles off her bleeding hands and tries to stand, looking around to see how many people saw. A few strangers slow down, but then continue when they see that she's getting up. Julie cups her elbows and helps her to her feet. Pain shoots through her right ankle, and she knows she's found the source of the popping sound. She shifts to the other foot. "Uh, it's ok. I'm fine. I think I twisted my ankle as I was falling or something. It hurts to stand on this one." She nods to the right side of her body and grimaces, leaning on Julie and hobbling onto the sidewalk.

Julie guides her to a stoop and lowers her onto a step. She examines Rachel's injuries, making sympathetic noises every time she finds a new bump, bruise, or scrape. Rachel feels herself shaking slightly, but she does nothing to conceal it, enjoying Julie's attention.

"It's fine," Rachel says. "I just need a Kleenex or something for my hands and knees. I think there are some in my purse." She looks around her, dazed. "Where's my purse?"

"Oh, I see it. Be right back." Julie jogs to the intersection and bends to pick it up from the gutter.

Rachel studies her hands, a burning sensation setting in now that the adrenaline is wearing off. She touches a finger to the edge of the road rash and winces.

"Lu?"

Julie's shadow falls over Rachel as she picks at the debris in one of her knees. "Yes?"

"What is *this*?"

Rachel looks up and inhales sharply. Julie is holding Rachel's card case and examining a Pennsylvania driver's license, brow furrowed. She pushes her sunglasses on top of her head and looks closer. "Why does this say your name is Rachel Adams?"

Rachel's mouth goes dry, and she tastes battery acid at the back of her throat. Her mind is blank. All of her instincts are misfiring, and the only impulse she can cling to is defensiveness. "Why are you going through my things?"

"Some stuff fell out when ya dropped it, and I was just puttin' it back in. I saw this lil wallet and figured we'll need your insurance card to getcha checked out and . . . what the fuck is this?"

"Julie, please just sit down. I can explain." Rachel pats the concrete next to her, remembering too late that her hand is sore. As Julie lowers herself onto the step next to her, Rachel racks her brain for an explanation that isn't the truth. She bites at a thumbnail, trying to focus.

"Is this *real*?" Julie asks. She drops the purse in Rachel's lap but keeps the card case and ID in her hands.

Rachel perks up. Once again, Julie has supplied the answer. "No," she says, "It's fake. I paid a guy to make it when I ran away from home. I was trying to protect my identity as much as possible because of my mother. I haven't had to use it, but I feel safer knowing it's there."

"Okaaay," Julie says, drawing it out as she raises her eyebrows. "So your real name is . . . ?"

"Louise, which I hate. Louise Danforth." Rachel flashes a nervous smile.

Julie continues to look back and forth between Rachel's face and the ID. Finally, she hands it to Rachel. "Ok, sorry. Didn't mean to snoop.

Is your insurance card in here, though? We should really take ya to the hospital to get that ankle looked at."

She turns her attention to the card case. Rachel's eyes bulge. "No!"

Julie freezes. "No, what?"

Rachel leans over and snatches the case out of Julie's hand. The health insurance forms required the name tied to her social security number and did not provide a field for a preferred name like the internal company paperwork. She considered going without coverage but thought that would only draw attention to herself. The card has Rachel Adams printed on it in all caps, impossible to explain.

"I, uh, hate hospitals. You know, with my brother and sister . . . "

"Right. Well what do ya wanna do then?" Julie asks, throwing her hands up.

Rachel looks up and down the street, trying to get her bearings. She remembers seeing a sign for a Minute Clinic in the window of the CVS a few blocks north. She assumes she can tell them she doesn't have insurance and just pay cash for care. "Just help me to the CVS. I'll let them clean me up and wrap this ankle or something. Really, though, I'm fine."

She stands and tries to descend the stairs without putting much weight on her right ankle. Every step makes her want to scream. She presses her lips together tightly, exhaling little moans.

"Yeah, ya look totally fine," Julie says, rolling her eyes and slinging an arm around Rachel's waist.

They stagger-step to the pharmacy, which turns out to be five blocks away. In the back of the store, Rachel leans against the clinic's kiosk and catches her breath, wiping sweat from her forehead with an index finger and wiping it on a thigh of the jumper. She rotates toward Julie and motions at the waiting area. "I've got this. You can have a seat."

She checks in as Louise Danforth, then sits next to Julie. When the nurse practitioner calls her name, Rachel puts her hand on Julie's arm. "Just wait here."

She shuffles toward the examination room, ignoring Julie's eyes on her back. The door to the room closes, and Rachel uses the privacy to take a deep shuddering breath. She climbs onto the examination table with help from the nurse, who introduces herself as Lisa. They work through the normal intake questions, Lisa tapping away loudly at the computer keyboard.

"Ok, then," Lisa says, spinning her stool around to face Rachel. "Before we get into what happened, I want you to know that this is a safe space. I want you to be honest with me. If there are any resources or help that you need, I can put you in touch with a case worker."

Rachel tilts her head, working at the coded message. It clicks, and she laughs nervously. "Oh, no one hurt me if that's what you mean. I wasn't paying attention and got bumped by a car. It knocked me down, and that's how I got all of this."

She holds up her raw hands and nods down at her scuffed knees. The story sounds made up when she says it out loud, but she has to convince this nurse that it's the truth. The last thing she needs is a case worker digging into her life.

Lisa pulls on a pair of latex gloves. "Ok, but if you remember other details . . . things that make you feel unsafe, just let me know. And if you'd feel more comfortable with your female friend in here-"

"Oh, that's my girlfriend," Rachel interrupts. "She was with me when it happened. I'm really embarrassed actually. Such a klutz."

"We see cases of domestic violence in queer couples too," Lisa says, handing Rachel a pamphlet. "Maybe just take this with you so you have it."

Rachel glances down at the face of a sad woman with the faint trace of a bruise on her cheek. Rachel lifts her head back up and smiles at Lisa. "Sure," she says, when what she really wants to ask is if every man that comes in with cuts and scrapes gets the same pamphlet.

Lisa cleans and dresses the wounds, placing large bandages over each knee. She then turns her attention to the injured ankle, which has swollen and turned a dark shade of purple. She carefully removes Rachel's sandal and bends down to examine the injury. "You really should see a doctor about this. They can take an x-ray and fit you for the right brace. All I can do is wrap it."

Rachel shakes her head. "I'm fine. Could you just wrap it and then I'll ice it when I get home?"

Lisa purses her lips. Her eyes dart between Rachel and the pamphlet that is currently crumpled in Rachel's lap. "Ok, honey, but have the pharmacist fit you for a pair of crutches and stay off it for at least a week. If it gets worse or you can't move it, promise me you'll go to the doctor."

Rachel nods vigorously, whatever it takes to get out of this place. She bites her lip against the pain as Lisa wraps the ankle with an Ace bandage and secures it in place. She slips the sandal back on and gives Rachel the total cost for the visit, an exorbitant amount for a saline wash and Band-Aids. Rachel hands her cash and watches her leave the room to get change. While Rachel is alone, she balls up the domestic violence brochure and tosses it in the garbage.

Lisa returns and hands her change and a receipt. She helps Rachel down from the table and holds the door open for her, flashing her a sympathetic face as one last parting barb. Rachel grits her teeth and limps back out to the waiting area where Julie is scrolling on her phone.

"What, no crutches?" Julie asks, standing as Rachel approaches.

"This will work for now. I don't have enough cash on me to afford crutches, so I'll just hobble up here tomorrow and buy some." Rachel hops the last few steps to Julie and leans against a chair, catching her breath.

Julie tilts her head to the side. "What do ya mean? Can't ya put it on a card?" Her eyes narrow. "Do ya not have a credit card?"

"No, I uh . . . just not on me . . . " Rachel stammers.

"Oh, for fuck's sake, Lu, let me buy ya the crutches, and ya can pay me back."

Julie approaches the pharmacy pick-up window. She talks to a technician, points over to Rachel, and then indicates Rachel's height against her own body. The technician disappears, then returns with a pair of crutches, ringing them up and handing them to her over the counter. She walks back to Rachel and thrusts them at her.

"Here. Let's getcha home."

As they approach the intersection where the accident happened, Rachel looks up at Julie. "Don't you want to get breakfast?"

"Let's save it for another day. It's probably best if ya rest, and I have some errands to run before work tonight."

"Oh, ok," Rachel says, realizing that Julie is leading them back to Rachel's apartment. When Julie said *home*, she assumed they were headed back to Julie's place.

Julie walks quickly, and Rachel struggles to keep up, the crutches jabbing into her armpits. The tension between them cuts deeper than any of the damage from her fall. A block from the apartment, Rachel pauses for a second to adjust the crutches. "These things hurt more than getting knocked over by a car," she says, laughing. Julie doesn't laugh, or smile, or react in any way. A hard knot forms in Rachel's stomach.

At the entrance to her building, Rachel fumbles with her key in the lock. She struggles to balance on the crutches while pushing open the door. Julie puts a hand on the glass to help and steps inside ahead of her to hold it open. Rachel lifts herself inside and positions herself between Julie and the stairs, blocking access. "Thanks, I've got it from here," she says. "I'm good."

"Ok, well I'm not," Julie says, crossing her arms.

Rachel stares at the sunglasses concealing Julie's eyes, trying to see an expression through the tint. "What do you mean?"

"We've talked 'bout this. It's clear ya have major trust issues, and I think I've been pretty accommodatin' so far, but where does it end?"

Rachel stands still, trying to process. There must be a misunderstanding. "Ok, but you said you were fine with taking things slowly. You said it was ok to keep some things to myself. I do trust you and-"

"I don't trust *you*," Julie interrupts, her voice flat. "I only learned your last name 'cause I happened to see it on your mailbox, and I only saw the mailbox 'cause ya live next to my nail salon. Honestly, after today, I'm not even sure I believe that's your name. I still don't know where you're from. Pennsylvania? I don't know the names of your siblings, or your birthday . . . I think I just need some time to think."

"What, like a break?" Rachel asks, suddenly frantic. Her eyes start to water, and she sucks in her quivering bottom lip to keep from falling apart. "But you *just* told me you loved me!"

Julie looks at the floor and nods. "I do. I regret tellin' ya that now 'cause of where we are, but I meant it. This is just startin' to feel like some codependent shit, and I don't wanna go down that path again. I think we need some space to figure things out on our own and then we can check back in with each other and see where things stand."

"How long will that be?"

"I don't know. I'll text ya." Julie makes a move toward the door.

Rachel's body is buzzing. It feels like a crack has opened in the universe, and the only way to prevent everything from being destroyed is to stop Julie from leaving. Julie pulls the door open, and Rachel clutches the edge. She drops the crutches and leans against the door frame, hopping on her good foot. "What about the money I owe you? And your romper? Just let me run upstairs real quick and get some things. I can come over, and we can talk."

Julie steps out onto the sidewalk and turns in the direction of her place. "Leave it at the bar like the first time."

Rachel shifts and the door slips out of her hand, slamming closed. She watches from behind the glass as Julie drifts away out of sight.

The world collapses.

CHAPTER 18

Rachel moves through each work day natural and confident, smiling through the brokenness. She covers her bruises and explains away the ankle sprain through various lies. These lies flow out of her with an ease that scares her, but she can't stop. She tells Jim that she went to pass the ball at her Sunday soccer match but slipped in some mud and injured herself. When Mr. Khaki, whose name is actually Jason, asks about the crutches, she describes a rugby injury. She tells Tamara that she drank too much at brunch with girlfriends and tripped on a step. She twists the story each time, daring people to compare stories and confront her.

The truth is too sad. When Rachel stopped by the bar to repay the loan for the crutches, Julie was working but refused to acknowledge her existence. Rachel stood at the end of the bar with the envelope extended, waiting for Julie to take it out of her hand. She wanted to force eye contact, to have a moment of shared devastation. But Julie never looked up or approached her, and Rachel was eventually forced to drop the envelope on the bar and leave.

The sympathy at work is intoxicating. Rachel includes Julie in her stories, reserving the news of the separation for the day her ankle heals and the compassion well runs dry. The photo of Julie remains pinned to the cubicle wall, and Rachel tries her best not to look at it a thousand times a day. Jim encourages her to work outside of the office when the weather's nice, so she reads manuscripts in Millennium Park on a bench near Buckingham Fountain, or at Museum Campus overlooking the lake, anywhere that puts distance between her and that photo. Inevitably, something she's editing will cause her to burst into random tears.

She cleans herself up in a public restroom and returns to the office at the end of the day, leaving an edited draft on Jim's desk with a toothy, everything-is-totally-fine smile.

She'd waited exactly three days before reaching out, giving Julie the space she requested. Every night on the commute home, Rachel stares at the unanswered texts on her phone. There's the nonchalant text asking Julie how her week is going. Silence. There's the apology text asking for a chance to explain herself. Silence. There's begging and excuses and finally, a promise to stop bothering her until she's ready to talk. That last one had coaxed out a blinking ellipses, but after thirty seconds it disappeared, leaving the loudest silence of them all.

After particularly good days at work, peppered with compliments and enjoyable reading, Rachel devotes her evening commute to scrolling up in the conversation and starting from the beginning. She witnesses the nervous, early flirtations deepening into real affection. And then the chasm of her own making, the desperation building. She tells herself this self-imposed torture is necessary, that she has to be a better version of herself for Julie's return.

She sleeps well at night. The nightmares have been replaced by the little voice in the back of her head. It's active these days, poking its way into random thoughts throughout the day. *She's never coming back.*

On the weekends, Rachel is drawn to Beatrix. She stands in front of her, presenting herself for confession, and Beatrix displays her sins for the whole world to see. In the beginning, Rachel comes to atone, divulging her missteps and detailing her plans for self-improvement. As August wanes and crisp September air approaches, the contrition turns to anger. Beatrix glows in her golden frame and stokes the flame. *Julie is a liar, incapable of loving someone else. How dare she throw everything away and completely cut off contact? She can't send a single text to check in? What if Rachel were dead?*

Rachel's ankle heals, but she waits an extra week to abandon the crutches. They lean against the wall next to the front door, a constant reminder that she, too, has been abandoned. Climbing the stairs to the train platform, Rachel enjoys her returned agility and tries to focus on the freedom, a clean slate. She walks into the office on Monday, smooth and unfettered. Coworkers drop by her office throughout the day to acknowledge her improved condition. She basks in the attention, squeezing every last drop out before it dries up.

"Size small?"

"Huh?" Rachel places her edits on the corner of Jim's desk. He opens a cabinet in the corner of his office and takes out a messenger bag, which he slings over his shoulder.

"T-shirts. I'm going to order some for Editor Row for the booze cruise next Friday to kick off Labor Day weekend."

"Oh, that's after work, right?" Rachel asks, constructing a lie to excuse herself.

"Nope, I booked the afternoon package. A bus is picking us up at 2:30 and taking us to Navy Pier. Boat leaves at 3:00. No excuses!"

"Fun," Rachel says through her teeth. She backs out of his office and returns to her cubicle, dropping into her chair and looking out the window. Labor Day. One more day without the distraction of work. And then her 30th birthday, alone.

She takes her purse out of her desk and digs around inside for her phone. No new notifications. Her hand drops, and she stares at the cubicle wall. There's Julie, smiling happily, promises in her eyes. Rachel rips the photo off the wall and shoves it into a drawer. She takes a deep breath and turns to leave. *Fuck her.*

"Headed out?"

Rachel freezes. Anna, the blonde Copy Editor with the undercut and septum piercing, is leaning against the edge of the cubicle wall, smiling to hide the questions in her eyes.

"Um, yeah, I was just tidying up a bit first." It sounds hollow in Rachel's ears, but Anna nods reassuringly.

"I just stopped by to see if you had dinner plans tonight. I know it's short notice, but a friend of mine just cancelled, and I don't want to go straight home. We haven't had a chance to get to know each other much since you moved to our side of the house . . . I thought maybe . . . if you're not busy."

Short notice is usually Rachel's favorite excuse; she can decline an invitation without guilt. But Anna's smile seems so sincere, and her desire for a night out is contagious. "Actually, I'd love that," Rachel says, pulling her purse over her shoulder. "Where to?"

* * *

Rachel steps into the restaurant and gives her eyes a moment to adjust to the darkness. It's an English pub with dark wood paneling and the smell of curry in the air. Anna returns a greeting to the hostess and then follows her to a booth toward the back of the restaurant. Rachel slides in across from her, placing her purse next to her, but not before taking her phone out and placing it face down on the table top. She realizes how little she knows about Anna and awkwardly tries to conjure topics for small talk.

"Have you been here before?"

Anna picks up the menu in front of her and flips it open. "Yeah, this is our regular spot, my friend and me. The food is pretty mediocre, but it's hard to screw up fish and chips, so I stick to that."

Rachel chuckles. "If the food isn't great, why do you keep coming back?"

"Pure laziness," Anna replies with a smile. "We can never decide where to go, so we just keep coming back here. It's halfway between our offices, so that's convenient too."

Rachel recognizes an opening and takes it. "Oh really? Where does your friend work?"

A waiter brings two pint glasses of water and asks if they'd like anything else to drink. Anna orders an ale that Rachel doesn't catch the full name of, but she echoes the order, uninformed about the different beer varieties. They mention that they're also ready to order food and place duplicate orders for fish and chips before handing over the menus.

Anna turns her attention back to Rachel. "She works as an admin for an architecture firm, but that's not what we're here to talk about. I want to know more about you. What did you do before Em Dash?"

The waiter brings the beers over and places them on the table. Rachel takes a long sip, trying to remember the specifics of her fake resume. "Oh you know, a little of this, a little of that. Mostly internships and freelance work after college. What about you?"

Rachel holds her breath, waiting to see if she'll be pressed for more details. Instead, Anna lets out a long sigh. "That's a long story. The short version is that I interned at Em Dash while I was in college and had dreams of using that experience to land a job in New York, but life had other plans." She takes a drink of beer before continuing. "My dad got sick, so I needed to stay close to home to help my mom with his care. Em Dash offered me a full-time position, and I couldn't refuse."

Rachel nods, familiar with the trap of family illness. "How long have you been here?"

"Oh god, it'll be . . . let's see . . . 15 years next May. Man, time flies."

"You must like it then, right?" Rachel asks. "You've been there so long, and surely there are other publishing companies you could take a job with if you wanted to."

Anna starts to speak, but pauses. She plays with an exposed edge of the napkin secured underneath her glass. "It's ok. I've worked my way up, and Jim is flexible with my schedule when I have to take my dad to appointments. It would be hard to start over somewhere else."

"Yeah, Jim seems great," Rachel says. "He's been so welcoming and truly seems invested in my success."

Anna sucks in her bottom lip and nods, staring at a spot in the distance, just over Rachel's shoulder. Her eyes drift back to meet Rachel's. "He's very friendly, for sure. Just don't fall into the trap of feeling too grateful for the opportunities he gives you. You got yourself promoted with your own talent and hard work. You don't owe him anything."

Rachel frowns. As far as she knows, it was Tamara who promoted her. Jim has never made her feel like she owes him anything other than a job well done because he's so supportive. She considers asking Anna what she means, but the food arrives so she picks up her fork instead. Maybe it's best not to press the issue when they're just getting to know each other.

The fish is greasy, and the French fries are a bit underdone, but Rachel picks at it anyway, still in the habit of avoiding waste. A chime dings from Anna's side of the booth. She opens her purse and digs out her phone. "Sorry," she says, reading something and then typing a long response.

"It's ok," Rachel responds, lowering her gaze to provide a semblance of privacy. She waits until she no longer hears the soft tap-tap-tap of Anna's thumbs against the screen to look up again. Anna tosses her phone aside and stabs at a flaky piece of battered fish.

"Sorry, I always feel so rude when I do that, but I'm basically on call 24/7, ya know?"

Rachel nods. "Everything ok?"

Anna chews slowly before answering. "Just the usual drama. My mom is freaking out over a hospital bill. Looks like I'll be spending my morning fighting with the insurance company tomorrow." She lowers her head, rubbing her temples with the thumb and forefinger of her left hand. She lets go of a long sigh. "Sorry. I didn't mean to monopolize the conversation with my personal life."

"Don't worry about it," Rachel says. "I underst-"

"So you're liking the new job then, huh?" Anna cuts in.

"I am," Rachel says brightly, attempting to cut through the tension that has settled over the table. "Everyone is so friendly, and I appreciate you inviting me to dinner. I haven't gotten to know very many people that well, so this is nice."

Anna looks up and flashes a tight smile. "Well you kinda keep to yourself, so that doesn't exactly surprise me."

Rachel feels her face flush and laughs nervously. "I know, I'm working on being more social. I'm just . . . not shy, but . . . "

Anna pushes her plate of half-eaten food aside. "You don't have to explain yourself to me. Personally, I think you're entitled to keep your personal life separate from your work life. I certainly don't want everyone up in my business all the time."

The waiter pauses at their table on his way back to the bar. "How are we doin'? Can I getcha ladies anything else?"

Anna reaches for her purse. "Just the check when you get a chance." She turns back to Rachel. "Sorry to cut this short. And sorry for being in kind of a foul mood. It's just been a stressful couple months."

Rachel puts what she hopes is more than enough cash for her half on the table and smiles delicately. "It's really ok. We'll have to do this again."

"Of course," Anna says, sliding the crumpled bills into her wallet and handing a credit card to the waiter when he returns with the bill. "And you're right about the office being friendly. I didn't mean to imply that you shouldn't make friends or open up to people. There are some great people at Em Dash."

Rachel watches as Anna signs the receipt and slides out of the booth. She follows her to the exit of the pub and out onto the sidewalk. "Thanks again for inviting me. Maybe we can have a drink together on the booze cruise."

Anna laughs. "You mean Jim's not so subtle attempt to get all the women of the office drunk?"

Rachel stiffens. "Oh . . . I . . . he's never . . . "

Anna touches Rachel's arm. "Don't worry. My sister's coming into town for the weekend, so I get a break from my tragic life for three days. Not only will I have a drink with you, but I promise that I'll actually be fun. Not like tonight."

Four men in suits walk side-by-side toward them, crowding the side-walk. The women step into the empty patio space to make room for them to pass. "Anyway," Anna continues, "I've got to get going, but I'll see you at work tomorrow, and we'll definitely hang on the boat. Just be safe!"

She's already halfway down the block before Rachel realizes that was their goodbye. Alone, in the shadow of the building, goosebumps ripples across her arms. *Be safe? From what?* Rachel checks her watch and realizes it's only 5:45 PM. She'd hoped this dinner would breathe life into the evening and distract her from the empty bed waiting for her. Now what?

Rachel walks to the Red Line and pushes into a crowded car, the post-work rush still in full effect. With each stop toward home, her chest tightens. She looks at the faces around her and feels completely unseen. Something that once would have been a comfort now feels like a death sentence. Her mind wraps around a thought. *What if I slipped back on that platform, hit the third rail, and died? What if I'm dead right now? What if I have to haunt this cramped, stained, rank train car for eternity?*

The doors open at an above-ground stop, and bodies slide past hers, making contact as they shove their way towards freedom. Rachel isn't sure which stop it is, but she follows the crowd off the train and down the stairs. Her throat is tight with tears, but she can't spend another night crying alone.

Further from the station, the sidewalk opens up a bit, and Rachel is able to slow her pace to a casual stroll. She blinks back tears and studies the businesses on this unfamiliar street. There's a coffee shop, a cat rescue that doubles as an arcade, a physical therapy office, and then, out of nowhere, a small storefront with black, iridescent bead curtains behind the glass. A neon sign flashes PSYCHIC READINGS – WALK-INS WELCOME.

Rachel pushes past the beads into the incense-heavy air before she even realizes what she's doing. A bell jingles, announcing her. There's an unmanned front desk covered in crystals, and to the side, a shelving unit with items for sale: books, dreamcatchers, bottled tonics, and more crystals. A red velvet curtain divides the waiting area from whatever is housed behind it. It parts, and a woman approaches Rachel.

"Hi, I'm Shannon. Welcome."

Rachel had expected something out of the movies, an old woman in witchy clothes and a head wrap, leaning over a crystal ball. Shannon is close to Rachel in age and dressed in jeans with a loose floral blouse. Her face is free of make-up except for two sharply-drawn, dark eyebrows and a bright red mouth. She pulls the curtain back and motions for Rachel to enter the back of the store.

Rachel steps through into a long hallway. Shannon brushes past her and leads them down the hall to a windowless room at the end. Inside is an oval coffee table surrounded by floor cushions. The room is lit by a rice paper floor lamp in the corner and dozens of candles, sprinkled about the room on floating shelves, the coffee table, and even the floor. Peppermint mingles with eucalyptus and sage.

"Have a seat where you're most comfortable."

Rachel settles onto a purple tufted square facing the door. Sitting in one big fire hazard, she feels more comfortable with an eye on the exit.

Shannon gestures to a pillow across the table from Rachel. "May I sit here?" Rachel nods and watches as Shannon crosses her ankles and slowly lowers herself onto the floor, her knees spreading as she goes. "Hello, companion. What questions do you have for the universe today?"

Rachel senses a laugh creeping up her throat, but what escapes instead is a loud sob. Tears immediately run down her face and drip into her lap. "I'm so sorry," she says between shuddering breaths. "I've never done this sort of thing before, and I don't know why I'm here. There's just a lot going on in my life right now, and I don't have anyone to talk to. I'm not sure what to do."

Shannon's face is soft and calm. Rachel suspects that she is not the first to cry in this room. She takes a Kleenex from the box extended to her and blows her nose. She takes another and dabs at her eyes, her cheeks hot with embarrassment.

"Let's keep it simple," Shannon says, shuffling a tarot deck that seems to have appeared out of thin air. "I'll do a three-card spread where we ask three questions. First, what has led to your current situation?" She lays a card face down on the table. "Next, what should we know about the current situation?" Another card is placed on the table. "Finally, what can we learn from this situation? Or sometimes I phrase it as, 'What is the outcome if you stay on this path?'" A third card is placed on the table, forming a neat row.

Rachel sniffles and leans closer, resting her forearms on the edge of the table. There's a flurry of wings in her stomach as Shannon flips the first card. It shows a bleeding heart, pierced by three swords.

Shannon clicks her tongue and looks across the table, eyes swollen with sympathy. "You've had your heart broken, poor thing. A true love is no longer part of your life, and you're struggling with grief as a result."

Stunned, Rachel stares at the card and wipes away fresh tears with the back of a hand. Shannon slowly turns the next card, a person sitting up in bed with multiple swords hovering above their head. Rachel recognizes herself immediately. "Nine of swords," Shannon says. "Have you been having nightmares?"

Rachel's body goes cold. She nods. Shannon closes her eyes and lets out a long breath. "I can see why you're so distraught. It's hard to move on when the past haunts us. There's also anxiety and fear with this card, so your feelings seem inescapable, day or night."

The third card is flipped to reveal a figure hanging upside down from a tree, suspended by one foot. "This is the outcome?" Rachel asks. "That doesn't look promising."

"Quite the contrary," Shannon says, sitting straighter. "The universe is asking you to give in to its will, to let go and let the spirits guide you." She takes an amethyst from her pocket and places it in Rachel's hand, closing her own hand over Rachel's. "You don't need to fight so hard. What will be, will be. You must find peace inside yourself and open your mind to the signs. The universe will point you in the right direction."

Shannon pulls her hand away and leans back, studying Rachel for a reaction. Rachel swallows and places her own hands into her lap, studying the crystal. Her eyes are heavy, and she has the sudden urge to crawl into bed and never come out. Finally, she looks up. "Thank you."

Shannon bows her head. "Of course. The reading is $15. If you'd like to purchase that healing crystal, it's $7. Place it by your pillow for a night of nourishing sleep."

Rachel puts the crystal in her purse and pulls $30 out, placing it on the table. She climbs to her feet and moves toward the hallway, mumbling another thank you. Her body is sluggish and disoriented. When she walks into the velvet curtain, she fumbles with it, searching for the opening. She emerges into the thickly incensed lobby and notices the darkness behind the bead curtains. The sun has already set. Rachel glances at her watch and is alarmed to see that an hour has passed since she entered the shop.

There are hurried footsteps behind her. Rachel moves in slow motion, reaching for the front door, stepping out into the night air. She takes a few deep breaths of fresh air, exhaling the many scents from the shop. She heads back toward the train, her mind clearing as she walks.

Rachel opens her purse and holds her phone in one hand and the crystal in the other. She concentrates on the photo of Julie currently tucked into her desk drawer. She wills the universe to bend in her favor. Timidly, she lifts the phone to illuminate it. No notifications. At the train station, she chucks the amethyst into a garbage can and stomps up the stairs to the platform. *Fuck the universe.*

CHAPTER 19

The forecast of rain that threatened to spoil the booze cruise turned out to be inaccurate. Rachel leans back against the railing of the multi-tiered yacht and watches the skyline drift away. Dance music pumps from the speakers. Young professionals from various companies wander up to the upper deck, posing for selfies and swaying to the music. Rachel notices that none of them have ridiculous matching t-shirts. Before boarding the bus, Jim handed out gray shirts with the Em Dash Publishing logo emblazoned across the chest. The back features an image of an alcohol bottle next to a manuscript with the phrase *100% Proof Pages* centered below, Jim's lame attempt at a joke.

A Copy Editor named Sarah walks up to Rachel and hands her a drink. "It's vodka. I don't know your drink of choice, so I went with the safe bet."

"Thanks," Rachel says, taking a long drink.

"Sorry to hear about your girlfriend. What an asshole."

Rachel nods and swirls the ice with the black stirrer. It took a few days for Jim to notice the missing photo, but word spread quickly once he knew the story. Soon, the whole office was whispering about Louise's girlfriend, the cheater.

"My ex cheated too," Sarah says, leaning against the railing next to Rachel. "Can I ask how you found out?"

Rachel turns around to look down at the water, making a show of tipping the plastic cup back to take two long pulls of vodka soda. "She works at a bar, and I stopped by at closing one night to surprise her. I knew the back door would be unlocked because she takes out the trash before she leaves, so I let myself in. She was with another woman on top of the bar."

The words spill out effortlessly. Rachel has envisioned it a million times. Every night as she walks home, the sign for Pale Gael's visible at the end of the block, she imagines a treacherous flirtation. As she lays in bed, staring at her phone and watching the time shift from 1:59 AM to 2:00 AM, she visualizes the betrayal in detail. These little deaths seep into her bones and bind to her DNA. This new truth is etched into her memory.

Sarah gasps and places a hand on Rachel's forearm. "That's awful! I'm so sorry that happened to you. I can't believe you haven't missed a single day of work! I would have been a mess."

"I am nothing if not a consummate professional," Rachel says, draining another drink.

"Want another one?" Sarah asks. "There's no way I'm going to use all of these drink tickets."

"Sure." Rachel hands the empty to Sarah and watches her walk down the stairs to the bar. She grips the rail and looks out at the skyline. Syncopated conversations from the couches behind her compete with the heavy bass beats. The boat turns, forcing her to close her eyes against the dizzying rotation.

Sarah returns with Elliot, a Junior Editor, in tow. "Tell Elliot what happened with your ex," she says, handing Rachel another vodka soda.

Rachel repeats the story, adding in more detail this time. She saw Julie's head between a pair of legs and cried out, causing Julie to look up from a stranger's exposed vulva. Sarah and Elliot's mouths drop open as she continues. She describes running out into the alley and waiting for Julie to come out to explain. She tells them that Julie never joined her in the alley, so she eventually went home.

"I sent a text that said 'obviously we're done,' and she never responded," Rachel says, lifting the drink to her lips to signal the end.

"Wow wow wow," Elliot says, clutching his chest. "So you never got real closure."

"That's what I was thinking," Sarah says. "I would need to tell her off and get an apology. She should be begging for your forgiveness instead of . . . what? Ghosting you?"

"See, this is why I don't fuck with bitches," Elliot says, twirling his straw.

"What the fuck are you talking about, El?" Sarah punctuates the question with her drink, spilling a bit onto the deck. "This is classic man bullshit. You've just never had a guy ghost you because you always bail before you even know their names."

Elliot gasps dramatically. "You whore!"

The two of them volley playful insults back and forth while Rachel empties her second drink. "Excuse me," she says, fishing a drink ticket out of her pocket and heading downstairs to the bar. The music is louder inside the cabin. She likes the way it drowns out her thoughts and makes conversation difficult. She orders a gin and tonic and drops the ticket into a fish bowl. The gin burns her throat and makes her nose wrinkle, a nostalgic feeling that brings a flood of tears to her eyes.

Jason is sitting alone at a table against the windows. He sees her at the bar and motions her over. Rachel makes her way over, smiling to herself at the site of his t-shirt tucked into khakis. She recently learned that he's colorblind, which is why his entire wardrobe is so monochromatic. She would feel bad about her secret nickname for him if his personality wasn't also 100% khaki.

Rachel fumbles with a banquet chair across the table from Jason. Once seated, he smiles at her and continues to drink his beer in silence, turning his attention back to the dance floor. He is perfect company. Rachel follows his gaze and notices for the first time that the dance floor is crowded with staff from other companies. They dance wildly, unbothered by the voyeuristic strangers around them. A woman in wedges does a high kick and Rachel snorts. Jason scrunches his face in thought and then holds up seven fingers. Rachel smiles, nodding in agreement with his score.

They continue this exercise of ranking people's drunken dance moves, communicating with facial expressions and hand gestures. A man in cargo shorts and a polo gets a two for his very loose robot movements. A couple receives a ten for the *Dirty Dancing* air lift that ultimately ends with both of them on the floor. When Jason stands and points to her nearly empty drink, Rachel nods and hands him a ticket. She can't tell if she's dizzy from the rocking waves or the alcohol or both.

Jason returns and shouts something about Jim and upstairs. He heads to the stairs with both drinks, so Rachel slides off her chair and follows him to the upper deck. At the top of the stairs, he hands her a drink and disappears. Rachel cups her drink in both hands as Jim materializes next to her. She lets him guide her by the shoulders toward the rest of Editor's Row, forming lines at the back of the boat, the skyline in the background. He places her in the front between Sarah and Anna.

"You doing ok?" Anna asks, placing a hand gently around Rachel's bicep to steady her.

"Never better," Rachel smiles, blinking rapidly against the sunshine.

Someone from another corporate group climbs onto a chair and lifts a phone in front of their face. "Smile!" Jim yells to the group. Rachel does as she's told. It feels good to follow instructions.

Sarah and Anna guide her to a recently abandoned couch. "Tell Anna," Sarah says excitedly. Rachel talks between sips, drawing out the story. This time, as Rachel is leaving the bar, she can't help but look through the front door, curling her hands around the sides of her face to block out the glare from the street lights. From this angle, she sees Julie's bare ass bouncing on the other woman's face.

Anna directs her to tell Jessica and the chain continues until Rachel is talking to an outsider in a white tank top. She feeds off the pity. More than that, she senses a form of admiration radiating from the wide eyes and agape mouths of her audience. She has a fan club now. They recognize her story, with its brutal details. It's a story of survival. She has lived to tell it, and that makes her brave.

As the boat returns to dock, Elliot takes her hand in his. "Some of us are going to get fucked up on margs and fried apps at Jimmy B's with the tourists. You have to come!"

"Yes, you *have* to!" Sarah echoes, forming prayer hands and pouty lips.

Rachel looks to Anna for consensus. "If you feel up to it, we'd love to have you," Anna says. "We'll understand if you'd rather go home. You've had a lot to drink already and-"

Elliot groans and steps in front of Anna, blocking her from view. He grabs Rachel's other hand and clutches both of them against his chest. "Doll, look at me. We've all been drinking. You have a long weekend to recover, and we won't have nearly as much fun without you. Come on. Ignore Miss Party Pooper over here."

"I'm not being a-" Anna tries to butt in, but Elliot closes his eyes and holds a long, continuous "please" to drown her out. His body starts to crumple as he runs out of air.

"Ok, ok, "Rachel laughs. She was never going to turn down the offer to stay out. The only thing waiting for her at home is crushing isolation. She follows the matching t-shirts ahead of her, gliding down the ramp to the pier. Her feet float above the ground as she weaves through the crowd, trying not to get swallowed up and left behind. Jim's head stands out above the masses, a bobbing beacon. She follows it through the glass doors of Margaritaville where she's ushered into a booth next to him, followed by Elliot, Sarah, and Anna.

"Is it just us?" she asks, looking around the restaurant for familiar faces.

"Honey, we only invite the cool kids to these things," Elliot answers over a menu. "It's bad enough that we have to see the rest of those basics five days a week; let's not extend that."

Rachel's eyes dart over to Jim, feeling secondhand anxiety for Elliot. But Jim tosses his hair and laughs before motioning a waitress over. He orders a round of appetizers and two pitchers of frozen margaritas for the table, tossing his charge card on the table. Rachel listens to conversations about terrible drafts and difficult authors, nodding and laughing at the right queues. Her margarita is sour, and the cold stings the roof of her mouth, but she smiles and drinks it. Food is placed on the table and she reaches toward a basket. Someone slaps her hand.

"Oh my god, Louise, how drunk are you? That's seafood!" Sarah yells, swapping the basket for one that holds tortilla chips and spinach artichoke dip.

Rachel crunches on a chip, trying to ignore the delicious smell of coconut shrimp. Jim takes her margarita glass and dumps the contents into his own. "Sorry, champ, we've got to cut you off until you get some more carbs in you. We're in for a long night and can't have you fading on us."

Rachel bites into another chip and tries to remember the plan for the rest of the night. She doesn't remember agreeing to anything else but knows she'll go along with it if there are drinks. She doesn't want to rise above the fog tonight. She wants to be so hungover tomorrow that the day slips away and gets her one day closer to the end of this long weekend. Anna says something across the table and Rachel smiles, trying to keep her eyes wide and sober. She eyes the pitcher of margaritas and eats another chip.

* * *

Rachel is surprised to see the sun setting when they walk back out onto the pier. She links arms with Elliot, her body jostling against his as they stumble toward downtown. The buildings glow orange. Sarah laughs over her shoulder, smiling back at Rachel, the pink clouds reflected in her eyes. *These are my friends.* Rachel laughs in return.

Jim points in the direction of a building behind other buildings and drops the name of a hotel that Rachel doesn't recognize. They follow the river, recapping highlights from the booze cruise. The pedestrian traffic thins as they cross Michigan Ave and curve toward the entrance of a boutique hotel with automatic doors. The doorman nods at them as they walk through into expensive air.

Rachel is led into an elevator, which opens onto a rooftop bar overlooking the river. The interior is decorated in lush wallpaper, modern chandeliers, and velvet chairs. The tin backsplash behind the bar sparkles in the sunset. Suits and blouses fill the space. Rachel looks down at her t-shirt tucked into belted paper bag pants and flushes. She turns to her coworkers, but they do not appear to be self-conscious.

"First round is on me," Jim says, striding to the bar.

Tumblers of clear liquid are passed back to Anna, Sarah, and Elliot, and then there's a glass of something dark in Rachel's hand, a skewer piercing a cherry and an orange peel. It matches the drink in Jim's hand.

"I think you'll like it," he says with a wink.

She shrugs and clinks her glass against his. It's smooth but unremarkable until she swallows and a bomb explodes in her chest, sending shockwaves of warmth through her body. She hums and lets her head fall back. She sees Jim smile through her fluttering lashes.

The group gathers around a table on the patio, adjacent to the floor-to-ceiling windows. The sky darkens to purple and a thin gray gauze shrouds the city. Dusk makes the city shimmer, lights blinking as the sun sinks. A slow synth-y pop playlist plays under the group's conversation. She catches bits and pieces of the others' plans for the rest of the weekend. The focus has shifted away from her and suddenly she feels placed in a moment that would happen with or without her.

Rachel slips away silently and orders another drink at the bar, holding up her empty glass to signal she'd like another of the same. Full glass in hand, she walks back outside to a quiet corner along the edge of the patio. She looks over the guardrail. The street below is luminous rust, and the river running parallel is inky black. She shivers and takes a long drink.

"Doing ok?" Jim places his elbows on the rail and looks at her. "The others told me about what happened with your ex. That must be hard to deal with."

Rachel nods. The square ice cube in her drink clinks against the side of the glass. "I turn 30 in a week."

"Oh shit! Happy early birthday!" Jim raises his glass and waits for her to return the cheers. "Thirty, huh? That's a big one. Got any plans?"

Rachel smirks and taps her glasses against Jim's. "Um, no. I fucked everything up, and now I'm going to die alone." The lights soften, and when Rachel blinks, there are halos around each one. She feels the pressure of the tumbler in her hand but not the individual sensations of glass and cold and condensation. The music is muffled in her ears. Her breath is deafening.

"You can't blame yourself," Jim says, wrapping an arm around her to squeeze her shoulder. "It's not your fault she cheated. You're an incredible young woman, and there's someone more deserving out there for you. When you're ready, you'll find them."

Rachel leans into the comfort of another body next to hers, the weight of a reassuring hand. She closes her eyes, trusting him to protect her while the night sky closes in around her. Her mind blurs, and she wavers between existence and nothingness.

Jim is behind her now, his hand dropping to her waist. "Louise is such a pretty name." He sets her glass on the ledge. He's pressed against her back, pulling aside her hair to kiss her neck.

Rachel's grip tightens on the rail. She stares at the lights below, the dark river water churning. She tries to find her footing.

"If you're looking for a rebound, we could have some fun together." He's hard against her hip. He lets her hair drop and moves his hand to her throat.

Rachel whirls around and pushes her fists against his chest. "N-no. Get away from me." It comes out as a high-pitched shriek, louder than she'd intended. She attempts to hold herself steady, to meet his gaze. *Fuck, I can't lose this job.*

His eyes widen, but then his mouth spreads into a wide grin. "Ok, you're drunk. Maybe another time." He kisses her cheek and walks back to the table where Elliot is shouting at Sarah about the merits of juicing.

Anna looks across the patio at Rachel and mouths *You ok?* Rachel slowly turns back to the ledge and collapses with her arms over the rail. She takes a deep breath and suddenly Anna is touching her elbow, asking the question out loud.

"I-I-I'm . . . I didn't . . . I don't."

"I know." Anna says, the knowing in her tone. "Let me just grab my purse from the table and tell them we're headed home. Do you live north of here?"

Rachel nods.

"Good. I'm in Edgewater. Are you anywhere near there?"

Rachel nods again. "Just south."

"Good! We'll split a cab," Anna says. "Just give me a second. I'm going to get you home safely."

The word *safely* is piercing. Anna says it delicately, with a certain understanding. *Does everyone know he's like this?* Rachel takes a deep breath and watches Anna scurry back to the table. Rachel wipes at her cheek with the back of a shaking hand. She blinks back thick, guilty tears, but they spill over, running down to her chin. Her tumbler is still sitting where Jim left it. She wants to take it and drop it over the edge, to hear the crash as it shatters. She envisions herself climbing up and over the ledge, feeling the wind tug at her, feeling the drop as she falls. Would she shatter into tiny pieces? Would she feel anything at all?

CHAPTER 20

The pain is sharp and piercing, nauseating. Rachel lays in bed staring at Charlotte, who died weeks ago, but stays put because Rachel can't bear to throw her out. Rachel still talks to her, sometimes imagining her as a zombie plant and other times as a ghost plant. Company is company.

Time is meaningless when there's pain. The hours are short but the seconds are long. It's Saturday morning, then it's Sunday night. An alarm goes off Monday morning, and Rachel is showered and dressed before she remembers the holiday, another day to dread the confrontation with Jim. The longer she's forced to wait, the fuzzier the memory becomes in her mind. Maybe he had something in his pocket. Maybe she misheard him. Maybe he didn't mean it to sound like a sexual come-on. But she can still feel his lips on her neck and his hand at her throat. She shudders.

Rachel cleans the apartment and organizes her desk. She makes her bed and does a load of laundry. She cooks a few meals that will be easy to reheat during the week. When there are no distractions left, she sits in the leather chair and props her feet up on the coffee table, lighting a candle that's supposed to smell like rain. It's time. She pulls up her conversation with Julie and types several drafts before tentatively hitting send. She holds her breath until it says delivered.

I hope you're doing well.
Couple things. I'm sorry
for everything. You deserve
the truth and I wasn't
honest. I want to make
things right. So if I were
to stop by the bar this
afternoon, would you be
there? And if I were to
stop by, would you talk
to me? Please?

Rachel waits a few minutes and then puts her phone down on the table. She stands in the middle of the room and stretches, trying to loosen the tension of expected rejection. An ache builds in her chest. She prays for any response, even a cruel one. Just one more interaction to bind her to Julie for one more day.

The phone buzzes, and Rachel lurches back to the coffee table. She sits in her chair with the phone in her hands, taking a centering breath. She does what she thinks is the sign of the cross and unlocks the phone.

No more lies???

Rachel pauses. She calculates the risk, accounting for her true identity and subtracting the omission of certain details.

I promise to answer any
questions you have. No
lies.

There's a blinking ellipse and then the bubble pops up. Rachel gasps.

Ok I have a break in 20.
Stop by then

Rachel leans over and drops her head between her knees. This is it. This is the chance. She struggles to breathe out between hungry, consuming inhalations. She conjures the memories of joking with Sarah and Elliot, and the moment with Anna. She tells herself that she's made friends, that she's capable of being liked, that maybe Julie can learn to love Rachel instead of Lu. *The Rachel your friends know is a lie.* She jumps up and goes to the kitchen for a glass of water, swallowing it down to drown the voice. She forms her lips into an O and blows out, long and steady.

Rachel waits until eighteen minutes have passed, then grabs her purse and walks out of the apartment. The key sticks in the front door, and it takes an extra second for the lock to click. The stairwell feels warmer than usual, causing the curls along her hairline to grow damp. The walk to Pale Gael's seems twice as long, and by the time Rachel reaches the entrance, she's certain she's late. This is not the way she wanted to start off this conversation.

As Rachel enters the bar, Julie is chatting with a woman over a bowl of Chex mix, and Rachel freezes. Julie looks up and points to the back exit. She finishes talking to the woman at the bar, then takes off her half apron and walks through the swinging gate. Rachel follows her to the back door and out to the alley. The door bangs closed and Rachel leans against the brick wall, arms folded, eyebrows questioning.

"Ok, first off, thanks for agreeing to meet me. Um . . . hi, I'm Rachel Adams." Rachel gives a half smile and an awkward wave with no response. "Louise Danforth is my mother's name, and I figured that if she was looking for me, she would never think to search under her own name. It's the name on my lease, and it's the name I go by at work, but obviously my real name is on official things like my driver's license and health insurance. I'm sorry I freaked out and lied to you. I've been lying for so long, and I panicked."

Julie stares back at her blankly.

"You can still call me Lu if you want, though. I actually kinda like it." Rachel chuckles and watches for a reaction from Julie. Julie runs her tongue along her teeth but says nothing. "Sooo . . . do you have any questions for me?"

"Where are ya from?" Julie asks in a declarative tone.

"Outside Pittsburgh. The address on my ID is real."

"Do ya actually work at a publishing company downtown?"

"Yes, it's called Em Dash, and I was on a booze cruise Friday with the rest of the editing team. I'd love to tell you about what a shit show that ended up being. I've missed talking to you."

Julie props a foot up on the wall behind her and stares back, unflinching. "When's your birthday?"

Rachel takes a deep breath. "This Friday actually. I'll be 30 and . . . I don't know, I guess it finally hit me how much I've isolated myself. Sure, my mother probably still hates me for leaving right after my brother and sister died . . . especially since she thinks it's my fault . . . "

"What were their names?"

"Rory and Regina. Samuel is my brother-in-law, and I owe him all that money, so he probably wants to find me, too. I'm just so tired of living in fear. I want to start over. I want an actual life. I want *you*."

Julie unfolds her arms and stands up straight, hands on her hips. "Your birthday is Friday?"

"Yes," Rachel says with a smile." I'd really love to have you over to my place . . . to prove to you that I'm not hiding anything there. It's just a shit hole. I'll get a cake."

"Oh my god, Lu, stop."

Rachel's spine stiffens, and her smile fades. Julie steps across the alley and places her hands on Rachel's shoulders. "You're not gonna buy your own fuckin' birthday cake."

Rachel laughs in a burst, exhaling as her eyes sting with tears. Julie pulls her into a tight embrace for a moment, but then pushes her away at arm's length. "To be clear, you're an idiot and I'm still mad at ya. But I love ya and can't let ya spend your birthday alone. Not when you're finally being honest with me."

Rachel nods and sucks in her bottom lip, sniffing hard to keep her nose from running.

"I'm off work 'round 7:00 on Friday," Julie says. "Should I just come by after?"

"That would be the best gift," Rachel says, blushing.

"Ok, I hafta get back in there." Julie jerks a thumb toward the door. "Have those crazy work stories ready for me. See ya Friday." She kisses Rachel's forehead and walks back inside.

Rachel's legs collapse, and she squats in the alley for a minute, wiping at her eyes and nose with a trembling hand. She stands slowly and places one palm against her forehead and the other on her stomach, grounding herself. She half expects to self-combust out of sheer gratitude.

* * *

When Rachel returns to work, Jim behaves as if nothing has changed. She's unsure if he drank too much to remember, or if he's just another predator. Either way, she focuses on damage control with her coworkers. As she bumps into people throughout the day, she repeats herself verbatim, sticking to a carefully rehearsed script. "Funny story, but turns out that wasn't Julie I saw in the dark bar. She didn't respond to my text because her aunt died unexpectedly and she had to leave town. She wasn't getting reception and I guess she emailed me, but it went into junk mail . . . isn't that funny?"

Everyone is visibly disappointed that they no longer have permission to hate this person they've never met, but no one questions the story. Rachel hopes it's enough to keep them from acting weird when she starts bringing Julie to work events. As Friday approaches, the passage of time grinds to a halt. Rachel distracts herself by reading every manuscript she can get her hands on during work and by window shopping fall fashion after work. She dreams of autumn leaves crunching underfoot while she and Julie visit apple orchards and pumpkin patches, sipping cider in sweaters.

On Friday, Rachel wears her favorite blue blouse and pulls half of her curls back with an antique comb she found in a thrift store. When she gets to the office, a cupcake is waiting for her on her desk. She sits down and stares at it, certain there was no announcement about her birthday. There's a knocking sound on the cubicle wall behind her, and Rachel spins her chair.

"Happy birthday! Hope you like chocolate." Jim smiles, his head cocked to the side.

"I didn't . . . I thought . . . "

"You didn't think I forgot did you? What kind of boss would I be if I forgot your 30th birthday? I assume you have plans tonight, but we'll have to get the gang together and go out for drinks sometime." He winks and walks away.

Rachel turns back to her desk and slides the cupcake into the trash. She grabs a manuscript and begins reading. Jim is a problem for another day. She's not going to let anything ruin this day. She keeps her head down and sneaks out a little early.

At home, she arranges the cheese board, laying the crackers in the shape of a big three next to a zero made of alternating salami and cheese slices. She pours expensive olives from the deli in a small bowl in the center of the zero. Shortly before 7:00 PM, Rachel looks at herself in the mirror, at the professional blouse and jeans. She takes off the blouse and flips through other options in the closet.

The buzzer echoes through the apartment, tinny and mechanical. Rachel looks down at her black lace bralette and closes the closet with a smile. She presses the door button on the intercom and unlocks the front door, opening it a crack so she can run into the bathroom to gargle some mouthwash. She hears the door open and then close as she spits in the sink and wipes her mouth on a hand towel. "You're early," she says, stepping into the hall.

A man stands in the entryway, peeking into her living space. "Excuse me," she says, "I think you have the wrong apar-"

Samuel turns to face her. "Sit down," he says, pointing to the bed.

Rachel feels like someone just punched her in the chest. Her heart thuds in her ears, and her hands clench, but she's glued to the floor. "Now!" he yells.

The volume startles her into motion. She runs to the bed and sits at the foot of it, closest to the windows, calculating how quickly she could open one and jump out. How badly would that injure a human body? She needs to distract him, get him talking. "Did my mother send you?"

Samuel scoffs. "Your mom's dead."

Rachel feels a small release in her chest. "What happened?"

"She killed herself in April, on April Fools' Day . . . Maxwell found her, and I thought they were playing a prank on me. Turns out, she tried to tell the cops what you did, but it sounded insane. Hell, I thought she'd finally lost it too, and now I'm sorry I didn't listen. It was too much for her."

"I've been cleaning up the house to sell it, and I went through the shit you left behind. I knew you were manipulative from the way you got all that money out of me, but yikes . . . your mom was right. You're an actual monster."

The hair on Rachel's neck stiffens. "I don't know what you mean."

"Cut the shit, Rachel!" Samuel drives a fist down on the desk, causing a row of books to tumble off the side. "I found the receipt for the mice."

Rachel looks down, her eyes welling. "It was just supposed to be a prank. He's scared of mice, so I dumped a bunch in there during the rehearsal dinner and . . . I didn't know they would chew up the wires."

"Well they did!" Samuel yells. "You put him in that coma and then you unplugged him. Were you afraid he'd wake up and expose you?"

"No." Rachel shakes her head, the tears falling freely now. "That just wasn't a way to live, hooked up to those machines. All the beeping . . . "

"Oh, did the beeping bother you? You murdered your brother because his heart was still beating? What about your sister?"

"She was sick."

"She was sick because you poisoned her with those smoothies. I found a big Ziploc bag of something tucked behind the tea, and I remembered you adding leafy greens to her smoothies from a bag like that. I figured it was some kind of kale, but then Rory died, and you disappeared, and I just knew you'd done something to Regina. I was walking through your grandmother's garden this summer, and I saw the rhubarb. It has that same leafy green top, and wouldn't you know it, rhubarb is poisonous . . . causes kidney failure."

"I'm sorry," Rachel sobs. "They left me there with my mother and then Rory skipped our Grandma's funeral, and Regina let Pellet die when I went to that therapy program for a week."

"What therapy program?"

"Remember," Rachel sniffles, "I told you I didn't want to publish my book, and you got really mad, so I checked myself into Dr. Smada's program for a week to get some help . . ."

"What the fuck, Rachel." Samuel steps toward her. "I was mad because you seduced me, then blackmailed me for money for your book. And then when I read it, it was total nonsense. It was psychotic rambling. You sounded like your mom."

Rachel leaps up from the bed and backs away from him. "What?"

"You never went to therapy. You sat in the attic for a week working on this self-help book that was nothing more than an incoherent diary. You had several pages where you just scribbled *What can we control?* over and over."

Rachel feels her head shaking back and forth, denying it. But she remembers the stack of notebooks she used to write in. When she tries to recall the layout of the clinic or retreat facility, she can't. She doesn't remember anyone else who was in the program with her. She can't picture Dr. Smada's face or his . . . her? . . . voice. The air is sucked out of the room, and Rachel reaches out to touch the wall, steading herself. "No," she whispers. "You're just trying to get in my head."

Samuel cackles. "*You're* the one who fucks with people's heads. I was happily married until you started putting all these thoughts in my head . . . asking when the last time was that Regina and I had sex . . . telling me she was pregnant when we got married and it wasn't mine. Then you started sending me nudes and suggestive texts. You stole my credit card information and used it to order a bunch of fucked up porn. Do you know how hard that was to explain to Regina? Did you have a job other than sitting around plotting how to ruin my life?"

"Yes, I-I- . . . " Rachel can't remember.

Samuel's eyes narrow. "You don't even realize how messed up you are, do you? Look at you! You're delusional; you're crazy like your mom. No, you're worse! *She* never killed anyone. You're a sociopath."

Rachel cups her face in her hands and cries so hard her entire body convulses. She knows her hand was forced, that her motivations weren't evil. But in the end, does it matter? She's losing grip on reality, and soon she'll be wandering the halls yelling at shadows like her mother. She squeezes her eyes tight and swallows hard. When she looks back at Samuel, she's composed. "How did you find me?"

"Turns out a buddy of mine is friends with someone you work with. He commented on a photo online, so it showed up on my feed. It was a bunch of people on a boat in Chicago, and there you were, front and center with the name of your company on your t-shirt. I expected you to look different, but you look exactly the same as the day you left."

"So you're here to get me to confess? To turn me in?"

Samuel snorts and rolls his eyes. "I could have just called the cops if that were the case; I have the evidence so I don't need a confession. But where's the fun in that? You killed the mother of my children. I wanted to see your face when you finally realize you aren't smarter than the rest of us."

He takes a step closer. "I called a sitter for the kids and drove straight here. It wasn't hard to find your address once I knew where you worked. Especially when I have a mutual friend with your boss. Good guy, that Jim. He seemed relieved that I was in town and you wouldn't have to spend your birthday alone."

Samuel pushes Rachel against the wall with unexpected force. She hits her head and slides to the floor. He steps closer, towering over her. "The car's out front. Time to go."

He reaches down for her, and her instincts kick in. She screams. She flails her arms and legs, connecting with his shin. He yelps and grabs at her with new rage. She cowers against the wall, covering her head. "Samuel, please . . . don't. Samuel!"

There's a loud thud, a moan, a sharp crack. His hands go limp on her arms. Rachel lifts her head, peeking out from between her forearms.

His eyes roll back, and he staggers to the side before collapsing on the floor. A small pool of blood begins to form on the rug. His eyes stare back at her, glassy and blank. Rachel covers her mouth and moans.

"Fuck, did I kill 'im?" a voice asks.

Rachel looks up, dazed. Julie is standing at the foot of the bed, a bloody crutch in her hands.

CHAPTER 21

Rachel pulls herself up and runs to the front door to close it, stepping over a discarded cake box and tote bag in the middle of the floor. Once the lock is latched, she turns back to Julie, who is frozen in the middle of the room. Julie's eyes are fixed on Samuel's body, her knuckles white around the crutch. "I followed one of your neighbors into the building, and your door was unlocked. I heard ya say his name . . . knew he must be here for the money. Lu, he was hurting ya and . . . his temper . . . ya said . . . " Her breaths are loud gulps.

Rachel pries the crutch out of her hands and tosses it near the body. She guides Julie to the bathroom and leans her against the sink, wetting a washcloth and dabbing at the blood spatter on her skin like scarlet comets shooting across her face. Julie stares ahead at nothing. Rachel lowers her onto the lid of the toilet and places the washcloth in her hands. "Start scrubbing those spots on your shirt. I'll be right back."

Rachel doesn't wait for Julie to answer. She runs back to the living room and kneels next to Samuel. She presses two fingers under his jaw and holds her breath. There's a pulse, faint and wavering. She glances back at the bathroom before straddling him, wrapping her hands around his neck, burying her thumbs deep into the flesh on either side of his trachea. The soft thump fades. Rachel holds steady an extra thirty seconds, just to be safe. She wipes at the sweat forming along her brow with a forearm and climbs back to her feet.

Julie is still seated on the toilet when Rachel walks back into the bathroom. The washcloth dangles from her fingertips, dripping swirly pink water onto the tile floor. "Listen to me," Rachel says sternly, cupping Julie's chin in her hand and scrubbing at a spot on her cheek. "You saved my life. He was going to kill me. You did the right thing. But now we have to get this body out of here. We only have so much time before he gets stiff, so we need to curl him up and find something to put him in . . . "

"Oh, god," Julie wails. She bats Rachel's hands away and covers her face with her hands. "I don't wanna do that. I can't. I can't touch 'im."

"You have to. I can't move him on my own."

"Can't we just call the police? It was self-defense."

"Julie, he wasn't attacking you. You can't claim self-defense."

"Oh, god, no," Julie continues to wail, rocking back and forth. "I just reconnected with my family. I was gonna go home for Thanksgiving. I can't go to jail."

"Ok, look at me," Rachel says, squatting between Julie's legs. "We just need to get a big suitcase or something. Do you have one of those big suitcases they make you check at the airport?"

Julie shakes her head. Rachel crosses her arms across Julie's knees, steadying them both. "Ok, maybe I can go buy one really quick. We'll get him in it and then wait until it's dark and drag him out the back to his car. I just have to figure out where to take him from there. We could dump him somewhere, maybe in the river somewhere. Or we could bury him . . . chop him up and put the pieces in grocery bags, then load them in that abandoned shopping cart in the alley and take him to the nature reserve near the lake. There are clearings under the trees, and no one is supposed to be there after dusk so if we wait a few hours-"

"Lu, stop!" Julie shouts, her voice breaking. "I can't touch 'im or lift a bag with a body in it, let alone . . . I just can't do it." She places her hands on Rachel's arms and looks at her with swollen eyes. Her cheeks are smeared with mascara and tears.

Rachel pulls in a long breath through her nose and leans forward. She kisses each of Julie's hands, slowly, deliberately, and whispers, "Do you have a better idea?"

Julie sighs and looks up at the ceiling. Rachel recognizes the emotional negotiation, the struggle in the silence. Once the unthinkable is spoken, it exists outside of you; it leads a life of its own.

"What if we burned the body?" Julie says, her voice even and clear. "We could get some gasoline and burn the whole apartment down so there's no evidence we were ever here. We could leave the furniture, but get all of your stuff outta here and make it look like ya already moved out. Like he was squattin' . . . "

"And set himself on fire?"

"No, of course not. Maybe we don't use gasoline. We make it look like a gas explosion instead. There's a gas stove right? We let that leak and then figure out a way to set a fire . . . "

"So the whole building explodes and kills all the neighbors?"

Julie falls silent. She rakes her fingers through her hair and leaves her hands propped on top of her head. Rachel stands and walks to the hallway. The sunset filters through the leaves of a tree and splashes across the living room floor. The pool of blood grows, reflecting the fading light.

"I'm sorry," Rachel says slowly, turning to lean against the bathroom door frame. "There's no other option. If we just leave him here, people will eventually notice the smell. Once they identify the body, they'll wonder why it's in an apartment leased under a dead woman's name. He got my address from my boss, and they have my real name on my new hire paperwork. It'll only be a matter of time before they piece things together and start looking for me. I have to get rid of the body and make sure no one thinks he's missing."

Julie's right knee jerks up and down and she taps a manicured thumbnail against her bottom teeth. The reckoning fills the rest of the quiet. "Ok," she says finally, hesitant. "What do we do?"

"We find a big bag to put him in and then clean the apartment until there's no sign that either of us were here. Then we wait until it's really dark. I'll find his car and park it in the alley. I just need help getting the bag down to the car and in the trunk. The crutches too."

Julie swallows and turns to face her. "Ok. Then what?"

"I'll leave. I'll pack up a few things and put an envelope with a month's rent and a note for my landlord in the rent drop. I'll email Jim and make up an excuse for needing some time away from the office. I'll dump the body somewhere far away with a good chance it'll never be found."

"Ok," Julie says, nodding, her voice more assured. "That makes sense. And then you'll come back, and stay with me. Camille won't mind."

Rachel knows her plan is solid. She's been planning escape routes for months, and although this isn't exactly how she thought things would end, she's ready for it. Except for this part.

"No, you're not listening, Julie." Rachel's voice quivers. "I have to go to Pennsylvania and make sure no one thinks he's missing. I can leave his car at the house like he never left, but I can't come back here."

"What?" Julie jumps to her feet. "Ya hafta come back, though."

Rachel steps closer. "It's too risky. I'll give it some time and then I'll tell Jim I have to quit . . . some family thing. But to protect you, I can't come back."

"I can't letcha do that," Julie says, barely audible. "I'm the one that killed 'im."

Rachel closes the distance between them and folds her hands over Julie's, bringing them to her chest. "You saved my life. Let me do this for you."

Julie drops her forehead to Rachel's. They stand in the middle of the bathroom, letting the moment draw out as long as possible, neither wanting to be the one to end it. Rachel closes her eyes and sees Julie behind the bar the first night they met. Memories come in flashes. The pasta night. Passionate nights in bed and the early morning scent of coffee. Julie standing over her as Samuel slumps to the floor. The body stiffening as they embrace.

Rachel pulls back and scans Julie from the ground up. The spots Julie missed on her clothes are barely visible against the black, but there's a smudge near her left ear lobe. Rachel rinses the washcloth and wipes at it gently. Julie smiles at her wearily.

"Alright," Rachel says, stepping back to check her work. "Let's find a bag and get this over with."

* * *

Rachel stabs a couple French fries dripping with cheese and lifts them to her mouth. She chews mechanically, trying not to think about the suitcase in her apartment, bursting at the seams with a stiffening body. Her hands are red and raw from scrubbing the floor with bleach. The rug had to be thrown out, but only after being doused in bleach and attacked with a brush typically reserved for cleaning the grout of her shower. When the fibers were worn and frayed, they rolled it up and tossed it in a dumpster at the other end of the alley.

"I still can't believe that bag was still there," Julie whispers, taking a drink of her Diet Coke.

Rachel hums in the affirmative. Something in Julie had shifted once they were out in the fresh air. She remembered seeing an old, dirty set of luggage by the dumpster behind her place but assumed someone had already taken it. They walked over anyway and were shocked to find two pieces still there, one an oversized roller bag.

"At least we've had one bit of luck tonight," Rachel says, trying to smile. She runs through the inventory of her apartment one last time, ensuring that all of her personal items made it into her duffle bag. Once the sky turns deep black and quiet, they'll load the car, and Rachel will drive away. The keys press against her thigh, a sharp ache. She lifts another forkful of fries to her mouth, savoring the crisp grease and dripping oil.

Julie pushes the contents of the basket around with her fork. "I can't believe this is it."

She drops the fork and props her elbows on the table, spreading her fingers across her face. Her nail polish is chipped and her hair is matted, strands of it falling from her tangled ponytail. The rancid smell of nervous sweat radiates off both of them, hovering over the basket of fries, reminding Rachel of the trucks of dead cattle headed to a rendering plant down the road from her childhood home.

"Hey," Rachel says, wrapping her hands around Julie's elbows, "I want you to know that I don't regret any of it. I'm glad I met you. You forced me to open up, and you made me a better person. I'll always love you for that."

Julie crosses her arms to intertwine her fingers with Rachel's. Her eyes glisten. "I love ya, too." She groans as she picks her fork back up and urges a single French fry toward her mouth.

"There you go," Rachel says with a short laugh.

They fall into a pattern of alternating dips into the basket, letting the sounds of clattering silverware and the sizzling cooktop fill in the gaps. They accept refills of their drinks and sip long after the check has been paid, avoiding eye contact. Traffic slows on the sidewalks and in the street. Rachel turns from the window. Julie nods.

Rachel pulls the car into the alley, a black Audi she knows Samuel can't afford. Couldn't. She turns the car off and joins Julie in the apartment. They put the newly cleaned crutches in the backseat and climb the back stairs one last time. The suitcase rolls easily enough to the door, but the stairs are difficult. Julie lifts the bottom end of the bag and struggles down the stairs backwards, one step at a time. Rachel struggles with her end, the strap of her duffle bag cutting into space between her breasts, the weight of it against her back, throwing off her balance until she's on level ground.

They whisper a countdown of three and thrust the luggage into the trunk, closing the lid with a thunk and a collective exhale. They lean against the side of the car catching their breath, stalling. Rachel fumbles for Julie's hand in the dark. She finds it, clutches it, gives it a squeeze, and then pulls away slowly, lingering. Rachel opens the driver's door, tosses her duffle bag in the back seat, and slides into the car. Her eyes begin to sting as she reaches for the handle.

"Wait." Julie steps forward, blocking the door. Her hand grips the edge, fingerprints forming on the glass of the window. Rachel makes a note to wipe them off before ditching the car. "I'm comin' with ya."

"Julie, you can't. Ultimately, this is my mess and you need to let me take care of the loose ends. This can't be traced back to you."

"Ya don't think I can handle it," Julie accuses, folding her arms across her chest.

A small laugh slips out before Rachel can stop it. "No, I think you've proven you can handle some shit. But that's not the point. I dragged you into this, and now you need to let me finish it. Go, live your life. Trust me . . . this shit follows you."

"Then it's too late, right?" Julie releases the driver's door and opens the rear one in a smooth motion. She scoots across the seat and climbs over the console into the passenger seat.

"Julie, I'm serious. You can't do this."

"Lu, let me help ya. There's nothin' keepin' me here. Not really. I know we've only known each other for, what, seven months? But you're my life now. If we do this right, together, there's no reason we can't stay together and move on with our lives."

Rachel shakes her head. "You don't know what you're talking about."

"I know I was scared at first, but I'm focused now. I know what we need to do. And you're gonna need me. He left his kids somewhere, right? I'm great with kids."

Rachel grips the steering wheel and leans her head against it. She weighs the risk. It's insane to even consider it. "You didn't pack a bag. You don't even have a toothbrush."

Julie reaches across her body and fastens her seatbelt. "Bitch, I killed a man tonight. We'll figure it out."

Rachel sighs and pulls the car door closed with a click. She starts the engine.

* * *

They avoid busy streets with traffic cams. They stay off portions of highways with tolls. They keep their phones in airplane mode and use the car's navigation system. Somewhere outside Angola, Indiana, they pull over on a dirt road and steal a shovel from an unlocked shed. In Ohio, a small town south of the road is illuminated only by the lights of the gas station. It's unmarked on the map.

"This is it," Julie says. "I can feel it."

They take the exit and turn down streets without signs. The road curves to a wooded area near industrial runoff ponds. They park at the edge of the woods and kill the lights. The woods are thick and overgrown, without paths or signs of human activity. It's difficult to drag the suitcase through the tall grass and bushes, or over the gnarled tree roots. The ground is wet from recent rain, and the wheels of the bag stick in the mud, but they manage to get to a very small clearing. They dig, passing the shovel between them so that while one of them works, the other stretches out her sore muscles. It takes hours, but they eventually have a hole deep enough that it's difficult to climb out of. They shove the bag in and repeat the process in reverse.

"That's good enough, right?" Julie asks, wiping her forehead and leaving behind a smudge of mud.

They slink back to the car and drop the shovel in the trunk. They climb into the car and Rachel rests her calloused hands on the wheel, staring into the woods. It really is the perfect spot. There's no reason for anyone to be near these woods, let alone in them. *Are we going to get away with this?*

"Lu, I think I'm broken," Julie whispers, fixated on her hands.

Rachel fights tears. She never meant for her life to impact Julie like this. It hurts to think that Julie will be forever changed because Rachel couldn't handle her own shit. She turns to Julie. "I'm sorry. I knew you must have been in shock when you insisted on coming with me. I should have pushed back harder. You don't deserve any of this."

Julie's head shakes. "No, that's not it." She looks over at Rachel. "This isn't your fault. Ya didn't ask for this to happen, and I'm glad I came with ya. I just . . . shouldn't I feel guilty or somethin'? I don't regret protectin' ya and I'm not sad that he's . . . gone."

Rachel touches Julie's hand. "I'm thankful you saved me, and despite what I said before, I'm honestly glad you're here with me. We're probably both in shock though. Let's find a place to sleep tonight, and we'll go over everything tomorrow."

Julie nods and gives a tired smile. She squeezes Rachel's hand and then leans back against the headrest as Rachel starts the car. Driving past Toledo, Rachel watches Julie's head droop toward the window and then snap back up. She pulls into the empty parking lot of a pawn shop and leaves the crutches and the shovel against the dumpster in the back before running back to the car and continuing on. Once the city lights have faded, she stops at a roadside motel and pays cash for a room just as the sun breaks over the horizon. She parks in front of the room and nudges Julie awake. The room is old and sparsely decorated, but there's a bed and blackout curtains.

They drop their muddy clothes onto the bathroom floor and stand together in the scalding stream of the shower, lathering hand towels with cheap soap and scrubbing the night off each other. They wrap their hair in towels and climb beneath the thin comforter covered in cigarette burns. The wall AC clanks to life and whirs, swirling air speckled with dust about the room.

Nose to nose in the double bed, Julie closes her eyes and is gone. Rachel listens to the sound of trucks barreling down the highway and struggles to relax. Her body aches for sleep, but her brain is circling around Samuel's accusations. Some moments in the past are frozen in time, so vivid she can still smell the dusty carpet or hear the soft, coded knock on her door. The rest are shadows in a murky pool. *That's what trauma does. You're not unstable.* She touches a blister on her thumb and tries to believe.

CHAPTER 22

Sirens approach, wailing toward her. Rachel flails her arms, crashing backwards into the headboard.

"Easy there," Julie says, standing naked at the foot of the bed. She brushes her teeth with an index finger and borrowed toothpaste. Rachel rubs her eyes, picking at the crust in the corners. The sirens recede into the distance. She hears the bathroom sink turn on and the sounds of Julie rinsing her mouth.

"Hey, what is this?"

"What's what?" Rachel groans.

Julie walks back into the bathroom with a notebook in her hand. She flips it open and reads aloud. "It has a list of stuff . . . from somewhere in western Nebraska . . . allergic to shellfish . . . is this *you*? Ya said you're from Pennsylvania"

Rachel sits up quickly. Her lower back seizes and she yelps.

"Lu, ya said you weren't gonna to lie to me anymore but . . . is this . . . you're not trackin' lies are ya?"

"Of course not," Rachel says with a casual laugh. "You told me I should write a book and I've been thinking about it. I started making character notes, and you know what they say, write what you know. Not that I know anything about Nebraska."

Julie snaps the notebook closed, and Rachel holds her breath. It's such an obvious lie and she braces herself for the fallout. Julie walks over to her and sits on the edge of the bed. "I'm so glad you're writin' again." She smiles. "And honestly, I can't be that mad 'bout the lies anymore.

I mean, clearly ya were right to fear your family. It's like ya were in the witness protection program."

Rachel smiles back, softening against the headboard as much as her sore muscles will allow. "No more lyin' though," Julie says, grabbing Rachel's duffle bag off the floor and placing it on the bed. She tosses the notebook inside and digs deeper. "Ya got anything in here that might fit me?"

Rachel throws the comforter to the side and takes the bag from Julie. She finds a pair of elastic-waist shorts and an oversized tank top for sleeping. Julie stands and pulls them on. Her breasts test the sides of the tank, and the shorts graze the tops of her thighs. "Ok, we're gonna need to do a little shoppin'," she says. "This place got breakfast?"

Rachel snorts and looks at the clock on the bedside table. "I doubt it, and it's 11:00 AM anyway. We need to get gas so we can grab something to eat there. Maybe they'll have t-shirts or something too." She stands, groaning against the stiffness in her back and arms. She pulls on a pair of jeans, coaxing her legs to bend against their will. Next is a t-shirt, harsh against her tender skin.

"Oh, come on," Julie whines. "Let's find a diner or somethin'. We're in the middle of nowhere and no one knows us. Let's go shoppin' and get some real food."

Rachel shuffles to the window and peeks out at the fully illuminated parking lot. There are two other cars and nothing but highway. "I don't think you understand small towns, Julie. No one knows us, which means they'll notice us. They'll all remember the two outsiders who were passing through in a muddy Audi."

"Ok, so a city. I just wanna buy a few things so I feel like myself again. And I want an actual meal so I feel like I'm on vacation instead of on the run."

Rachel releases the curtain and makes her way to the bathroom. She bends with effort and picks up their dirty clothes, stuffing them into the trash can then lifting the liner and placing it on the bed. "Fine. We've got to get rid of these first, then get gas, then run the car through a car wash, and *then* we can find an outlet mall or something and a place to eat. Let's head toward Cleveland and stop there."

Julie smiles and wraps her arms around Rachel's neck. The tank top lifts, exposing small bruises along her stomach from the jostled luggage as they struggled down the stairs last night. Rachel looks away, burying her face in Julie's shoulder. "Julie, you know this isn't a vacation though, right?" Rachel asks, squinting against the deep throb in her temples. "We need to be careful. We *are* on the run."

"I know," Julie says softly, "but we're not bad people, Lu. It just happened and we shouldn't punish ourselves for that. We dealt with it and now we're gonna move on. Someday, it'll be that thing we laugh 'bout, in secret."

"I don't know that good people laugh about murder." Rachel smiles against Julie's collarbone.

"Ya know what I mean," Julie says, giving her a playful smack. Rachel grimaces against the pain, but relaxes into the comfort of the mundane, the ordinary routines that suggest everything might work out.

They slip on their shoes and sunglasses, grab the bags, and step out into the sun. Gas stations litter the sides of the highway. They pull into the first one with a car wash next door and spray the remnants of Small Town, Ohio off the Audi. Julie walks over to a burn barrel beside the gas station and drops the bag of yesterday's clothes into it, along with a small duffel bag they'd found at the back of the trunk, containing a fresh set of clothes and some essentials that Samuel had packed. Near Cleveland, they follow the navigation to an outlet mall and park at one end.

"You can't use your cards," Rachel says, turning to Julie. "Do you have any cash?"

"I've got . . . one hundred and . . . seventy-four dollars," Julie says, counting a stack of cash she pulled from her purse.

"Why do you have so much cash on you?"

She shrugs. "I haven't gotten around to depositin' my tip money in a while. And don't even start 'bout how I could get mugged. I know ya only carry cash, and it's a good thing I have this so I can help pay for things until we figure out our next move. How much do *you* have?"

"A lot," Rachel says, pulling a large tote bag from the duffle and clutching it protectively against her chest as she climbs out of the car. She locks the car behind Julie and drifts past stores, falling back quickly to let Julie take the lead. They enter a Gap Factory and Julie sifts through the clearance rack. She pulls a pair of yellow pants and a white t-shirt with thin rainbow stripes from the rack.

"Color?" Rachel raises her eyebrows.

"I'm tryin' to look like someone else," Julie says. She grabs a pair of light indigo jeans and a shirt with a foiled pineapple print, and heads toward checkout, fishing a few thongs and a pink bra out of bins along the way.

"I saw a Famous Footwear on the other side," Julie says. "Let's go over there and get new shoes since these are beyond gross." She stomps her foot lightly to illustrate. Bits of caked mud and grass fall onto the store's carpet.

Rachel agrees and feigns interest in the jewelry racks while Julie pays. They jog across the parking lot to the next store and purchase new sneakers, dumping the old ones in the trash. Julie goes into the public restroom to change. She comes out twirling and Rachel can't help but laugh. The pineapples flash in the sun as they walk back to the car.

"Food, please," Julie sings, fastening her seatbelt.

Rachel starts the car, but hesitates. "Julie, I know you're trying to make this fun, but I want to make sure you're doing ok. It's a lot to process and I know *my* nerves are shot-"

"Ok, but the hard part is over, right?" Julie interrupts. "He's gone and now we just hafta cover our tracks and figure out what to do with the kids. That feels easy after everything else. Right?"

Rachel leans over and kisses her. "Sure." She knows the hard part is just beginning. When everything is checked off the to-do list and there are no required actions left to keep your mind busy, that's when the real work begins. That's when you second guess every decision you've made, and the pressure of constant scrutiny grows suffocating.

* * *

"Isn't this nice?" Julie smiles before biting into a dripping cheese-burger.

Seagulls circle overhead, waiting for crumbs to fall on the patio. The tables are full of families and tourists. Rachel looks out over Lake Erie and stirs her salad. "You'd think they'd have fish on the menu, being lakeside and all."

"Why?" Julie asks, eyes narrowing behind her sunglasses. "I thought ya couldn't have seafood."

"Shellfish. You know, crab and shrimp. I love fish. Doesn't this seem like the kind of place that would have fish?" Rachel takes a bite of salad and forces herself to swallow against the rising bile. *It's just one lie.* Her hand trembles slightly beneath the weight of the fork and the other, bigger deceptions – too big to be called lies.

Julie shrugs. "At least it's a beautiful view. I can't believe Toronto is over there on the other side of the lake. Maybe we should go there after everything is settled. Chill in Canada for a bit."

"Toronto is too expensive," Rachel says, relieved that they've already moved past the allergy lie. She scans the menu to see if she missed an alcohol section.

"We'll get jobs," Julie says.

"Without visas? We'd have six months to survive on the cash we have and then we'd be there illegally."

"Ok, ok. You're clearly more experienced at this than I am." Julie says as she dunks a French fry in mustard and takes a bite.

Rachel tenses at the implication, but then she eases as she watches Julie eat, carefree. It's the truth; she *is* better at this. Running is second nature. Hiding is reflexive, like breathing.

"Ok, new idea," Julie says, pulling her hair back. "A friend of mine used to vacation with her family in Gulf Shores. I think it's in Alabama. They have those brightly colored houses on stilts, ya know? We could hang out on the beach, the perfect place for your writin'. There are plenty of bars so I could get a job pretty easily. Ooo . . . we should figure out how to get fake IDs!"

Julie plucks a strawberry from Rachel's salad and pops it in her mouth. "I just need to text Mike and Camille soon. I can tell them somethin' happened with my parents and I had to go to Iowa on short notice. I'll wait a week and then tell Mike I quit. I'll hafta figure somethin' out with Camille though. She'll think it's weird if I never come back for my stuff."

Rachel nods, relieved to have someone else worrying about the details. "When we're done at the house, we can walk to the bus depot and take that to Pittsburgh. We can buy some new phones so you can call people . . . I need to do the same with Jim. Then we'll take a train to DC. I think there's a train from there that will get us to Jacksonville. There's gotta be a bus or something to . . . what was it? Gulf Shores?"

"Really?" Julie beams. "Oh, Lu, you'll love it. I promise!"

"You're right about the fake IDs," Rachel continues. "Once we have those and we're settled, I probably need to go back to Chicago to get my last paycheck and quit in person so Jim doesn't think anything is off . . . you know, show him some tears over family drama and whatnot. I'll rent a truck and swing by your place to pack up your things while Camille is at work. Just let her think you were the one there and write a note for me to leave behind that says you're moving back home to be with your family. I can leave some rent money, too."

Julie nods, wiping mustard from her mouth with a napkin. A toddler erupts a few tables over, kicking and screaming. She looks over her shoulder then turns back to Rachel. "What are the kids' names?"

"Maxwell, Olivia, and Hazel."

"Cute! Do you want kids someday?"

Rachel picks around the almonds of her salad and pierces a couple blueberries with a bunch of spinach. She chews and watches a family at another table. The father cuts food into manageable bites for a small child while his own food grows cold. The mother discreetly breastfeeds an infant, sweating under the weight of the blanket. Rachel studies them, the unconditional love involved in putting another human's needs before your own at all times. "I don't know. I've never really thought about it."

"I love kids," Julie sighs. "I was lookin' forward to Thanksgiving so I could finally meet my nephews. Do you think it'll ever happen now?"

"Maybe," Rachel says, meaning it, surprising herself in her conviction. "We're never going to have fully normal lives, but I don't see why we can't travel to Iowa every so often to see your family."

Julie freezes, a fry halfway to her mouth. "Really? Isn't it too dangerous?"

"Maybe," Rachel repeats. "But I don't have anyone left. I don't want that for you."

"But what 'bout your sister's kids? They're your family."

"I barely know them," Rachel says. "I don't think they'll even recognize me when we get there. And they're Samuel's kids, too, so . . . "

Julie nods, and they finish eating in silence. They pay the check and decide to walk around downtown Cleveland, stretching their legs before the drive ahead. They walk hand in hand, pointing out interesting buildings or familiar landmarks. It's routine, and Rachel feels herself adjusting to the normalcy, only to remember the high stakes in shocks and jolts. It's jarring, but in a way that also feels familiar, a return to the intimacy of anxiety. If this were a truly normal trip, they would spend the day at the Rock & Roll Hall of Fame or the International Women's Air & Space Museum. Instead, they'll eventually head back to the car to tie up loose ends.

In Cleveland Public Square, they wander down a path, pausing to study a public art display of tall rotating prisms made of iridescent panels. Each is identical enough, but they stop in front of each one, stretching time to avoid what's ahead. "I bet these are beautiful at night," Julie says.

Rachel nods. "It looks like they light up."

She starts to move to the next one, but Julie pulls her back. "Lu, we're gonna be ok, right?" There's a quiver in Julie's voice that wasn't there before.

Rachel slides Julie's sunglasses up on her head and sees her eyes shifting nervously. "I don't know, but I think we hid him as best we could. And if we get caught, I'll take the blame. I'll tell them-"

"That's not what I mean," Julie interrupts. "I'm not nervous 'bout gettin' caught. Wait, should I be nervous 'bout gettin' caught?" Her eyes drop. She turns around, but Rachel sees the doubt flash across her face before it's out of sight.

Rachel steps closer and wraps her arms around Julie's waist, resting the side of her face against Julie's back. She's glad her expressions are obscured as she fumbles for the right reassuring words. "No, you don't need to worry. We covered our tracks really well." She feels Julie's arms fold over hers. "But hold on," Rachel continues. "If you're not nervous about getting caught, what did you mean?"

Julie turns slowly, careful not to break Rachel's grasp. "Us. I mean are we gonna be ok? I knew we'd have some shit to work through when we got back together, but then this thing happened. I feel like we're stronger than ever, but I know we didn't get a chance to talk things out, and I don't wantcha to feel like you're stuck with me."

"Stuck with you?" Rachel asks, reeling. She rocks forward onto her toes and gives Julie a quick kiss. "I was devastated when you asked for a break, and I was terrified that I'd never get you back. My greatest wish is to be with you forever. I know this is messy, but I *choose* this."

Julie sniffles, but a smile spreads across her face. She looks up and wipes at the wetness under her eyes, groaning, "Ugh, I swear I never get emotional like this. Sorry, I'll get it together."

Rachel rubs the small of Julie's back. "Don't apologize. This is a lot. But you were patient with me while I was struggling, so it only seems fair that I return the favor."

"Jesus, we're quite the pair," Julie says, laughing. She lowers her sunglasses and grabs Rachel's hand, pulling her toward an exit from the Square. "Get me outta here," she says. "I need a toothbrush."

They walk toward the parking garage, stopping at a Walgreens along the way so Julie can purchase a toothbrush and some toiletries. Rachel uses the bathroom and then wanders the aisles, looking for Julie. She finds her in the make-up section with a half-full basket. "What have we got here?" she asks, sifting through the contents of the basket.

"Just essentials," Julie says, tossing mascara and lip gloss in next to a toothbrush and toothpaste, mouthwash, deodorant, shampoo and conditioner, a hairbrush, facewash, moisturizer, body wash, razors, and a loofa. She studies the items in her basket then looks up. "I got store brand where I could, but I might need to borrow some money."

"That's fine," Rachel says. "I'm going to grab a bottled water. Want one?"

"Can I get a Diet Coke?" Julie asks, wandering over to the body lotions.

They meet back up at check-out. Julie pulls a crumpled pile of small bills from her pocket, but Rachel waves it away, taking a stack of crisp twenties out of her bag and handing them to the cashier. Julie gives her arm an appreciative squeeze and gathers up the plastic bags. They find the car in the garage and Rachel types the address into the GPS.

"Is that it? Home?" Julie asks, pointing to the screen.

Rachel nods. "Not sure I think of it as home, but yes, that's our final destination."

Julie's eyes widen. "What 'bout your mom?"

Rachel frowns for a moment before realizing that Julie doesn't know. They were so concerned with cleaning up a crime scene that she never thought to share the things that Samuel told her. Or rather, the one thing she could tell Julie. "She died in April."

"I'm sorry," Julie says with a questioning lilt at the end.

"Don't be," Rachel responds, putting the car in reverse.

CHAPTER 23

Rachel drives along the lake, settling back on the road. They cross the Pennsylvania border, tunneling into forest that grows thicker by the mile. Julie brushes her hair back and applies mascara in the visor mirror. Finished with that, she stares out the window, pointing out hawks and deer. Rachel laughs. "Are you nervous or something?"

"What? Why?" Julie asks.

"You had trees and wildlife in Iowa, right? Seems like you're trying to keep busy."

"Nothin' like this. And I've lived in Chicago so long that I forgot how nice nature is," she says, reaching for the scan button on the radio. She cycles through static, Christian preaching, old honky-tonk, and more static, before turning the radio off and leaning back against the window in silence.

Rachel reaches over to give her knee a squeeze. "We're kind of in the middle of nowhere now, but we're almost there."

Despite the calm front, Rachel feels her chest getting tighter as the miles tick by and the distance shrinks. Each curve in the road is a relief and a trap. After a sharp curve, she slows, looking for her turn. It's set back in the trees, but she finds it through instinct. She turns into the driveway and edges toward the front of the farmhouse, rehearsing her lines in her head—lines designed to alleviate any suspicion the sitter may have.

A light blue hatchback is parked in the driveway. The children are playing on a new wooden playset next to the hill on the side of the house. The sitter stands watch in torn jeans and a t-shirt featuring the local community college mascot, her long blonde hair spilling over her shoulders. She looks up and waves toward the car, the darkly tinted windows concealing its inhabitants. Rachel scowls at this idyllic childhood scene. She looks for signs of the darkness she remembers, the sound of blood pulsating in her ears.

"Oh my god, they're so cute," Julie says, pressed against the car door, forehead against the glass.

"Remember the plan," Rachel says, her tone serious. "We came back with Samuel, but he had a meeting with the realtor in town so we dropped him off, and he'll find a ride home."

"Yeah, yeah, I've got it," Julie says, opening the door with a wide smile. She waves at the sitter and strides confidently toward her. Rachel turns off the car and sits for a moment, listening to the engine click and settle. She stares at the house where she was trapped for so many years. It seems smaller than she remembers.

Julie motions at Rachel to join her and then wanders off toward the children. She kneels, listening to Maxwell describe the toy dinosaur in his hand, clearly excited to have a new audience. Rachel opens the car door and steps out, forcing a tight smile. She walks over and extends a hand to the sitter. "Hi, I'm Rachel. Thanks for watching after the little ones."

The young woman smiles brightly and shakes Rachel's hand. "Katelyn, but everyone calls me Kate." She pulls Rachel into a hug. "I'm so glad Samuel managed to track you down. He was, like, crazy upset after your mom died and wanted a chance to tell you in person. So sorry about your mom by the way."

Rachel squirms in Kate's embrace. She closes her eyes and compels herself to return the hug, awkwardly patting Kate's back. "Yes, I'm glad he found me too. It's nice to be around family during these times." She pulls away and motions toward the children. "I haven't seen these three since I moved away. I'm not sure they even know who I am."

Kate calls for them and turns back to Rachel. "I mean, they're young, but they know you. I've, like, been telling them about you, so they're excited you're back home. I didn't know about your girlfriend, but, like, I'm sure they'll love her, too."

Maxwell walks over to them, holding Julie's hand and still engrossed in his conversation with her. Olivia and Hazel continue to play in the dirt beneath the swings. "Girls," Kate shouts, beckoning them with a stern index finger. They stand and run toward her, dusty and giggling. Each grabs one of Kate's legs and stares up at Rachel from the safety of Kate's body.

"Girls, this is your Aunt Rachel. Remember we talked about how she was coming to visit?"

They smile shyly and glance over at Maxwell for direction. He looks up at Julie. She grins down at him and tousles his hair. "Hey buddy, this is my good friend, Rachel. She's really nice, and I'm sure she'd like to hear 'bout your dinosaur, too."

Maxwell looks at Rachel suspiciously and hides the toy behind his back.

"They're just shy," Kate says, dismissing them with a hand toss. "You should come inside and see the changes to the house. Samuel has been putting, like, sooo much work into it. You might not recognize it."

Rachel follows her toward the house, anxious to be rid of her but also nervous about how much she may know. Julie lifts Maxwell onto her back, holding him in place with one arm while she reaches out to Olivia and Hazel with her free hand. They take it without question and stumble along next to her.

"So do you know Samuel?" Rachel asks Kate. "Or did he hire you through a service?"

"Oh he's, like, my professor for my Intro to Business course at the community college. I mentioned that my work study job got, like, cut or something so he hired me to watch the kids while he works on the house."

Rachel is not surprised that Samuel was drawn to a job where he had an excuse to spend time with young women. "That makes sense," she says. "So you didn't know my family before you met Samuel?"

"Oh, like, everyone knows about your family," Kate says. Rachel's jaw drops before she can stop herself. Kate blushes. "Sorry, was that rude? I just mean that there's been so much, like, tragedy in your family . . . there's sorta this rumor that the house is cursed or something."

Rachel feels the tension in her shoulders soften a bit. "That might be true." She shrugs. "It certainly felt cursed while I was living here." She watches Kate for signs that she's heard specifics about Rachel, but as they walk up a couple steps to the patio, Kate turns her attention to moving the group indoors.

The worn wooden front door has been replaced with a blue steel door. Kate opens it and ushers everyone inside, instructing the children to take off their dirty shoes. She closes the door and turns to Rachel and Julie. "You know, I wouldn't mind, like, staying until Samuel gets back. They can be a real handful."

Rachel frowns, realizing for the first time that Kate calls her professor by his first name. Maybe it's because she's also the babysitter, but it strikes her as odd. "Oh, we don't want to take you away from whatever other plans you probably have. It's Sunday night so I'm sure you have homework or studying to do."

Kate laughs. "It's only 6:30. Like, how long could Samuel's meeting possibly take? I can hang out until he's home. He hasn't responded to my texts in a while so I just want to, like, touch base before I leave."

Rachel shoots a worried look at Julie. It's obvious to her that Samuel and Kate have some sort of relationship beyond teacher-student and that this woman isn't going to leave until she has the chance to say goodnight to her lover. Julie's eyes flicker ever so slightly as she turns to Kate. "Ya know what, that would be really helpful, actually. Why don't we order pizza and have dinner together? Then ya can give us a tour and show Rachel all the updates."

Rachel's eyes are daggers. She wills Julie to look at her, but Julie is focused on Kate. Kate's face lights up. "Really? That sounds great. But, like, nothing delivers all the way out here."

"Oh, that's not a problem," Julie responds with a wider smile. "Rachel and I will go grab somethin' in town and come right back.

We'll check in with Samuel while we're there. I think his phone has been actin' up lately."

"Ok, yeah, great!" Kate says, clapping her hands four times in quick succession. "I'll get the kids washed up real quick and in their PJs so you don't have to mess with that later. I'm sure you're all, like, real tired from the drive."

Kate collects the children and herds them upstairs. Julie grabs Rachel's arm and pulls them out the front door. "What are you doing?" Rachel hisses through clenched teeth. "We don't need a stranger hanging around here."

Julie rolls her eyes and heads toward the car. "She was makin' a big deal out of stayin', and it would look really suspicious for us to be so against it. Now we have time to come up with a plan. We can say we talked to Samuel and he told us that he ran into a friend and now they're havin' dinner together. We'll say he's gonna call Kate tomorrow. That should get her off our backs."

Rachel walks around to the driver's side of the car and hesitates before opening the door. It makes sense. She climbs in and closes the door behind her, letting the soundproofing muffle the outside world. "You're right," she says, turning to Julie. "I'm sorry I freaked out. It's so weird being back here, and I'm just not thinking clearly."

Julie smiles and buckles her seatbelt. "Apology accepted. Let's get some pizza."

As they drive into town, Julie brainstorms details for their cover story out loud. She points out that they shouldn't mention specific people like the realtor because Kate might approach every realtor in town when Samuel never turns up. She creates a story of bumping into Samuel and a pretty brunette outside the pizza place. Julie's eyes sparkle as she describes that they were holding hands and said they had plans so Samuel wouldn't be home until morning. "Do you have his phone?" Julie asks.

Rachel hums. "It's tucked under the lining in the trunk."

Julie sucks in her bottom lip and nods to herself. "Ok good. We'll turn it on later tonight and text Kate a breakup message. We can make it seem like he's runnin' away with one of his other students so she doesn't look for him or report him missin'."

Rachel feels a smile spread across her face. Julie is a natural. Maybe they really will make it. She turns onto Main St. and reaches for Julie's hand. "Thanks for all your help with this. We can call our bosses and Camille from the land line in the house tonight. We'll just use *67 so Caller ID is blocked." She lifts Julie's hand to her lips and kisses it. "You really were great back there with the children. They trust you."

Julie squeezes her hand and leans her head against Rachel's shoulder. "Yeah, what's the plan for them, Lu? We hafta make sure they don't get separated."

Rachel pulls into a parking spot in front of Pat's Pies and kills the engine. "I haven't worked it out completely, but I promise we'll keep them together." She isn't ready to tell Julie the entire plan. Not yet.

"Should I go in by myself?" Julie asks, pointing to Pat's. "Just to make sure no one recognizes ya?"

Rachel shakes her head. "People around here haven't seen me since I was a little kid. We should be safe." She steps out of the car, pulling down her sunglasses, just in case.

They buy two pizzas, cheese breadsticks, and a 2-liter of Coca Cola. Julie insists on one pizza being pepperoni and that they buy a half gallon of chocolate milk for the kids. They return to the house and let themselves in, balancing dinner and the bags of their belongings. Rachel walks to the kitchen and almost drops the pizza boxes. The counters are clean, and the drop-leaf table that used to sit in the corner, covered in trash, is gone. In its place are shelves that serve as an open pantry, every container and bin labeled and organized precisely.

"We're all set up in here," Kate yells from another room. Julie heads off in that direction. Rachel shuffles along behind her, disoriented. They enter a formal dining room with a long banquet table and ten matching chairs beneath a large chandelier. There's a sideboard on one side of the room and a matching hutch on the other. Fine china and servingware are displayed neatly behind the glass of the hutch.

Rachel sets the boxes down on the table and spins around in a complete circle. It hits her that this is the room her mother used to use as an office. The hideous paisley wallpaper has been replaced by a deep blue that compliments the chestnut furniture. The burnt-out bulbs in the chandelier have been replaced, and there isn't a speck of dust visible. The stacks of old magazines and newspapers are gone. The cardboard boxes that used to line every wall have been thrown out.

"It looks so good," Rachel says softly.

"I know, right?" Kate takes paper plates from a stack on the table and makes a plate for each child, cutting Hazel's into bite-sized pieces. They wait patiently in their booster seats.

Julie takes a seat next to Maxwell and across from Olivia and Hazel. She pours them each a cup of milk. "You kiddos are so well-behaved!"

"Oh, don't let them fool you," Kate says, taking the head seat closest to the children. "They're a little slow to warm up to new people, but once they do . . . oh, shoot . . . " Her eyes dart over to Rachel. "Sorry, didn't mean to imply that you're, like, new to them."

Rachel gives a half smile and sits next to Julie. "It's fine. It probably seems that way."

They turn their attention to the food, everyone eating while Rachel nervously picks at a slice. All three children babble away with Julie about their interests: cartoons, games, and outdoor activities. She keeps them distracted while Rachel runs through the Samuel story one more time in her head.

Rachel clears her throat, summoning a confident but natural voice, when Kate jumps in. "Did you see Samuel in town while you were getting the pizza? I'm, like, kinda worried. He never ignores my texts like this."

Rachel takes a deep breath and shapes her face into a sympathetic look. "Actually, I'm not sure how to tell you this." She leans onto the table, towards Kate, and drops her voice closer to a whisper. "He was having dinner with a young woman. They seemed . . . intimate."

Kate's face falls, her lips pressing into a straight line. "What's she look like?"

"Tall. Thin. Long brown hair."

"Really pretty," Julie adds.

Kate's face twitches, clearly trying to keep herself from crying in front of strangers. "That sounds like Alexis. Ugh, she was in my class this spring and, like, always hitting on Sammy."

Rachel cringes at the pet name Kate throws out so nonchalantly. She feels a new rush of anger towards Samuel and imagines punching him in the face until she remembers he's already dead. "We don't want to get in the middle of anything," she says, watching Kate blush. "He should be the one telling you all this since he hired you, but he's not coming home tonight."

"Oh." Katie stares down at a half-eaten slice of pizza. She starts to pick it up, stops, lifts it again, stops, lets it hover near her mouth, and then drops it back to the grease-stained plate. "So he'll be back in, like, the morning?"

Rachel shakes her head slightly, and Kate's eyes begin to blink back tears. Julie reaches over and takes Kate's hand. "I'm sorry. We sensed that maybe there was somethin' special between you two. Am I right?"

Kate nods, biting her bottom lip. Julie makes a clicking sound with her tongue. "Ya deserve better, honestly."

One of the little girls spills her milk, causing Julie to jump into action, creating a dam of napkins. Kate continues to stare down at the table. A narrow river of milk creeps toward her, but she does not move. Julie tosses a fresh napkin on the mess in front of Kate, which jolts her back to life. She slowly looks up and locks eyes with Rachel. "When's he coming back?"

"I'm not sure," Rachel says softly. "He and . . . Alexis, was it? They're going away together. He asked that we stay here with the children until he's back. I'm not sure how long that will be."

"But his car . . . He barely packed anything when he left for Chicago . . . "

Rachel nods, picturing the bag in the bottom of the burn barrel in Ohio. "I don't think he's really thought this through. We can take it from here, though."

Kate pushes her chair back and gathers up the used plates, cups, and soggy napkins from the table. She disposes of everything in the kitchen and walks back into the dining room, eyes red. "Kids, why don't you go watch cartoons while I go over everything with Rachel and Julie."

The three of them clamor down from their chairs and run or toddle out of the room. Their feet can be heard pattering down the hall, and then the loud sounds of an animated show blare from an unknown room.

"Not so loud," Kate yells, but she does not enforce the directive. The volume remains unchanged. She sighs and motions for Rachel and Julie to follow her into the kitchen. They gather around the long counter that juts out into the center of the room like a peninsula. Kate reaches for a binder near the landline and opens it up in front of them. "This has, like, everything you need to know. Sleep schedules, allergies, favorite toys. Diapers, wipes, and clothes are in their room. And here's my contact information." She turns to the last page and points to a phone number. "Could you let me know when he's back? I, like, hate to ask, but I just want to know what happened."

"Um . . . " Rachel delays. Her frustration centers itself in her palms as a burning sensation. She opens and closes her hands into fists, fighting a growing urge. *Just go the fuck away.*

"Sure!" Julie jumps in, brightly. "Do the kids have any activities or appointments we should know 'bout?"

Kate closes the binder with a loud snap and walks to the entry where she gathers her things. "Not that I know of." She bends down to tie her shoes. "Like, as far as I can tell, they never leave the house. They probably do for doctor appointments, but you'll have to ask Samuel about that. I think he, like, said something about a therapist after his wife, your sister, died. I don't know. I started coming here after your mom died."

She points her chin at Rachel each time she mentions the dead. It feels like a threat. Rachel forces a small smile and follows Kate to the front door. "Well, thank you for helping us out tonight. We'll call you when he's back, but I wouldn't hold my breath if I were you."

Kate's eyes widen, but she quickly shakes her head and composes her face. "Wow, uh, yeah. Let me know."

She starts to step out onto the front porch, but Rachel grabs her arm to stop her. "Kate, if you could keep all this between us, that would be great. I don't want anyone to think he abandoned his own children."

"Didn't he, though?" Kate's eyes are daggers. Rachel squeezes her arm, maybe a little too tightly. Kate yanks her arm out of Rachel's grip and walks down the front steps. "Don't worry," she says over her shoulder. "I don't want anyone to know either. This is, like, the most embarrassing thing to ever happen to me."

CHAPTER 24

With Kate gone and the front door locked behind her, Rachel leans against the cool, blue steel and breathes deeply. She allows the smiling, cordial mask to drop. Her face aches from the strain of the performance.

"Wanna show me around?"

Rachel rotates her head to look over at Julie. She loves her, but she can't summon the strength to show it right now. When she speaks, her voice comes out raspy and harsh. "Not really; this isn't my home. I'd rather just call it a night."

"Ok," Julie says, lifting her hands in surrender. "Let's get those sweet cherubs in bed."

She walks toward the sound of the television and Rachel follows with the bags of their things, floating down the hallway that is both familiar and strangely foreign. The children are in the old living room, but Rachel barely recognizes it. The carpet has been torn out, and there's new furniture. Maxwell and Olivia sit side-by-side, too close to the TV. Hazel is asleep on the couch, one pudgy arm hanging off the side.

Julie sits down next to Hazel and gently scoops her up. "Come on, Sweet Pea, time for bed."

Hazel's eyes open and flutter. "Where's daddy?"

"He's on a trip," Julie coos. "We're gonna stay with you until he's back."

She waits for a response, but Hazel has already fallen asleep in her arms. Julie whispers for Maxwell and Olivia, who begrudgingly pull themselves up from the floor. Rachel spots the remote on the matching loveseat and turns the TV off. The room goes dark except for a sliver of moonlight emanating through the curtains.

They form an awkward caravan, maneuvering down the hall to the staircase, using the limited light from the kitchen. Maxwell leads the way up the stairs to the second floor and down the hallway to the door at the end of the hall that Rachel still thinks of as Grandma's. It's the only door on this floor that's open.

The other doors are tightly closed, either to conceal unfinished remodeling or to confine the ghosts to their respective spaces. Rory and Regina both died in their rooms; Regina was too stubborn to go to the hospital, and everyone around her was too in denial to force her. Does the shadow of Rachel's mother lurk behind her bedroom door? It suddenly dawns on Rachel that she doesn't know where her mother killed herself, which room she might have settled into for an eternal haunt.

Rachel drops her duffel bag and the plastic bags of Julie's belongings along the wall and watches as everyone files into Grandma's bedroom. She takes a moment to get her bearings, then turns and twists the doorknob to Grandma's bathroom. The big bulbs around a brand new vanity slowly brighten. The wallpaper is gone and the toilet tank lid is bare.

Rachel looks for a medicine cabinet, but that, too, was removed. Without thinking, she frantically pulls out drawers and opens cabinet doors, searching for some small reminder of her grandmother. Beneath the sink she finds it—a small basket filled with old decorations. Squatting lower, Rachel reaches into the basket, hunting through the dusty trinkets for treasure. She spots the familiar ceramic and grabs for it.

"Fuck!" Rachel sinks to the floor in pain. She slips a bleeding finger into her mouth and examines the baby bunny in the palm of her uninjured hand. It looks as though its chipped ear is bleeding, too, a slow trickle flowing down to one beady, black eye.

"You always were a fighter," Rachel whispers softly. As she brings it closer, the lights dim and the pipes begin to groan. The bunny tremors in her hand for a few seconds, then implodes into a million tiny shards.

"No!" Rachel cries, "No, no, no, no, no." She cups what's left in her hands. It amounts to little more than ceramic dust. The lights brighten and the noise ceases. Rachel scrambles to her feet and shoves her hands under running water. Her hands shimmer from the dust.

Rachel rushes out of the bathroom, slamming the door behind her. She slowly creeps toward her grandmother's bedroom and hears humming as she approaches. She tenses, stopping outside the doorway to look in from the safety of the hallway.

Julie hums a lullaby as she changes diapers and pulls pajamas back onto squirming bodies. She moves about the room like it's hers, like these are her children. The room has been converted into a shared space with three small beds in a row. One is a twin bed with a dinosaur-themed bedding set, and the other two are cribs with matching Minnie Mouse sets. The walls are covered in framed art, mostly thick finger paintings created by the small hands that now occupy this room.

Julie sits on the edge of Maxwell's bed and begins to read from a children's book. Rachel recognizes the cover. It's a story she edited about bunny pirates, which seemed cute at the time, but now makes her shudder. Rachel looks down at her finger but is startled to see there's no sign of injury.

The room goes dark, a heart shaped night light glowing red from an outlet next to the changing table. "Goodnight, peanuts," Julie says softly. She pulls the door behind her, leaving it cracked an inch. She listens at the door for a moment before turning to Rachel and sliding an arm around her waist. "Where are we sleepin' tonight?"

Rachel can't imagine falling asleep in this house. Beneath the fresh paint and clean surfaces, something sinister lurks. She feels it in her quickened pulse and her sore finger where a cut once was. The storm cloud energy that followed her to Chicago is dangerous here, amplified at the source. "My room is up another flight," she says cautiously, unsure what awaits her there.

Julie's eyes dart to the children's door. "I really think one of us should stay closer to 'em. Is it ok if I find a bed in one of the other rooms on this floor?"

Rachel knows the question is asked out of consideration for her feelings and not out of fear or hesitation. Julie has no idea what monsters might hide behind these doors, and Rachel envies her for it. She leans her head into Julie's shoulder and points to Regina and Samuel's room. "That one is probably your best bet. I'll see you in the morning?"

Julie kisses her forehead and gives Rachel a squeeze. "Yeah, I'll make breakfast, and we can talk through our next moves."

She grabs a Walgreens bag from the floor and disappears into the bathroom. Alone, the darkness of the hall feels navigable to Rachel; her instincts guide her like sonar over to the stairs, up to the next floor, through the blackness to her bedroom door. She twists the brass door knob, feeling the antique filigree pattern against her skin. The door opens, and a flick of the light switch reveals boxes of family heirlooms, each one labeled with Samuel's block lettering.

It does not surprise Rachel to discover that her room continues to be used for storage, but one box stands out, a small one on the bed labeled "Evidence." Rachel sits down next to it, her weight lifting a puff of dust off the comforter. She reaches for one of the tucked flaps but hesitates. Maybe there's a chance to pin this all on Samuel. She runs a calculation in her head; they'll need to know how much the children know, how much they remember. It could work.

Rachel surveys the room. The smell of it is cold and damp like wet earth. She feels no trace of herself in it. *Unless this is my scent. Death.* She pulls back the comforter and flicks a spider from the sheets. She'll need to sleep, to clear her mind so that the plan is perfect.

Rachel walks to a stack of boxes and lifts the top two, grunting under their weight. She opens the bottom box, which is filled with Grandma's jewelry and knick-knacks from her vanity. Her eyes scan the contents until they land on the desired target, the purple velvet of a Crown Royal bag. Rachel sifts through the bag, looking for the familiar pink tablet. She pulls one out, checks for the AMB 5 stamp, and swallows it dry.

Rachel drops the Crown Royal bag onto the bedside table and crawls between the thin sheets, fully clothed. The pillow case scratches against her cheek, clawing against her attempt to rest. Rachel stares at the towering boxes surrounding her. They close in around her, suffocating her. Her eyes fight the medication, trained to stay alert in treacherous situations. She blinks slower and slower. She sleeps.

* * *

Rachel is floating down the hallway. She leans against the banister and looks down. Her mother, draped in funeral blacks, paces back and forth on the landing below, wringing her hands. Rachel grips the newly sanded wood until the blood drains from her hands. Her fingers become skeletal, much like the dry, white bone of her mother's exposed hands. The pacing quickens, becomes frenzied. Suddenly it stops, and her mother looks up at her from two vacant sockets in rotting flesh. Rachel's blood turns to ice, her fingers now icicles frozen to the banister. A beam of light splashes across the staircase, and Rachel's mother disappears out of sight.

Rachel feels faint. She leans against the banister and closes her eyes for a moment. When she reopens them, she's standing in the doorway of Rory's room. She somehow knows it's Rory's room even though the patriotic plaid wallpaper has been replaced with a soft blue paint color. The far wall has been turned into a library with gorgeous walnut bookshelves stretching from one corner to the other. Academic texts crowd the shelves, clearly placed there as props for Samuel's second life as a professor. A large executive desk sits in the spot where the hospital bed used to be. Its size and curved maple edges are too reminiscent of a coffin. Rachel backs out of the room, pulling the door closed behind her.

All signs of Regina have been erased from her room. Samuel painted the walls charcoal gray and added a slat wood accent wall behind the queen bed, which is covered in leather throw pillows and fur blankets. Over the bed, a deer's lifeless, glass eyes stare down in judgement. Rachel finds herself drawn to this butchered head. She inches closer and closer, never breaking eye contact.

Something flashes in the deer's dark pupil, and Rachael gasps, backing away slowly. Ice-cold hands settle around her waist. She feels her body scream but the sound is trapped in her throat.

"Good mornin', Lu." It's Julie's voice behind her. Rachel spins around to face her, to make sure she's actually there. "I didn't know you were awake. Sorry if my hands are cold. I just washed 'em and the water in this house takes *forever* to warm up. But ya probably know that already."

Rachel's brow furrows, still not completely convinced that Julie is real. This was supposed to be a dream; she saw her mother. Julie walks over to a leather chair in the corner where she's placed her belongings. She takes out her make-up and walks toward the bedroom door. "The kiddos are eatin' breakfast downstairs. Can ya keep an eye on 'em while I put my face on?"

Rachel pinches her arm, feels the sharp pain. She stares at the white spots her finger and thumb left behind and watches them return to pink. Head dizzy with confusion, she pushes herself out the door to the staircase. At the top of the stairs, she pauses, her eyes sweeping the area for signs of familial apparitions.

The children are seated at the dining room table, Maxwell across from his sisters. Bits of egg, bacon, and toast spill from their plates onto the table and floor beneath each of their chairs. There's a coffee mug and a facedown cell phone next to Maxwell, reserving Julie's spot. Rachel goes to the kitchen, pours herself some coffee, and returns to the dining room, taking the seat at the head of the table. She sips her coffee, hoping it will clear her head and bring her fully back to real life.

"You ok, Aunt Rachel?"

Rachel looks up from her mug to find three sets of eyes on her. Olivia tilts her head, waiting for a response to her question. Maxwell takes a bite of bacon and turns to his sister. "I think she's just sweepy, Liv."

Rachel hums in agreement, but the conversation has already shifted to Hazel's messy face. It's as if Rachel isn't present at the table, and she feels the creeping chill rise up her spine. *Maybe I'm not here.*

"Hello, beautiful people!" Julie walks into the room, bright and fresh. The children giggle and begin to recount all of the things she missed in the five minutes she was out of the room. She nods excitedly, eyes wide and eager. Rachel watches the scene without listening. Everything is high-pitched noise. She takes another drink and urges herself to wake up, to start the plan.

"So, Maxwell," she begins, "does your dad ever take you into town?"

He swings his legs beneath his chair, grinning at the creaking noise it emits. "Town is just on TV, silly."

Rachel smiles. "What about the doctor's office or the library? Do you ever see other adults? Other big people like Julie and me?"

Maxwell lifts a hand and uses the finger of his other hand to count off. "We know you, and Julie, and Kate, and Dr. Stephens . . . he comes here when my tummy hurts."

Rachel's smile widens. "Do you go to school? Do you have a teacher?"

He shakes his head. "Daddy says I so smart, I no need a teacher. Daddy teaches us colors, and letters, and dinosaurs. Wanna see my dinosaurs?"

Julie stands and begins to clear the table, using the side of her hand to scrape food bits off the table and onto a plate. "Maybe later, bud," she says sweetly. "Why dontcha guys go watch some cartoons for a bit, and then we'll play outside."

There's a chorus of excitement for cartoons as they clamor out of their booster seats, Olivia helping Hazel down from her chair. Julie waits for them to leave the room before turning to Rachel. "They're gonna need baths tonight for sure."

Rachel leans across the table toward Julie. "Leave them dirty. I've been thinking, and if we contact CPS anonymously, they'll come out and find the children all alone. We can take Kate's information out of the binder and replace it with my cousin Stacie's. I'm pretty sure she's godmother to one of them."

Julie freezes in the middle of cleanup. She leaves the pile of dishes in the middle of the table and sits back down, picking up her mug and slumping low in her chair, staring at the surface of her coffee. "Yeah, I guess that makes the most sense. I hate to think of where they'll live before your cousin gets here. You're sure she'll take all three of 'em?"

Rachel nods. "I'm positive." She watches Julie's face relax. Julie doesn't need to know that Stacie threw herself in front of a train three years ago. "We just need to figure out what to do about Kate, then I'll make the call to CPS, and we can hit the road."

Julie brightens, leaning forward to pick up the cell phone from the table. "Oh, I already took care of Kate. While you were still sleepin', I found her conversations with Samuel . . . that guy was so desperate for love that I almost felt bad for 'im. Anyway, I sent her a message about findin' someone new and insinuatin' that she would look real desperate if she didn't just move on. I was really mean."

Julie lifts her eyebrows to emphasize the last sentence, daring Rachel to imagine her cruelty. Rachel feels a warm tingle between her thighs for the first time since Samuel showed up. This could work. They sip their coffee in silence, shooting reassuring smiles across the table.

When they've drained their mugs, Rachel collects everything from the table and takes it to the sink while Julie gathers the children and herds them out to the yard. When Rachel walks out the front door, the four of them are running barefoot in circles around the playset in a game of tag. Julie moves in slow motion, pretending that she's having trouble catching Hazel whose toddler legs stomp in jerky movements.

Rachel folds her arms and rests against a porch column, watching as Julie lifts Olivia and Hazel into swings. Maxwell pushes one swing and then runs to the other to give it a shove, revelling in his sisters' delighted squeals. Julie trudges over to Rachel, wiping sweat from her hairline. "They have so much energy!" she pants as she slips behind Rachel and slides both arms around her waist.

Rachel leans back into her damp embrace and takes a deep breath. Soon they'll be on their way to a new place, to a new life. She feels a flicker of hope growing but tempers it. The past has taught her better.

"God, they really are the cutest," Julie says. Her arms tighten against Rachel's hips. "Lu, we can't just turn 'em over to CPS. We don't know for sure that your cousin will take 'em, and if they stay in the system, they'll get split up. What if we took 'em with us?"

Rachel's spine locks in place. "What are you talking about?"

"You've lost so much, but this is your chance to have a family. And they deserve someone who's gonna love 'em . . . someone like an aunt. Or we could just stay here and raise 'em. This house is beautiful and has more than enough room."

Rachel's mouth twitches. *I thought she understood.* Her hands tingle and burn. She can feel her mother's presence in this house, mocking her. *You don't get a happy ending.*

The sound of tires on gravel steals Rachel's attention. She twists toward the driveway and sees a familiar light blue hatchback approaching. She feels Julie's arms drop. "Why is Kate here, Julie?"

"I don't know," she says. Her voice trembles, revealing her true bewilderment.

The car parks near the front of the house and Kate jumps out before the engine has stopped rattling. She marches toward them, her face rest, her hands balled into fists. "Where the fuck is he?"

"Who?" Rachel asks, backing toward the front door.

"Sammy! He sent me, like, the *worst* message this morning and I want to make him say it to my face!"

"Kate, I'm sorry," Julie says in a soothing voice. "We told you he left with Alexis. He's not here."

"Bullshit!" Kate's face darkens. "He sent it through the app we use and it shows his location as being here. So, like, where the fuck is he? Stop protecting him!"

Waves of emotions course through Rachel's body. Surprise changes to fear, and from fear to resolve. Rachel is centered under the heat of newly found rage. She feels a switch flip, her body shifting over to muscle memory. Something in her settles, the chord resolution after dissonance. *What can we control?*

Rachel walks around Julie, down the stairs, close enough to Kate that she can speak in a low voice. "Ok, you're right. He's inside in the children's room, packing some things for them so they can come back to Chicago with us. They don't know yet so please stay calm. Come inside and we'll let you confront him."

Kate clenches her jaw and pushes past Rachel toward the front door. Rachel turns to Julie. "Grab the kids and bring them inside."

Julie doesn't question. She knows she made a mistake with the phone. She jogs over to the swings, gathering the three of them. Rachel looks up at the windows of the second floor. A shadowy figure is staring at her from behind the reflective glass. She squints against the morning sunlight and lifts a hand above her eyes, but the figure is gone.

* * *

One highway blurs into the next. Rachel counts street lamps, the signs, the taillights of the cars ahead . . . anything to stay awake. She turns the AC up and yawns. An exit for Chicago looms in the distance and she smiles. One last detail to handle and then a moment to relax. She runs through the plan for tomorrow. She'll go into the office and clean up her office space for the next occupant. She'll take down the photos and discard them, slipping the one of Julie in her back pocket. She'll walk into Jim's office and tell him she has to move back home to help Samuel with the kids. *Oh Julie? We broke up again.* She'll ask if he's free for dinner with a wink, one last hoorah before she leaves forever. She'll give him the address to Julie's place then wait for him to buzz.

Rachel takes the exit for Lakeshore Drive and whips around its curves. It will be nice to sleep in Julie's bed tonight, to smell the rose water one last time, the lock of hair next to her on the pillow, still silky smooth. She needs that photo though, a memento of how Julie looked before everything took a turn. Before they murdered someone together. Before it became apparent that Julie didn't understand the rules—She'd wanted an impossible life in that house.

Rachel shakes her head, trying to dislodge the memory of her cursed childhood home. Samuel did so much work to hide its terrible secrets, but in the end, it was clear what she needed to do. All of it had to be destroyed.

Rachel rubs an itch under her nose. She can still smell the butane under her fingernails and feel the heat from the flames. The fire spread quickly to the bedrooms, erupting when it got to the children's room at the end of the hall where the gasoline was most concentrated. Rachel watched it burn from the driveway until the screams subsided. Then she climbed into the hatchback and drove away.

She smiles now as she pulls onto Julie's street and parks across from a late night pizza shop. She takes a tube of lotion from the middle console and rubs it on her calloused hands. It really was harder to tie everyone up than she had expected. But it's comforting to think of those charred, little bodies snuggled next to Julie's. It's what Julie had wanted after all; this way the children will never be separated. And Kate will forever be out of their way because Rachel thought of everything. She took the time to drag Kate's bludgeoned body out to the staircase before the first match was struck. Kate can keep her mother company.

Rachel walks into the shop and approaches the counter. A middle-aged man looks up from a copy of the Reader and hovers a hand over the register. "What can I getcha, sweetie?"

"Can I get a small pepperoni pizza and a Diet Coke to go?"

"Sure thing. Can I get a name for the order?"

"Julie," Rachel says, handing him a credit card.

ACKNOWLEDGEMENTS

I could not have written this book without the support of those closest to me. Thank you to everyone who pushed me along the way. I am grateful beyond words.

To Lauren, for encouraging me when I was only three chapters in and doubting myself. You were my biggest cheerleader and motivated me to keep churning out chapters.

To my wonderful partner, Nick. Thank you for letting me disappear for hours to write, and for doing the first round of edits. I'm so happy I get to celebrate this book with you.

To the friends who read early drafts and offered feedback. Kasey, Amber, Jane, and Holly, I owe you all a round of drinks!

To my editor, Emily. You're an amazing editor and an even more amazing friend. Thank you for removing all those extra commas and helping me craft this into the story it was meant to be.

To my therapist, Hannah, who coached me out of a Covid slump and convinced me that even one sentence a day was a victory. You changed my life for the better.

And finally, thank you to my family whose teasing "when ya gonna write that novel" comments kept the fire lit.

Kelsey graduated from The University of Kansas with a bachelor's in English - Creative Writing and a master's in Higher Education. She has written many short stories over the years but These Little Deaths is her debut novel. She resides in Chicago with her partner and their cats. Visit booksbykelsey.com for contact information.

CPSIA information can be obtained
at www.ICGtesting.com
Printed in the USA
LVHW080359120522
718055LV00003B/3